‖‖‖ W9-AOS-976

No polite society could impart all the lessons she needed to be a love poetess....

Ivy had heard the expression "to tumble a maid" but until now had had no idea how literal and apt a phrase it proved. She decided she would rather like to be tumbled. Often.

Her arms wound around Roger's neck and she savored the feel of his body against hers, a sensation she'd been dreaming about as she penned poetry that should be for her eyes alone. Writing words of longing entertained her, but not nearly so much as living the fulfillment of that longing.

To kiss him in the garden the first time had sparked sensual dreams she couldn't escape. But to kiss him now, clad in the thinnest of linens, her mind still reeling with provocative visions from her poem...*this* was pure madness.

And yet she did not think about letting go. She would finally receive that education she needed as a love poet— a keen understanding of the physical hunger, the carnal craving, the sweet torment of real passion.

* * *

The Knight's Courtship
Harlequin® Historical #812—August 2006

Praise for Joanne Rock

"Joanne Rock's heroes capture and conquer in just
one glance, one word, one touch. Irresistible!"
—*USA TODAY* bestselling author Julie Leto

The Laird's Lady
"...classic battle of wills plot, fiery repartee
and feisty heroine."
—*Romantic Times BOOKclub*

The Wedding Knight
"*The Wedding Knight* is guaranteed to please!
Joanne Rock brings a fresh, vibrant voice
to this charming tale."
—*New York Times* bestselling author Teresa Medeiros

The Knight's Redemption
"A highly readable medieval romance with an
entertaining touch of the paranormal...."
—*Romantic Times BOOKclub*

**DON'T MISS THESE OTHER
NOVELS AVAILABLE NOW:**

#811 THE RUNAWAY HEIRESS
Anne O'Brien

#813 WANTED!
Pam Crooks

#814 THE BRIDEGROOM'S BARGAIN
Sylvia Andrew

Joanne Rock

The Knight's Courtship

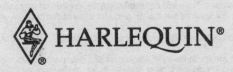

HARLEQUIN®

TORONTO • NEW YORK • LONDON
AMSTERDAM • PARIS • SYDNEY • HAMBURG
STOCKHOLM • ATHENS • TOKYO • MILAN • MADRID
PRAGUE • WARSAW • BUDAPEST • AUCKLAND

If you purchased this book without a cover you should be aware
that this book is stolen property. It was reported as "unsold and
destroyed" to the publisher, and neither the author nor the
publisher has received any payment for this "stripped book."

ISBN-13: 978-0-373-29412-1
ISBN-10:   0-373-29412-3

THE KNIGHT'S COURTSHIP

Copyright © 2006 by Joanne Rock

First North American Publication 2006

All rights reserved. Except for use in any review, the reproduction or
utilization of this work in whole or in part in any form by any electronic,
mechanical or other means, now known or hereafter invented, including
xerography, photocopying and recording, or in any information storage
or retrieval system, is forbidden without the written permission of the
publisher, Harlequin Enterprises Limited, 225 Duncan Mill Road,
Don Mills, Ontario, Canada M3B 3K9.

All characters in this book have no existence outside the imagination of
the author and have no relation whatsoever to anyone bearing the same
name or names. They are not even distantly inspired by any individual
known or unknown to the author, and all incidents are pure invention.

This edition published by arrangement with Harlequin Books S.A.

® and TM are trademarks of the publisher. Trademarks indicated with
® are registered in the United States Patent and Trademark Office, the
Canadian Trade Marks Office and in other countries.

www.eHarlequin.com

Printed in U.S.A.

Please address questions and book requests to:
Harlequin Reader Service
U.S.: 3010 Walden Ave., P.O. Box 1325, Buffalo, NY 14269
Canadian: P.O. Box 609, Fort Erie, Ont. L2A 5X3

This book is dedicated to the bold strength of the feminine spirit that transcends time and resonates through historical figures like Eleanor of Aquitaine. The story of this fearless queen assures me that women were forces to be reckoned with—even in the Middle Ages, when the historical record often paints a more docile picture of femininity. Thank you, Eleanor, for lifting your voice across the centuries.

And to Dr. Helen Taylor of Louisiana State University at Shreveport, who brings to life these voices across time for her students. Thank you for sharing your time and expertise with me, and thank you for taking my hopes and dreams seriously even before I published so much as a word.

Chapter One

Poitiers, France
Spring 1174

"...married for money, bred for heirs,
She wept in shadow, burdened by cares."

Ivy Rutherford read her new poem aloud, hoping the freshly penned words would touch the hearts of the jaded court ladies who filled Queen Eleanor's garden bower. She took a calming breath before continuing her recitation.

"Til a Knight arrived, his honor well-proved,
Who spied her tears and his soul was moved.
Love's keen lance soon pierced her heart—"

Lady Gertrude snorted as she patted the head of

her obnoxious little lapdog. "I'll bet that's not all love's lance pierced."

Feminine twitters rippled among Eleanor's courtly crowd, which was gathered in the shade of the vine-covered wooden arbor for their afternoon entertainment.

Ivy stared down at the costly parchment, the words she had labored over crumpling slightly with her tightened grip as laughter erupted from the queen's cronies. Eager to put the awkward moments of reading her new creation behind her, she continued as soon as the noise abated.

"And Venus revealed her comely art—"

More laughter.

"Enough!" Marie, Comtesse de Champagne, rose from her bench amid the flowering foxgloves, silencing the assembly with one censuring frown. Tall and elegant, Marie wrote poetry herself and perhaps understood the difficulty of creative endeavors more than did her peers. "Ivy has been gracious enough to amuse us this afternoon. We can at least extend her the courtesy of silence."

Although she appreciated the comtesse's efforts, Ivy sensed from her brief time at court that the queen's ladies would swarm like vultures around any creature weak enough to require another's defense. Their unspoken scorn reverberated in her ears as clearly as the chirp of the lone meadowlark fluttering about the bower's eaves. *How dare she, a mere merchant's daughter, give herself noble airs?*

From the front row, stout and stalwart Lady Gertrude appealed to the queen. Latticework shadows flickered across Gertrude's sullen features as her dog growled. "Since when have any of us in Your Majesty's illustrious court had to feign enjoyment of inferior art?"

Ivy flinched at the cruelty—and accuracy—of the jab, regretting her vulnerability to the criticism. Her poems meant the world to her. Life at Queen Eleanor's court gave Ivy the chance to indulge in the most important thing in her life—her art.

Lifting a censorious brow in Gertrude's direction, the queen peered down her nose. "Do not attempt to flatter me. There is no excuse for coarse manners at my court."

Ivy ducked to hide her smile. Not that she cared so much about Gertrude being put in her place, but because Ivy loved to see the queen in action. Few could match wits with Eleanor of Aquitaine.

The woman was everything Ivy longed to be—independent, confident, talented. Besides, at fifty-two years old, having served half that time as queen of one realm or another, Eleanor had never shed a tear in public, even when her husband was rumored to have been conducting a flagrant affair under her nose. Ivy braved a glance at her sovereign, who was seated in the bower's only chair in the midst of her ladies. All of Europe stood in awe of her audacity in starting her own royal court in her family seat of Poitou on the wrong side of the English Channel. She had astonished the western world by defying her adulterous husband, an English king no less.

"I apologize, Your Majesty." Gertrude bowed her head in deference to the queen.

Other women who had laughed at Ivy's poem now dipped their heads, too, though Ivy suspected their motives had more to do with securing the queen's good graces than actual remorse. Knowing that didn't squelch a brief sense of victory.

"And, Gertrude, you are wrong to say Ivy's art is inferior." Queen Eleanor turned indulgent eyes toward her newest troubadour.

Thank heaven the queen appreciated her efforts. As long as Ivy pleased the monarch, her position at court remained secure. Ivy could not help the fanciful dream she had of rising in station one day thanks to her art. A foolish notion, no doubt.

"She has written poetry to make my spirit soar," Eleanor continued, "and she will do so again."

Ivy almost burst with pride. The queen did not praise idly.

"Her failing today resulted not from inferior art," the queen continued, "but from lack of life experience in regard to the nature of love."

No one dared laugh, yet Ivy imagined they wanted to. Her utter lack of knowledge about men had been brought to her attention on several occasions since she had joined the court a fortnight ago.

The queen swept the room with a shrewd and level glare. "I chose to bring Ivy to Poitiers because she is a brilliant thinker. While most of you belong to this court by chance of birth, Ivy is here because she has made something fine and noble of herself in spite of her heritage, tainted by her noble mother's marriage to a commoner."

The other women looked down at their colorful, silk-covered laps while the soft hum of honeybees drifted on the breeze.

Mon Dieu. The ladies-in-waiting would definitely resent the merchant's daughter now. But the queen's brief words had given Ivy more confidence in her art than her father had bothered to engender in her in a lifetime, and for that, Ivy would be forever grateful.

Perched on a stool only slightly lower than the queen's chair, Comtesse Marie nodded, clearly approving of her mother's speech.

"How might we assist Ivy in her love poetry, Mother?" Marie interjected after an appropriate silence. "You yourself have noted it is not as strong as some of her other pieces. Must we marry off young Ivy to give her some notion of love?"

The queen laughed. "I think most of us can attest to the fact that marriage does not teach a woman about love."

Amen.

From Ivy's observation of her parents' disastrous marriage, she knew the Church-sanctioned union of man and woman did little to foster tender feelings between them. Yet she nurtured a secret hope that one day she would experience the rare gift of true love—the kind troubadours described in their ballads. The kind that made Ivy's wishful heart sing like the bird fluttering overhead.

Marie winked in Ivy's direction, then turned back to the queen. "Yes, but once she is married, other men can woo her openly without the constraint of her maidenly status."

Several women nodded.

They could *not* truly mean that.

Unrealistic as her dreams might be, Ivy wanted no part of a loveless marriage. Not even for her art's sake would she suffer a husband who cared naught for her. She'd sooner endure a spinster's fate.

"Perhaps…" Eleanor tilted her silver-threaded head to one side. "Perhaps Ivy might join our Court of Love proceedings for the next moon or two."

A low murmur of surprise—or was it disapproval?—rumbled through the group. Eleanor's courts of love were entertaining gatherings for the diverse travelers and guests who populated Poitiers at any time of year, but especially during the spring. Lovers brought their romantic problems before the judgment of the ladies at court, a practice that provided amusement as well as enlightenment, since the assemblies were forums for discussing the ideals of romantic love that regional troubadours struggled to express to the world in their beloved art form.

Marie smiled. "What a wonderful idea, Mother.

She could find no better place to learn about passion…outside an ardent man's arms, that is."

Lady Gertrude spluttered her indignation, her chubby fingers tightening around her scrawny dog's head while the animal yelped. "But you said yourself the girl knows nothing of love. How would she contribute to our discussions?"

"She does not have to contribute. She will merely observe." Eleanor cast a knowing glance toward Ivy. "Our Ivy likes playing the quiet role of spectator, do you not, my dear?"

Was this crowd of worldly women determined to make Ivy feel inferior? Without question. She cringed whenever her new troubadour position forced her to read her labors of love aloud. Today, she was stuck in front of everyone, a defenseless target of their scrutiny.

"Yes, Your Majesty."

"Then it is settled," the queen announced, smiling. Her beauty, only slightly faded with age, sparkled with her pleasure. "We meet tomorrow morning to review our next case. Who is it to be, Marie?"

Ivy fought the urge to clap her hands together in delight. The Court of Love enjoyed notoriety across the land, and now she would witness it firsthand. What wonderful fodder for her poetry.

"Lord Roger Stancliff, my lady, newly arrived from England."

A collective squeal arose from the younger women of the party.

"Come to seduce the ladies of the court and drink the gentlemen under the trestle tables, I suppose?" The queen hissed the question, ignoring the rising tide of whispers and giggles among her ladies.

Marie laughed, her joyous spirit a colorful contrast to her mother's sparse wit.

"His vices render him a challenging test of our powers, Your Majesty. If the Court of Love can turn Roger Stancliff into a courteous *chevalier,* then our skills will become as legendary as Lord Roger's reputation."

Ivy gasped, shocked the countess would be willing to support such a risky endeavor when the troubadours all worked diligently to infuse the notion of courtly love with the idea of unselfish devotion and admiration in its purest form. Roger Stancliff was obviously a craven scoundrel—the antithesis of the romantic ideals Ivy held dear.

The queen narrowed her gaze on her daughter. "Have you fallen prey to Stancliff's charm?"

To Ivy's amazement, sophisticated, worldly Marie de Champagne blushed.

"Of course not." With an airy gesture, the queen's firstborn waved away the matter. "My heart lies elsewhere."

"I am not concerned where your heart lies, my dear, only your person."

The comtesse stiffened. She followed the progress of a hummingbird with her gaze until she finally responded, "Then you may ease your mind, Your Majesty. I only wish to test our abilities by transforming one of Christendom's most heralded lovers."

The queen grumbled but did not argue. She dismissed the royal company, freeing her ladies to walk about the gardens or retire indoors.

Ivy lingered, as did a few others. Gathering her parchment, she overheard Marie's words of reassurance to her queen. "He is here to change his ways, my lady Mother."

Lady Gertrude coddled her ill-bred pet as she brushed past Ivy, muttering under her breath. "He is more likely here to change mistresses."

Long after the other ladies had departed the queen's bower, a delicate young woman remained. Graced with pale creamy skin that glowed with good health, she sat alone.

Roger Stancliff counted his blessings as he studied her.

Her pale blond hair escaped its circlet in the slight spring breeze. A white kirtle embroidered with ivy made her seem a part of her surroundings, at one with the encroaching greenery. Her angelic profile drew him as much as her solitude.

The fact that she sat unaccompanied told him several things. Either she was not well-connected at court or she was somewhat of a rebel. Both scenarios suited his purpose, for he needed to befriend someone at Eleanor's elegant court to feed him the information he sought.

Befriend.

The word had an awkward ring. A year ago he would have seduced the girl in question.

Now, thanks to the king's orders that Roger cultivate a more sedate reputation in order to be accepted at Eleanor's court, Roger would have to try to befriend this innocent.

Damn Henry.

The king had been adamant, however. Roger wouldn't inherit the full family holdings if he didn't investigate the possibility of sedition at Poitiers beneath the pretense of courtly love, refinement and heightened attention to manners. Roger could retain the earldom, but the majority of the Stancliff lands would go to their neighbor, William Montcalm, if Roger failed in this. Montcalm had a strong claim to them, after all. And his family's thirst to wreak vengeance on Roger seemed insatiable.

Recalling Roger from his somber thoughts, the delicate blonde arched like a sleepy cat and slumped against the garden bench.

Now or never.

The king's order gave him a chance to prove his worth. To make something more of himself than the dissolute scoundrel the world had believed him to be ever since his betrothed had died.

He stepped closer, considering how best to approach a befriending. The girl's head tipped back in abandon to the day. Eyes closed, a peaceful smile playing about her lips, she looked as if she couldn't be more content.

Damn.

Why couldn't his first official befriending involve a less appealing female? From her full pink lips to her gently upturned nose, this young woman looked like a Dionysian reveler, caught up in the magic of a lovely afternoon, drunk on nature and life.

Taking a deep breath, he committed himself to the cause. "Is this bower your own, lady? Or might another rest here, too?"

Heavy dark lashes fluttered open. Startlingly green eyes peered back at him, the same color as the white kirtle's intricate vine pattern.

She said nothing. Only stared, unblinking.

"My lady?" He prompted, amused. He hadn't struck anyone speechless in more years than he could count.

"I am Ivy, my lord," she responded, her color heightening as she straightened herself.

Her name matched the gown, Roger noted. "May I join you?" He did not offer his name, preferring to delay a revelation that could send her running. Perhaps she would be too tired—or too polite—to remark on his omission.

"Please do." She sounded as if she had just woke up. The smokiness in her voice sent a jolt of awareness through him.

He sat across from her, stretching his legs just enough to make his presence known, but not enough to brush against her.

Befriending only.

The parchment she clutched seemed a good opening. Nodding at it, he asked, "You are an artist?"

Still she stared at him, dazed. "Oh." She waved her long quill, as if only just remembering she held it. "I am a troubadour, sir."

"A poet?" Maybe she was not the innocent she seemed. "I dare say you don't fit the traditional mold for a troubadour."

"No?" Her spine straightened. A quarrelsome note crept into that smoky voice.

"No offense, but most troubadours I have met have been amorous men looking to seduce their lady listeners with their words." He wondered if she would be interested in seducing him with erotic lyrics.

Her green eyes grew even rounder before her chin flew up. She didn't look too amenable to seduction at the moment.

"There may not be a great number of practicing women," she huffed, "but I assure you, there are many of us who enjoy poetry. And Queen Eleanor is the greatest patron of our art, so it is no surprise there are so many poets in residence at Poitiers."

Roger rejected this route as a way to befriend a temperamental poet. He decided to try again.

"Would you care to take a turn about the gardens, my lady?" He extended his arm to her.

A timid soul might refuse, but Roger suspected Ivy the troubadour was accustomed to defying convention now and then.

"I would enjoy a walk." She smiled briefly before

masking her eagerness. She accepted his arm, her gentle touch generating a wave of keen hunger in him.

"Might I inquire what kind of poems you write, Lady Ivy?" Once out of the arbor, he released the soft enticement of her slender fingers. He didn't wish to make his task more torturous for himself.

"Please, my lord. You must call me Ivy." Her face flushed pink as they reached the entrance to the small labyrinth.

"As you wish, Ivy." She wished to be on such familiar terms? This innocent? He guided her into the winding maze hedge, careful not to touch her any more than necessary.

No sense courting temptation.

The girl stayed close to him as they strolled through the narrow tunnel of green hedges. When the garden maze grew darker and more intimate, Roger attempted to draw her into conversation. He had to start his search for information somewhere.

"Tell me about your poetry."

"I experiment with all different forms." Her voice was warm. "But I came from England to see the ideals of courtly love enacted. That is what I enjoy writing about most."

Roger groaned inwardly. She couldn't be propositioning him. Courtly love was a polite term for adultery, as far as he was concerned. The rebellious women who congregated at Eleanor's court could romanticize the notion all they wished with their ideals of admiration from afar, but too often such affairs led to men and women seeking love outside their marriage.

Not that he wouldn't relish the chance to spirit Ivy away and give her more material for her damn poetry than she knew what to do with. But he needed to be discreet. If he expected to keep the Stancliff lands out of Montcalm's vengeful grasp, he couldn't fall prey to a shapely troubadour.

"Courtly love?" Perhaps his safest reaction was to be obtuse. Pretend he didn't hear the blatant proposition associated with any talk of courtly love.

"Yes." Stopping alongside a boxwood hedge, she squeezed his arm. "I want to see love in its purest form, then transfer that experience to parchment and create poetry to inspire people."

Her touch sent unwanted heat through him. A year ago he could have whispered in her ear that he would take her to a place where they'd find love in its purest form. And he'd certainly be inspired.

Not anymore.

"How exciting." He tugged on the collar of his tunic, surprised at how warm a French spring could be. That sounded trite at best, but his brain stopped functioning when she touched him.

Her hands slid from his arm as she resumed walking. Now he could breathe again.

"I suppose it *doesn't* sound exciting to other people. But it is my dream." Ivy sighed.

Damn. He had hurt her feelings when he was supposed to be befriending her. The slump of her shoul-

ders saddened him. He much preferred her more enthusiastic mood. "Perhaps I would understand more
clearly if you read your poems to me one day."

She stopped.

Silently, he willed her to keep her hands to herself. To save him from the idiocy her touch seemed
to precipitate.

"Truly?" She squeezed his arm in an effusive
gesture.

Roger could not help but notice the undulation of
the golden necklace that rested on her breasts. An unfamiliar emblem scrolled across the surface of a
small medallion that dangled from the chain. His
hand itched to touch it. Or any other part of Lady Ivy,
for that matter. Despite his reputation, it had been a
long time since he'd indulged himself.

"Certainly. I would love to hear your poems."

Her expression clouded. "I read at court from time
to time, of course, but it is always difficult in front
of such a large group."

She wouldn't cease, would she? The little minx
sought to meet with him alone.

"Maybe you would find it in your heart to read just
for me one afternoon this week."

Ivy gifted him with a pretty smile. For a delicate
thing, she lit up like a warm flame with a bit of coaxing. "I would like that." She was all blushes again,
as if a stranger to this game. Roger had never seen a
more convincing innocent act.

He conducted her out of the maze, opting for the

quickest route back to safety. He did as well as could be expected in his first befriending, but he needed to escape this artful creature before she started clamoring for lessons in "pure love" again.

"Then I shall call on you tomorrow afternoon, Lady Ivy." He bent over her hand and kissed it with quick efficiency, ignoring the warm lavender scent of her skin. "You may depend upon it."

Ivy watched the most beautiful man in the world walk away, knowing her feet wouldn't hit the ground for a fortnight. It took a Herculean effort not to release a dreamy sigh.

The man embodied every romantic fantasy she had ever penned about a chivalrous knight. Dark hair framed a face that only God could have dreamed up. And, honest to heaven, the man possessed silver eyes. As surely as she stood there, they were silver and not gray.

His height had forced him to bend slightly when he entered the archway of the garden bower, and his sudden presence had filled the space with a tangible, dynamic aura.

Watching him cover the ground between the bower and the keep, and knowing he was beyond earshot, Ivy submitted to the inevitable sigh. Tomorrow afternoon couldn't possibly come soon enough.

He'd shown interest in her art. The Court of Love's morning proceedings paled in comparison to the promise of reading poetry to the silver-eyed man.

Even if he weren't incredibly handsome, he would have stolen her heart with his request to hear her poems.

As soon as the queen's ladies were finished making mincemeat of the scoundrel Roger Stancliff tomorrow, she would wait for the man of her dreams.

Chapter Two

Dearest Daughter,
Your letters do not discuss your progress in finding a noble husband. Do not forget your purpose. I have financed an expensive endeavor for you, and I expect to be repaid with a lofty connection to expand my trade. You must discover the lowest nobles in need of coin or I will find it necessary to marry you to someone of my choosing—someone who might lack nobility but who is wise in trade. I am content either way, but I wish to hear of your progress with all haste.
Love, Father

Even now Ivy burned with indignation at her father's missive, hours after she'd received it. The shame she'd felt at his mention of money and marriage had caused her to shred the letter into the flames of her solar hearth that morning and had remained with her until she sat in the great hall before the afternoon's Court of Love proceedings.

She had come to the court for the sake of her poetry. Indeed, her talent alone had brought her to Queen Eleanor's attention, not her father's wealth. But he refused to acknowledge her role at Poitiers, preferring to hound her about his own agenda for her time among the nobility.

She deliberately shoved aside thoughts of the marriage she would not make. Noble or merchant, she would not care, so long as she were wed for love and not as part of a political barter. Failing love, she would as soon remain at court. She allowed the hum of anticipation in the air to draw her in and thrill her poet's soul. Protocol for the Court of Love dictated Ivy sit behind and to the side of the most eminent noblewomen. Far from feeling slighted by the placement, Ivy chose to enjoy the fact that she could be here at all.

The day stretched before her, full of infinite possibility as long as she put her father's urgings far from her mind. She would find a way to repay him for his generosity before she left Poitiers, but it would *not* involve bartering her own marriage contract.

As much as she anticipated seeing the silver-eyed knight again, she was grateful for the opportunity to watch the world's most famous queen reign over her court first. This was no smoke-filled great hall full of errant knights and slobbering hounds. Poitiers had been renovated to become an elegant haven fit for a sovereign who relished her role as queen.

Ivy could not blame the king for wishing his wife would come home now that his kingdom had splintered in the wake of the archbishop's death and power struggles among Henry's sons. Eleanor was an asset, and the people admired her. But why should the queen scurry to fulfill her husband's wishes when he accused her of conspiring with her sons against him?

Dipping her quill for the tenth time in the last few minutes, Ivy hoped she had brought enough parchment for all the notes she wanted to make. Her troubadour status gave her license to write while in the queen's presence, though Ivy sometimes struggled to do so without a table beneath her. She steadied her ink on the floor at her feet. The rest of the company sat upon plush pillows scattered around the center of the sprawling chamber.

The hall had filled to overflowing long in advance of Lord Stancliff's appearance. Women of every rank and position circled the doors, hoping for a glance at the man whose legend had preceded him.

But no matter how often Ivy told herself the man must be a first-rate scoundrel, her heart softened toward anyone forced to face the stalwart row of queen's cronies who waited for Stancliff with all the patience of hungry wolves.

As Ivy scribbled impressions on her parchment, she savored the tableau, eager to relay them in detail to the gentle knight who had plagued her thoughts since yesterday afternoon.

Lady Gertrude sat front and center before the small dais, prepared to taunt and leer at Stancliff, no doubt. Or perhaps she would just release her smelly lapdog on the man, since the creature enjoyed taking a nip at any person not to Gertrude's liking. Comtesse Marie, who never needed an audience but whose charm attracted one anyway, held court with her favorites at one end of the hall.

The queen's throne, with its high, straight back and jeweled legs, remained empty. Carved with ornate details from the queen's pilgrimage to the Holy Land, the chair loomed over the floor pillows in constant reminder of the court's strict observance of social rank and order.

Rank and order.

Ivy stopped scribbling for a moment to contemplate that last thought. Glancing down at her blue silk kirtle with her recurring wardrobe theme of beaded green ivy creeping up one side, it struck her that no one would ever know by looking at her that she was not nobly born on both sides.

Her manners were refined. She sang, played the lute and wrote articulate, if not brilliant, poems. Her father had seen to it that she could also read Latin, calculate mathematics and execute the steps to every conceivable round or processional dance known to mankind.

Yet everyone at Queen Eleanor's court, except

perhaps for the silver-eyed stranger, knew Ivy Rutherford to be an interloper. No matter how lofty her mother's birth, her father's lowly origins tainted Ivy as far as the rest of the world was concerned. She was a merchant-class trespasser on the holy ground of nobility.

A fraud.

"Ivy, pay attention." Lady Katherine wrenched Ivy's quill from her hand. "If you do not put that feather down, you will miss all the fun."

The highest ranking woman at court aside from Marie and Queen Eleanor, petite and headstrong Lady Katherine de Blois possessed an exotic beauty and a dowry of solid gold that assured her social acceptance despite her friendship with a woman of more humble parentage like Ivy.

Katherine didn't mind sitting off to one side to be with her friend. She thwarted protocol at every opportunity. Ivy adored her for it, even if—at times, such as now—Katherine insisted on having her own way.

Ivy snatched back the quill, comfortable enough with Katherine to discreetly elbow her in return. "I am not missing a thing. And I am writing it all down besides."

Later, safe within the privacy of her small chamber, Ivy would scrutinize every detail of her notes, reliving each glorious moment. Then, one day, she would use her scribbles as the basis of a poem.

Peeking over Ivy's shoulder, Katherine clucked her disapproval, her long dark hair slipping loose of its thin veil as she bent closer. "But think what subtleties you miss when you bow your head to look at the parchment, Ivy. A telling smirk or a teasing wink. Trust me, you do not want to miss a moment of Lord Stancliff."

Slowly releasing the quill, Ivy regarded England's wealthiest unwed heiress with interest. Intelligent Katherine might be intractable in her opinions, but she was seldom wrong.

"Is he that handsome?"

Katherine's ready grin unfurled as she straightened. "Is Eleanor a queen?"

"Two times over."

"You take my meaning then."

Ivy laughed. Her anticipation grew, though she knew the reprobate Roger Stancliff couldn't touch the man she'd met in the bower. But if Katherine thought him that handsome…

"Do you admire him as a potential suitor?"

Gasping in mock horror, Katherine swatted Ivy lightly on the shoulder. "My father told my sister he would disown her if she so much as smiled at Stancliff last summer." Fluffing her silk veils, Katherine feigned indifference. "He is certainly not for me."

Ivy saw right through the act. "But you will smile at him anyway if given half the chance."

"Wait until you see him, and you will know why." Dropping her detached façade, Katherine squeezed Ivy's forearm. As two of the few unwed women at court, Katherine and Ivy had often discussed the merits of various men at Poitiers, debating their perspectives on what made the ideal courtly lover. And while they always weighed a man's intellect and deference to women in their accounting, even the most discriminating woman could not help but note a man's aspect.

A cry went up outside the hall, and Katherine released Ivy to peer toward the doors. Ivy had never seen such a frenzy, though she had once watched a pilgrim cavalcade carry a sliver of the True Cross back from the Holy Land and cause quite a stir. Maids and servers, peddler women and wet nurses from throughout the castle thronged around the man who attempted to shove through the doorway.

With a jaunty nod to his low-born admirers and a full-fledged bow to the noble ladies of the court, the Earl of Stancliff stepped into the room.

Ivy did not realize her mouth had fallen open until Katherine gently cupped her friend's chin to close it.

Roger Stancliff, the most notorious womanizer in Christendom, had heart-stopping silver eyes.

"I cannot believe it." Betrayal slammed Ivy in the belly. The knave had been toying with her yesterday. And she had fallen for him without so much as a blink.

"Did I not tell you?" Katherine giggled, unaware of her friend's anguish.

The pang in Ivy's heart radiated through her body until she became one pulsing ache of anger, embarrassment and disappointment. Her eyes burned, but she would not allow herself to grieve a lesson well-learned. Better that she discovered Stancliff's nature now, before she pinned any more romantic yearnings on a man who did not deserve them.

He hadn't seen her, at least. Sir Roger seemed too preoccupied with a bevy of admirers to notice Ivy Rutherford off to one side. As handsome as she remembered, he looked more colorful and animated today, having traded yesterday's subdued black silks for rich burgundy. He still wore a silver medallion, only now the chain that held it also secured a formal surcoat over his tunic. The subtle differences rendered him far less approachable and infinitely more high ranking than he had appeared the previous day.

Heavy eyebrows animated his countenance—lifting in wry humor one moment, furrowing in concentration the next as he listened to the whispered words of one eager woman or another.

Ivy's dreams—her own dreams and not her father's—of being courted by a chivalrous gentleman disintegrated in a heartbeat. Not only was Roger Stancliff too far above her station in life, he was also a renowned knave. Any sympathy she might have felt for his plight at court vanished along with her romantic fantasies.

She hoped Gertrude unleashed her nasty beast of a dog on him.

"Back to your duties, girls." Queen Eleanor's

words resounded outside the doors as she chastised the flock of gathered women. Breezing into the hall, the queen nodded curtly to the newcomer before taking her seat.

Thrusting all thought of Stancliff and her lost dreams aside, Ivy concentrated on Eleanor. Although Ivy's romantic notions might be crushed, she would at least derive some enjoyment from watching her idol in action.

After clearing her throat, the queen glanced at Lord Stancliff and then focused upon her daughter. "And who do we have before us today, Marie?"

The queen had deliberately slighted him.

Good for her.

Yet Stancliff grinned. Perhaps he had no idea he stood at the mouth of the lions' den.

Marie gave her mother a reproving look, but her tone remained deferential. "Lord Stancliff, Your Majesty, who is newly arrived from England."

"You have left my husband's court in England to join mine?" The queen studied the man, as if she had never seen him before. As if she hadn't gossiped about him just yesterday. Arching an eyebrow in his direction, Eleanor leaned forward in her chair.

Bowing before speaking, Stancliff seemed to know all the rules of etiquette despite his scandalous reputation.

"King Henry's court has deteriorated in your absence, Your Majesty. I come seeking diversion and entertainment, for which the Court of Love is notorious."

"As well as its ladies," the queen replied, gesturing to the overwhelmingly female populace.

Stancliff grinned. "Another commodity I have been known to appreciate, Your Majesty."

Ivy winced. The lout.

How could she have ever thought him the epitome of knightly chivalry? She turned to Eleanor to see if the queen would condone such behavior. With immense satisfaction, Ivy observed a storm cloud settle on the royal countenance.

"We are not chattel at Poitiers, Stancliff, and I defy any man to say otherwise at my court."

"Precisely, Your Majesty." The man on the stand shook his head with remorse that might have appeared sincere had Ivy not spied the dimple that flashed in his cheek. "That is my other reason for following you to France."

Just what was he about? Did he think it a grand game?

"To insult me and my good ladies?" the queen prompted.

"Nay, Your Majesty. I seek the court's guidance to become a better man. A chivalrous gentleman, in fact." His grin probably set every female heart aflutter. Stancliff was absurdly handsome. "All of Christendom whispers that your refined ladies specialize in just that sort of thing."

A muted roar rose from the benches as the women

muttered mixed reactions—some flattered to learn of their court's fame, others annoyed at Stancliff's audacity.

Katherine nudged Ivy. "Roger Stancliff, a gentleman?" She sounded almost disappointed.

"Perhaps your father would find him suitable then," Ivy whispered back.

Katherine snorted.

"Ladies, please." The queen's raised voice brought immediate silence. She turned toward Stancliff. "Are you suggesting we teach you the art of courtly love?"

"That is what you are noted for, is it not?"

Marie looked to her mother for permission to speak. At the queen's nod, the comtesse stood. "We are noted for our discussions and debates about the nature of courtly love, sir. We have not necessarily taught it as an art form before."

"Then I hope you will decide to put your theories to the test." Stancliff rocked back on his heels, the picture of masculine arrogance.

Ha. The man was beyond help. A courtly hero he would never be.

"Such a project as your education would be a full-time effort, sir." Queen Eleanor shook her head, causing her sapphire-covered crown to shoot refracted beams of blue light about the hall. "The Court of Love could not focus all of its efforts on you."

"A skilled tutor perhaps," Comtesse Marie ventured, blushing ever so slightly.

Lady Gertrude stirred, bumping the women on either side of her pillow with generous hips as she wriggled. "Any tutor we give him would only be seduced within the sennight, Your Majesty. A man of his reputation would corrupt the woman in no time."

Ivy flushed, thinking how easily she could have been the corrupted woman. She would have been thrown out of court. Her father would have been devastated if she had been sent home in disgrace. She would never be able to repay him for his generosity in sending her to court if her honor was compromised. Glancing toward the queen Ivy was surprised to see a look of deep contemplation on her sovereign's face.

"Unless…" The queen peered around the hall.

Marie sat up straighter in her seat.

Roger Stancliff cocked a lazy eyebrow.

Ivy was memorizing every detail of the scene, eager to commit it to parchment, when Queen Eleanor's roving gaze stopped on her.

Merchant's daughter Ivy Rutherford, lurking in the shadows with her quill.

Silence reigned as queen and troubadour stared at one another. All eyes turned to them. With dawning realization, Ivy caught her breath.

No.

A triumphant glow lit Eleanor's features. "Unless someone like young Ivy Rutherford were to serve as his tutor."

Mon dieu. How could she? Ivy's heart sank to her feet while all the heat in her body raced to her cheeks.

Why would the queen do this to her? Were her poems that bad?

Lady Gertrude spluttered. Katherine de Blois gasped.

"Me?" Ivy squeaked the question past stone-dry lips.

Marie de Champagne clapped her hands together. "A virgin!"

Ivy's mortification now complete, she prayed for a hole to open beneath her feet and the ground to swallow her up.

Queen Eleanor nodded. "Even Lord Stancliff poses less of a threat to such an innocent. Not even he would be so brazen as to steal a young woman's first time, since he knows well the condemnation he would face from the whole court."

For an instant, Ivy's eyes met Stancliff's. An expression of mild horror furrowed his face. Though he quickly schooled his features into a semblance of good humor, he evidently thought the situation as much of a punishment as she did.

Humiliated by the frank discussion, Ivy turned her gaze to the queen, longing to see a change of heart.

"But she is a merchant's daughter," Lady Gertrude complained, her whine slicing through Ivy's already frayed nerves.

Unfazed by the hubbub around her, the queen rose from her throne and walked toward Ivy. Eleanor extended her hand to her troubadour, a look of satisfaction upon her face. "Which means I will not have to worry about an overprotective papa lamenting that I have entrusted his coddled little girl to the clutches of a notorious heartbreaker, will I? Besides, her mother outranked even you, Gertrude. Let us not forget that."

Too disillusioned with the monarch she had admired so much, Ivy could not even enjoy the vindication of her mother. Ivy dutifully took the queen's hand, allowing Eleanor to lead her where she might. The great hall became a blur of curious feminine faces on one side and *his* on the other.

Dear God.

Drawing Ivy across the hall and toward the dais, Queen Eleanor spoke sharply to Stancliff. "Even so, I want your word that you will not disgrace this innocent girl, Stancliff."

Everyone in the hall gasped. The queen could not have insulted him more if she had slapped him.

"Of course, Your Majesty, you have my vow."

Surprised at the cool tone of Stancliff's voice, Ivy braved a glance at him. He stood a few hand spans from her, all trace of the dimple vanished as his jaw flexed with tension.

The queen laughed as if she played a great jest. Which, in fact, she probably had.

"Then that settles our business for today, ladies and gentlemen," she announced, prodding Ivy to stand closer to the dark-haired Titan on her left. Ivy stumbled until he caught her elbow, his touch inciting an unwelcome warmth all over her skin.

"I do not bite, I swear it," he whispered, a devilish glint in his gaze making her question the truth of the statement.

Was it only yesterday she had clutched his arm with such fervor, her heart on her sleeve for him to crush with one heavy boot? Her foolishness flashed in her memory with embarrassing vividness.

He would pay for humiliating her.

Eleanor swept her arm toward the couple at the head of the hall. "Our own Ivy Rutherford will undertake to transform the wayward Lord Stancliff into the epitome of courtly knighthood."

When dragons are lapdogs.

Ivy fumed while she numbly accepted the well wishes of the court members on their way out of the hall.

Stancliff seemed to have recovered from his initial annoyance. He shook hands and kissed cheeks as various female acquaintances greeted him, handsome and courteous as ever.

The fraud.

His attempts at chivalry were a lost cause in Ivy's eyes. The fact that he had not even come before Eleanor's court with a sincere heart made his request for a courtly education all the more ludicrous. How could the queen have believed his request?

Usually slow to anger, Ivy had exceeded her personal boiling point this afternoon. Of course, getting mad wouldn't solve anything. She knew that firsthand from having witnessed too many arguments in her parents' home as a child.

There must be an intelligent way to exact an ounce of revenge on Roger Stancliff for his careless attempt to turn her head, to crush her foolish notions of romance with his cavalier approach to love. Although he might not have slighted her directly, she understood he'd tarnished many a maiden's reputation and broken plenty of tender hearts.

Vowing to teach the scoundrel a thing or two, Ivy lifted her chin and began to plot a tutoring strategy the earl would never forget.

Chapter Three

Amazed he had ever found court life remotely amusing, Roger Stancliff bowed politely to Queen Eleanor's hall of ladies despite the slow trickle of sweat that eased down his back.

These women could scare the wits from a man.

Why hadn't he ever noticed the bloodlust in their eyes before today? They were out to make his life miserable, to seek vengeance for any petty slight they had ever dreamed him guilty of, and he had just given them the perfect outlet for all their grievances. Last night his plan to throw himself on the court's mercy had seemed like an appropriate tactic for acceptance here. How could Eleanor be suspicious of a man who'd come for love lessons? Now, he realized how much more he'd be scrutinized with Ivy at his side.

Curse the king. This was all Henry's fault.

"You two will certainly need to become acquainted." Queen Eleanor leaned close, ignoring the curious stares of the court members filing out the doors. She looped a velvet-draped, protective arm around the troubadour who would be his tutor.

Lady Ivy, technically no lady at all as a merchant's daughter, stood with polite stiffness under Eleanor's show of affection. Although the young woman had managed to accept well wishes with diplomatic grace, her rigid grip on a small sheet of parchment conveyed her fear.

Poor Ivy.

His sense of honor moved him to address the queen. Clearing his throat, he spoke in the deferential tones long years of court attendance had pounded into him. "I do not complain on my own behalf, I assure you, Your Majesty, but this seems a cruel trick to play on a naive girl."

The girl in question and the queen straightened their shoulders in absurdly similar gestures. On second glance, Roger detected more than just fear in Ivy's rigid posture. The sweet flirt, who only yesterday had bubbled with delight at his interest in her poetry, now seemed to seethe with cold outrage.

At him? Or the queen?

"Ivy is stronger than she appears, Stancliff," Eleanor said, her tone conveying a clear note of warning. Her sapphire-encrusted crown looked heavy enough to break a normal woman's neck, yet Eleanor wore it with the grace of one long accustomed to her position. "And," the queen continued, winking at Roger, "she is in as much need of the education she will receive as the one she will bestow."

Ivy blanched, but her chin remained high. From the way the queen's embrace seemed to bolster her courage, Roger guessed Eleanor was not the target of the young woman's anger.

He was.

The idea intrigued him as much as it bothered him. He had thought of "Lady" Ivy repeatedly since meeting her yesterday afternoon. His shameless mind had schemed to somehow accept her flirtatious overtures without allowing the king to discover the lapse.

Obviously, that was no longer a possibility. Ivy's virginal status was well-known, so she certainly hadn't been making the advances his lustful mind had imagined yesterday.

The next few weeks in Ivy's company promised to be very interesting. Perhaps unraveling the mystery of her contrary behavior would make his spying assignment a shade more tolerable.

If it didn't torment him too much.

The queen glanced toward the remaining crowd in the hall, then turned back to Roger and Ivy. "You may conduct your daily lessons in my bower. It is quiet enough, yet permits the court to chaperone your activities. Perhaps they will even wish to contribute to your discussions."

"Very well." Roger itched to return to his rooms and throw off his practiced court façade for a few hours. His reputation weighed on him, demanded too much exertion. "Shall we say midmorning for this first meeting?"

Eleanor turned to Ivy, allowing her to decide. The girl blushed and nodded. "That would be acceptable."

"As long as you keep your word to me, Stancliff," Eleanor interjected, "I have every confidence that you and Ivy shall get on famously."

"Indeed we shall."

Roger bowed, wondering if the legendary queen had seen straight through him and partnered him with a woman outside Eleanor's inner circle in an effort to keep him at arm's length.

He departed as soon as he could, eager to withdraw from the oppressive atmosphere of the court.

Fleeing the keep, he shrugged off his restrictive formal mantle. Another warm day beckoned, and he greeted the queen's gardens with relief.

Escape.

Rolling his shoulders to ease the tension knotted in his back, he crossed the neatly maintained lawns to the private bower where he had met Ivy yesterday.

Where he would meet her every day.

Thick ropes of green vine encased the graceful framework of the arbor. Inside, the dense plants gave guests the illusion of privacy without really obscuring the view of passers-by. It would be a convenient place for curious court members to watch over his lessons, yet it was intimate enough to put him far too close to the tempting Lady Ivy. He sank onto one of the hardwood benches and recalled her words yesterday.

You must call me Ivy.

He hadn't understood her at the time, thinking she meant to allow him a familiarity by using her first name. *Idiot.* How could he have been so lack-witted?

Ivy was obviously at court because of her poetic talent and not by birthright. He had to admit he had never met such an articulate and unassuming merchant's daughter before. Most rich merchants who nursed noble hopes for their daughters trained them to be quite forthright with men. Many of them were happy to be accepted as a nobleman's mistress.

Not Ivy.

Her innocence was well-known here, yet the queen herself had commented that Ivy needed the type of education Roger could give her. Now what in Hades had that meant?

The pounding in his head doubled. Spying did not agree with him, and his assignment had only just begun. Soon, he would have to discover Queen Eleanor's most closely guarded secrets. How could he accomplish that when simply becoming a part of her court made him more tense than a stag in hunting season?

Restless, he stood. The outdoor air hadn't alleviated the tension wrought by the she-devils of the court. No wonder he was one of the few men at Poitiers. How many men could withstand their scrutiny?

Departing the bower for the stables, Roger hoped a ride might clear his head. He had one day to determine how to proceed with Ivy before their lessons began. Could he extract information about the Queen from his alliance with the prickly troubadour? If the outrage in her eyes earlier was any indication of her revised opinion of him, it might not be easy to wear down her defenses.

Somehow, he had to find a balance between the circumspect attitude that had won Ivy's admiration yesterday and the more rakish aspect the nobility had come to expect from him over the years. Too much of a departure from his notorious self might raise Eleanor's suspicions about his purpose.

He hastened his pace to the stables.

His plans taking shape in his head, he resolved to flirt with Ivy to a certain extent, so as to seem as if he really did need her instruction, but to keep his word to Eleanor about leaving her innocence intact.

Resisting Ivy would be a supreme test of will, but he intended to do just that. He *would* reform his ways.

The ache in his back climbed up past his neck to gnaw at the base of his skull. After plowing through the stable doors, he grabbed his horse and swung a leg over the animal's back.

For a few hours at least, he could escape the cursed spying mission. And the crafty queen who saw too much. And the innocent troubadour whose opinion of him could make or break the future of every Stancliff dependent.

* * *

With a vicious jab of a hairpin, Ivy rearranged her stubborn tresses for the fourth time.

It would be nice to look somewhat presentable today, when all of Eleanor's court would probably descend on the bower to watch the first day of "love lessons" in progress.

Although Ivy held no illusions that her limited attractiveness would make an expert like Roger Stancliff take notice, she wanted to at least appear neat and competent.

The court ladies had teased her mercilessly the previous night about her new position as tutor. Ivy knew they wouldn't miss a chance to watch the prim little tradesman's daughter fall under the spell of Stancliff's charm.

Little did they know she had already steeled herself against it. Having been taken in by his too-handsome appearance and charming manners before, Ivy would not be fooled again. Inside, the man must be cold as stone. No one with a pinch of sensitivity could break as many hearts as the earl's reputation suggested.

But his days of heartbreaking were over if Ivy had anything to say about it. She had devised a set of lessons—rules for love—that would limit his philandering, and she planned to share the plan with anyone and everyone at court so they would help her keep an eye on him.

It was no more than he deserved.

Tearing the pin out again, she tossed it on the wardrobe chest and rearranged the silver circlet and sheer white veils to encompass all of her hair. No matter how she pinned it, the silky strands slid from their confinement to frame her face.

So be it. The whole mess would have to remain as nature intended. Grabbing her scrolled notes for the day's lesson, Ivy hurried through the door.

And ran straight into Stancliff.

Hard.

"Oh." Dazed to meet him in the middle of the corridor, she dropped her parchment on the floor.

"I was just coming to escort you." He looked relaxed and amused, his garments as perfectly arranged as his straight white teeth.

Her face heated as he took in her appearance with slow consideration. Still flustered by her failed attempts at hairdressing and annoyed by his perusal, she frowned. "You didn't need to. I was just coming down."

"So I gathered." He stooped to collect her scroll, seemingly oblivious to his crimson silk tunic brushing the dusty floor. Handing her the fallen parchment, he straightened. "I thought I would take some initiative to become more chivalrous, however, by accompanying you." With a wink and a bow, he offered his arm.

Mon dieu, he possessed some expertise at this game. If Ivy hadn't known he had cultivated his charm with an eye toward seducing women, she would have been touched by his simple gallantry.

"Very well, then." Reluctantly, she accepted his arm.

They walked through the keep and out the northern doors together. Stancliff made polite conversation while she recalled how different it had been yesterday to stroll with him. Then, she had thought him the embodiment of her dreams. Today, she knew him to be the exact opposite of her fanciful notions of love and romance.

"Here we are." He stopped in front of the empty bower, staring at it with what seemed like a trace of the same trepidation that gnawed at Ivy. "Eleanor must have warned off observers for our first day," he remarked, glancing around the quiet lawns. "How shall we proceed from here, Mademoiselle Tutor?"

Extricating herself from his arm, she stepped through the grapevine-covered arches that provided the framework of the bower. She fiddled with her notes to avoid his gaze and took a seat on one of the wooden benches. Even without an audience, she still found the earl intimidating to be around, but she was determined not to let her discomfort show.

She imagined herself as Eleanor, imperious and unflappable. She could do this, curse his eyes. "Join me, sir, and I will try to teach you as the queen has bid me, whether we appreciate the situation or not."

"Eleanor has quite the sense of humor, doesn't she?" He ducked between the low-hanging arbor vines, sauntered toward her and then sat, leaving naught but a hand's span between them.

Sighing, Ivy moved to the bench across from him,

censuring him with a look. She agreed with his assessment of the queen but was unprepared to take his side regarding anything. "She is no doubt trying to do what is best for you."

He met her gaze. "And for you, if I recall her words."

Ouch. Ivy had gone over that aspect of Eleanor's speech time and time again. *She is in as much need of the education she will receive as the one she will bestow.* Ivy had rather hoped Stancliff had not heard that remark. "Yet you were the one who approached the court with the desire to learn."

"And I am certain you will fulfill my desire."

The words sent a wave of unwelcome heat through her. Apparently, he'd not yet made any real progress toward reforming himself if he could reel off suggestive comments so smoothly. "Then let us begin."

"As you wish, Lady Ivy."

She ground her teeth. "You now know, sir, that I am not entitled to be addressed as such."

"But I respect you as much and more than any noblewoman in my acquaintance." He leaned forward on his bench.

Ivy fought the urge to lean away from him. She refused to let him unnerve her any further.

"It is a title that suits you well," he continued, "and I think the queen must agree, to give you charge of such a reprobate as myself."

"Unless she meant to punish me in some way."

Stancliff stiffened.

Ivy experienced a moment of triumph at the flash of surprise in his eyes. She would not be trifled with again. Her method of retribution for his deceit when they first met would be slow and subtle, but she had no doubt it would be effective. She planned to hit Roger Stancliff where it would hurt him most.

His legendary libidinous urges.

"I think not, though it may seem like a punishment," Roger replied. He crossed formidable forearms over his chest, as if taking stock of her.

"I am sure we will manage, once we understand each other."

"Indeed." He nodded, as if conceding the point in their silent war of wills.

Good. Now she was ready to begin her campaign to tame him. Her mission to curb his lustful ways. Her crusade to reform him.

In other words, her lessons.

Affecting the no-nonsense posture of her intimidating dancing instructor Mistress Drusilla, Ivy straightened her spine and lifted her parchment notes. "I thought a logical place to begin would be for me to relate some of the qualities I think are essential in a chivalric man."

"You mean a courtly lover."

"I imagine they are much the same thing." She had used the phrase in poems before, to refer to people who were in love. Yet she knew he thought of the words in more earthy terms.

"I disagree, which is why I make the distinction."

He tapped one thoughtful, rhythmic finger against his lips. "It is not my role as a man that I am concerned with, but my role in relation to women…as a lover."

Her breath caught. He possessed a certain intensity—a power to make a woman feel like the only person in the world who mattered. His strength of personality filled the bower, while hers…

Damn the man.

She took a deep breath and closed her eyes. That always helped when her papa became too pushy.

"Let us dispense with issues of terminology for at least today, my lord, so that we might make some headway. I'm sure we will develop a greater level of comfort with this as we progress, but let us focus on getting through this first day, shall we?"

"Of course, you are right. I am listening." Roger straightened, the barest hint of a smile playing on his lips.

"Excellent." Growing more eager to flay Roger Stancliff with her tutoring, Ivy launched her first weapon. "Lesson number one is to keep your distance from any woman who isn't your beloved."

"That doesn't eliminate very many." The slick smile he had flashed all over court yesterday resurfaced.

The knave.

"That in itself is a contemptible thing to admit, sir."

"A poor joke, Lady Ivy, and far from the truth." The grin vanished. "I apologize."

She stood, annoyed with her pupil and frustrated at the prospect of meeting him every day. The task would be less disagreeable if she hadn't had such stars in her eyes when she first met him. The memory embarrassed her. Looking at Stancliff meant facing up to her rampant fancifulness—the daydreaming quality her father condemned as useless and unbecoming in a lady.

How could she ever write affecting love poetry if she admitted that perhaps her father had been right in this much, at least?

"You think I am too forward with women?" The earl rallied from the bench behind her.

She made no reply as she peered out of the bower to the gardens. Slowly filling with nobles seeking the sun's warmth, the rolling lawns were the perfect place to spy courtly behavior in action as the queen's guests sought afternoon amusement. A couple strolled arm in arm. A band of five ladies whispered and pointed at various groups of people. Comtesse Marie laughed at something Lady Katherine had just said.

She would not fail in her duty to teach Roger Stancliff the art of chivalric romance, because she refused to leave behind the most elegant and refined court in Europe. She'd worked so hard for her place here, honing her craft as a wordsmith with endless drafts of poems. And now that she'd secured her spot, no number of snide remarks from Gertrude or suggestive comments from Stancliff would deprive her of her dreams.

Ivy considered how to make her lesson understood.

"You've a habit of making casual contact with nearly every woman who passes you," she said, finally.

"I do?" He sounded surprised.

Ivy left the arbor archway and sat across from him. "After the Court of Love proceedings yesterday, you clasped hands with most women when a bow would have been sufficient for all but the closest of acquaintances."

"I guess you are right." His forehead furrowed.

"And you sat much too near me today when you came into the bower."

He cast a sly glance in her direction. "I thought to win over the teacher."

"There is no need to come in such intimate contact with any lady who is not the woman of your heart. It shows more respect to give a woman some space." She plucked at the pattern of embroidered greenery on her yellow surcoat. "And keeping your distance avoids raising a lady's hopes that you might be interested in her."

His gaze flew to her face. Ivy's words echoed in the air between them as he stared at her with questioning eyes. The heat of embarrassment threatened, so she peered out of the bower again. It seemed an auspicious time to change the subject.

"That having been said, perhaps I may illustrate a few things using the couples walking along the path."

Ivy pointed to an isolated section of the grounds. Romantic and tree-lined, the nearby path was an escape for courting couples—still within view but considerably quieter than the rest of the gardens.

Stancliff joined her on the bench that faced the path, though Ivy noticed he kept a respectable distance between them. Of course it wasn't far enough to keep Ivy from sensing the allure of the man. The warmth of his presence, the scent of sandalwood, made her very aware of his nearness.

"Do you note the room Lord Maven allows between himself and Lady Helen?" She pointed to a strolling pair, both widowers.

"He is just waiting to get her behind the next tree," Roger observed. "I'll bet he picks that fat oak."

"Not Lady Helen." Apparently Stancliff imagined the rest of the world to be as immoral as he. "Honestly, I can't imagine why you would think—"

Once behind the tree, the couple did not emerge.

Ivy waited. "Perhaps Lady Helen tripped and has hurt herself—"

"By all means, let us wait for them to emerge." His smirk was evident even in his voice.

"Maybe we should seek other examples, then." Ivy searched the gardens for a man and woman she knew without doubt abided by the rules of courtly love. "Over there." She pointed to a couple walking toward each other from opposite ends of the lawn. "Lord Barrington and Lady Anna."

She sneaked a glance at Stancliff's profile as he watched the scene unfold. His chin rested in the crook of his elbow, propped by the low wooden wall that encircled the western portion of the bower. As always, he looked at ease, a natural part of the glittering world Ivy would never truly belong to.

"Barrington has quite an eye for Anna," Roger noted, a hint of amused warning in his voice. "They may not be as circumspect with one another as you think."

Confident in Anna's adherence to social rules, Ivy ignored his comment and watched the pair meet in the middle of the spring grass.

Barrington bowed low, then took Anna's hand. With gentle reverence, he lifted it to his lips for a kiss before escorting her about the lawn. Yet he did not touch her again as they promenaded about, walking beside her with companionable respect.

"You see?" Ivy turned to her companion, unable to suppress the victorious note in her voice.

"Oh, I saw, all right." Stancliff quirked a cynical brow. "I just wonder if we noticed the same things."

"What was there to notice but the polite, restrained regard of a man for a woman?" How dare he try to see something sordid in that lovely exchange? It was just the sort of scene Ivy might choose for a poetic image.

"Did you even note the kiss?" He edged closer to her. Not enough to break the rule she had imparted today, but enough to make her think quite suddenly what it would be like to exchange a kiss with him, to be the object of warm regard for him. She shivered pleasantly at the notion.

"Perfectly chaste and completely appropriate."

His eyes widened. "Did you note *where* he placed that kiss? Or *how* he placed it?"

Ivy struggled to comprehend his meaning. What was there to miss? "He kissed her hand. Of course I noticed."

"And you thought the kiss chaste?"

This conversation served no purpose that Ivy could discern. She would not be intimidated by Roger Stancliff. She had observed the tableau with her own eyes. "Positively."

"Then it would be admissible for me to kiss another woman in that fashion?" A triumphant gleam lit his gaze.

Warning bells tolled in her head, but she couldn't think how to abandon the discussion without losing credibility. She had no choice but to defend her position.

"I don't see why not. It is a common enough way to receive a lady."

"But I sense undercurrents in that greeting that may have escaped the naive eye. Allow me to show you what *I* saw in that greeting, Lady Ivy." He reached for her hand. "Or, at least, what I suspect happened."

"As you wish." Her heart raced. Nervous flutters worried her stomach. But she couldn't back down now. How could she maintain integrity as a teacher if she did?

With the same tender care she remembered Lord Barrington demonstrating, Roger enveloped her hand in his. The gesture proved much more intimate to experience than to observe. His fingers ran a soft, sensuous pattern over hers, imprinting their warm texture on her skin and in her memory.

The earl's gaze absorbed hers, increasing the jerky rhythm of her pulse. He leaned over their joined hands.

Ivy held her breath. Braced herself against the temptation of his touch.

Just before his lips met the back of her fingers, he turned her hand over, and placed his kiss in the sensitive flesh of her palm.

Startled, she could only stare down at the black sheen of his hair in the bright spring sunlight. Barrington had surely not done that. Yet Stancliff saved the biggest surprise for the next moment, when his tongue snaked out to caress her flesh in swift, charged contact.

The whole of her being seemed to contract and concentrate into that one small space of skin where her nerve endings sang with awakened vitality for a singular moment. Surely this feeling was special, unique.

Her breath released on a gasping little sigh at about the same moment he grinned.

His words silenced the sweet croon of her senses.

"I think that was enough of a first lesson for both of us, Lady Ivy."

Chapter Four

I have heard no whispers of plots against Your Majesty, only plots against men in general. The women here are outspoken and bold with the queen's blessing, but they spend far more time debating the merits of one kind of poetry over another than they do discussing political affairs. At least as far as I have been able to discern—

Roger tossed his quill aside and watched it skitter across the stone table before floating to the floor of his solar in the sprawling household of Poitiers. Unable to focus on his first missive to the king, he found his memory turning to disillusioned green eyes, reminding him what a miscreant he had been.

What had possessed him to kiss Ivy Rutherford with such blatant disregard for his mission? The king had instructed him to mend his wayward ways. And damn it, he really wanted to. Yet he had been powerless to stop himself from tasting the soft flesh of Ivy's palm when she naively presented him with the opportunity.

He lifted a heavy chalice of mulled wine and took a long drink. Staring down at the parchment in the flickering torchlight, he wondered if he could be slipping back into old habits.

He had no excuse now. He had recovered from the numbing grief and anger that had driven him to dally with many an eager woman. In the wake of his betrothed's death he had been inconsolable, his certainty that he could have prevented her death by marrying her sooner rendering him sleepless and guilt-ridden. But then, when the rumors of her condition had surfaced…

Had Ivy heard those rumors? Would she shun him completely once she knew? He held no illusions that her peers would protect her from the truth—or, at least, the truth as they knew it. Gossip abounded in any court and this one most especially, given Eleanor's preference for conversation and entertaining.

Of course, it hadn't helped that Roger had done nothing to deny the ugly whispers about his relationship with his betrothed. If anything, by immersing himself in a continuous drunken revel, he'd only solidified the commonly held view of his character.

His impropriety had enraged both his king and his fiancée's father, William Montcalm. But Roger was not the same reckless man he'd once been. Alice's death had filled him with regrets, and the events that had unfolded in its aftermath had taught him the high price of indulging his own wants. Why then, should he find it so damn difficult to walk away from the temptation of Ivy? He should have been quizzing her about court gossip—the kind that didn't involve him—instead of indulging a personal interest.

Slamming the chalice on to the table with undue force, he splashed a bit of wine on the parchment. In his frenzy of sopping and cursing, he did not notice the door to his chamber open until he heard someone clear his throat behind him.

"Pardon, my lord, but are you that unwilling to abide a guest?" A tall, fair-haired stranger stood in the entryway as Roger's most recent oath waned in the air between them.

The newcomer was immaculately dressed in the quiet colors of a mere knight—dark blue, a bit of silver trim. His posture was unassuming, but the sword at his side resided in easy reach and his burly physique suggested he'd grown well accustomed to using the weapon. He looked to be a few years older than Roger. As he peered about the chamber with assessing eyes, his squire stood beside him, weighed down by several bags.

Roger swiped the remaining spots of wine from his missive before shuffling another piece of vellum on top of it. "The curses were not intended for you, I assure you." It wouldn't do to raise the man's suspicions, even if he'd been rude enough to enter without knocking. "Did you wish to see me?"

The stranger laughed as he directed his squire to set down the bags. "No more than you wish to see me, I'll warrant, but according to our good queen we have no choice but to share these accommodations. She had Lady Gertrude show me the room earlier today. She said you were out. Learning a lesson, I believe."

"Of course. I'm Roger Stancliff." Roger swallowed to tamp down a sudden bout of queasiness. How could he conduct secret business with the king when he had to share his chamber? Did the queen suspect his motives? Striding forward to greet his guest, he told himself he would have to be all the more discreet.

"James Forrester. A pleasure to meet you, my lord." They clasped hands briefly before James peered across the chamber to where Roger had been sitting. "I apologize if I have caught you at a bad time—"

"Nay," he protested, all the more suspicious that Eleanor had sent this man to keep an eye on him. Certainly there were other rooms available at Poitiers. "Lady Gertrude must have shown you the other bedchamber attached to this solar. It is a family suite, I suppose."

"Aye." After pointing the squire and the bags toward the bedchamber, James wandered about the solar they would share.

Roger itched to run to the table and yank away his parchment papers from potential prying eyes, but resisted the urge.

James paused before the painting that dominated

one wall of the chamber and appeared to study the detailed hunting scene. "You are being tutored by Mistress Ivy, I hear."

"Lady Ivy," he corrected without thinking. But then, what harm did he do to bolster Ivy's status with his show of respect? Not that his name for her would change anyone's opinion about a merchant's daughter, but the title suited her perfectly. He'd never encountered a woman so concerned with propriety. Indeed, he knew many well-bred ladies who cared naught for decorum, a thought that still had the power to anger him even after all this time.

"She indeed seems all that a lady should be," James agreed, running a finger over the vivid colors of the painting, as if to test their freshness. Roger had done the same thing himself when he first arrived. "I met her briefly this afternoon and I must say I was rather enamored. It is not often one meets a young woman so self-possessed yet utterly modest."

"Really?" Roger ground his teeth. "I found her a bit too rigid."

"Ah." James met his gaze and seemed to study him for a moment before ambling away from the painting toward his chamber door. "Then it is a good thing we will not be vying for the same woman's affections, I suppose." He flashed Roger an amiable grin. "Refined as she is, 'Lady' Ivy is still closer to my rank as a lowly knight." He bowed to Roger. "I'm sure I will see you later. I hear the Court of Love is to entertain questions from courtiers after the supper."

The newcomer closed the door between them, leaving Roger to plot ways to keep Ivy's virtue safe from the obvious knave who now shared his solar.

The scoundrel. Who did he think he was, spouting Ivy's virtues in company like that? All of Poitiers would be abuzz with gossip if the dolt continued to spew such lovesick drivel about her.

He must warn his comely tutor to be careful around such men. Ivy and her romantic fantasies would probably be beguiled by James Forrester in a trice unless Roger intervened.

Which he would, by God.

Congratulating himself on his new, nobler duty where Ivy was concerned, Roger collected his quill and missive and hastened to dress for the meal. He needed to arrive in the hall before James so he could secure a place near Ivy.

And although an emotion oddly akin to anticipation filled him for the first time in years, he assured himself his eager pace was merely the result of an unselfish desire to protect an innocent.

He had robbed her of her innocence.

Ivy sat alone in the great hall before supper and fumed as she stared down at her blank parchment, unable to fill it with pretty words or romantic speeches. With one molten kiss of his lips, the infamous Roger Stancliff had divested her of her naive notions of love.

Cursed reprobate.

Why did he have to touch her, taste her? His kiss had not only awakened a wellspring of desire she had not known she possessed, but it had spoiled her pristine idea of what lovers shared. She had believed romance was a pleasant, but ultimately benign condition—something noble that would bind a woman and man in a relationship of unswerving loyalty.

But Roger's kiss had wreaked havoc with her tame vision. Ivy now understood more clearly that romance led to passion, which was obviously not a civilized emotion at all. The ardor that Roger had inspired in her left her with a gnawing ache for more and a liberal dose of shame for her wanton thoughts.

She didn't even *like* Stancliff, after all.

As the great hall began to fill with guests of the court, Lady Katherine's voice filtered through Ivy's recriminations.

"Your muse seems to have deserted you, Ivy." Katherine nodded toward the blank parchment as she slid into the seat beside her at a long trestle table. "I cannot recall a time when I have discovered you without your quill in motion."

Looking up from her frustrated creative efforts, Ivy realized the hall was now quite full. A laverer already scurried from table to table, offering water for washing before the servers began their rounds.

"It is a long story—" Ivy's words lodged in her throat as she spied Stancliff, thief of her romantic dreams.

He breezed past the other trestle tables, ignoring

several women who vied for his attention. His hurried pace and steady gaze seemed to indicate he was intent upon reaching her side.

"Good evening, Lady Katherine. Lady Ivy." He bowed formally to them both, but his attention never strayed long from Ivy. He gestured to the bench near her. "May I avail myself of your company this eve, my lady?"

She nodded, wordless, and watched him take his seat on her other side.

His interest unsettled her. Why was he not flirting with every other woman in attendance? Apparently other people wondered the same thing, as their meeting attracted notice from all sides of the hall.

Undaunted, Katherine greeted him with her usual aplomb. "Good evening, my lord. I trust your day's lesson was enlightening?"

Leave it to her outspoken friend to drive to the heart of the matter. Ivy had a sudden urge to scribble marginalia on her blank parchment—or to do anything else that would rescue her from this conversation.

"Actually, I sat beside my instructor this eve so that I might show her how well I have learned it," Roger responded. He leaned forward to converse with Katherine, but did not crowd Ivy in the process. No doubt that was the lesson he thought to exemplify.

Katherine nudged Ivy beneath the table as she smiled at Roger. "I will wager Lady Ivy is not easily impressed."

"I have no doubt that you are right, but I am determined to win her favor."

Ivy struggled to find words that would divert attention from herself and was saved by a pleasing masculine voice.

"Might I join you, ladies? My lord?" Sir James Forrester bowed before them. A handsome man with wavy fair hair and dark brown eyes, Forrester had dressed immaculately in a white tunic and blue silk surcoat. A colorful heraldic device bearing a lion was embroidered into the indigo fabric.

Ivy had met him that afternoon and liked him immediately. He did not put her on edge the way Roger could with one smoldering glance or one brush of his hand along her arm.

"Of course. We would be pleased for your company." She gestured to the seat on the other side of Katherine before she noticed her friend looked less than pleased to have the newcomer join them. The notion puzzled Ivy, as Katherine always seemed to enjoy new faces and conversations.

Forrester bowed again. "If it pleases Lady Katherine?"

Ivy observed the interchange with interest. For a long moment, the two of them seemed to take one another's measure. Finally, Katherine nodded, but said nothing to reassure the man.

She prepared to launch into a discussion with James to conceal her friend's unusually cool behavior when Roger's fingers claimed her hand and speech became impossible. Heat streaked through her, reminding her just how potent his kiss had been earlier that day. James and Katherine forgotten, Ivy turned toward the source of that heat.

"I thought you were taking your lesson to heart and allowing women some distance, my lord?" She strove for just the right note of detachment as she met his silver gaze.

A smile twitched his perfect lips as his hand fell away from hers. "Aye. But I sought to seize your attention on behalf of the laverer." He nodded toward the young serving girl who carried a carved aquamanile for pouring water and a small bucket.

Embarrassed, Ivy submitted her hands for washing. She stared down at the water sluicing over her fingers to avoid Roger's amused expression, until she noted the aquamanile was carved in the shape of a disrobed woman riding on an equally unclad man's back.

Why did her whole social life have to be a series of one awkward moment after another? At least her father was not present to urge Ivy to wave her jewel collection beneath Roger's nose in an attempt to display her material worth. For that, she was grateful.

Roger's voice threaded through her discomfiture. "It seems Eleanor is quite fond of amorous themes in her decorating. But then I don't suppose they call this the Court of Love for naught."

"The longer I stay, the more I wonder if it is not misnamed. It seems they would have been more accurate in designating it the Court of Lasciviousness or perhaps the Court of Licentiousness." She dried her hands on the laverer's linen before turning to face Roger.

His grin displayed none of the deliberate charm he seemed to don for his court appearances. Instead, his smile appeared spontaneous. "The Court of Lewdness and Lechery, mayhap? Or perhaps the most precise of all—the Court of Lust?"

Ivy smothered a laugh. "You must admit it is unusual to find as many statues and paintings of unclothed people as at Poitiers."

"Perhaps I am accustomed to a different sort of company than you, because I don't find it at all peculiar." He accepted a trencher from the server, then carefully moved Ivy's parchment aside before situating the bread between them. "Poitiers might be different only because here it is a woman who accumulates such art, whereas in my experience it is usually men who gravitate toward depictions of nude figures."

Their conversation was wholly inappropriate, yet she did not let the topic unsettle her. Perhaps she'd grown more accustomed to Roger's manner. Besides, although they might make light of the court's earthy side, Ivy fully appreciated that Eleanor's court was a creative wellspring for the many poets, artists and musicians she'd met while in residence.

The meal passed pleasantly enough once she steered the conversation away from nudity, although Ivy remained aware of the silence between Lady Katherine and Sir James. Yet every time she thought to intervene, Roger claimed her attention with a comment.

James Forrester leaned forward to speak to Ivy as the servants cleared the trestle tables and moved the furnishings to accommodate the court assembly. "Will you be entertaining us with a poetic reading tonight, my lady?"

Ivy marveled that all of Poitiers seemed to follow Roger's directive and refer to her as "lady." Even Katherine had adopted the title. Ivy's father would be overjoyed. "Nay. Her Majesty has extended me a creative reprieve while I tend to Lord Stancliff's education."

"And her own," Roger added, rising to his feet. "Shall we sit closer to the dais?" He offered her his arm.

Did she imagine it or did he seem eager to draw her away?

Katherine hastened to stand. "Ivy, would you attend me first?" Perhaps seeing her confusion, she added, "For but a moment?"

"Of course." Ivy read the command in her friend's gaze. Clearly something was amiss.

The words had scarcely tumbled from her lips when Katherine yanked her away, pulling her across the hall and into the corridor.

"Pray, do not leave me with him," she whispered once they reached a corner of relative privacy.

"Leave you with whom?" Ivy had never seen her spirited friend so distraught. While Ivy could shed tears at the slightest instigation, Katherine had always seemed unflappable.

"James Forrester." Katherine seized Ivy's forearms. "By the saints, could you not tell I do not like him?" Her voice held a note of desperation.

"How could you not like such a perfectly agreeable man?" James Forrester put Ivy more at ease than any of the other court *chevaliers*. He was unassuming and humble. And while he looked strong enough, his manner remained gentle. Deferential.

"If you like him so well, *you* sit beside him." Katherine released Ivy's arms before stalking back into the hall in the opposite direction of Sir James.

A bell tolled to indicate the beginning of the proceedings, preventing Ivy from pursuing the matter. Decorum told her she should reclaim her seat beside Roger and James, but the notion intimidated her. She found an unobtrusive place behind the queen and settled in to watch the events.

As Marie, Comtesse de Champagne, and the queen exchanged formal pleasantries, Ivy cursed her lack of parchment. She had left her quill and vellum behind when Katherine had whisked her away. Now she would have to rely on her memory alone to capture the details.

Marie's words snagged Ivy's attention away from parchment worries. "…And tonight Sir James Forrester seeks the court's opinions, Your Majesty."

What question could Sir James possibly have? He appeared to be the consummate chivalric gentleman. He was nothing like Roger, whose court appearance had set noble jaws flapping days before he arrived.

She watched as James stood and bowed—both formally and a bit awkwardly—to parties on all sides. Ivy sought out Kathcrinc to gaugc hcr rcaction to Sir James. Would she march out of the hall?

"'Tis a small matter, really," Sir James began. His wavy fair hair fell over his forehead in slight disarray.

Ivy finally spied Katherine among the assembled guests. Her friend gazed up at Sir James with an expression far from dislike. In fact, the unflappable Katherine looked almost...dreamy.

"I wonder what the court's position would be on loving beyond class barriers, Your Majesty?" James continued.

At once, Katherine's features lost their wistful softness. Ivy could practically feel her friend's consternation from across the hall.

Katherine might not have been pleased by the subject matter, but James had Ivy's complete attention. The notion of love beyond social bounds had always pervaded her life. If her father had not wed a woman so far above his station, he would have saved his family immense heartache. But Ivy had been torn between two worlds from the day she was born—half her mother's daughter with a preference for all that was refined and elegant, and half her father's offspring, embracing hard work as a means to an end.

"It is only natural to admire someone in a more preeminent social class," Marie observed. "It is preferable, even, as it encourages the lower classes to adhere to the more civil conduct modeled by the nobility."

"It is to one's social edification," agreed the queen.

"But what of marriage?" queried Sir James.

The Court sputtered its collective dismay.

"A man should certainly try to obtain a woman with lands and title that will benefit him," Marie proffered. "But we do not usually concern ourselves with such mundane matters as marriage in the Court of Love. We have made clear in other discussions that marriage and love do not coincide."

"But you would agree that a man may love a woman above him," James continued, leaning forward. "And can even try to wed her?"

"I disagree." Roger stood as he delivered his dissension.

Ivy stiffened. But then it made sense Roger would not think there should be love outside class barriers. He would not want his lofty peers snatched by upstarts like lowly Sir James.

Like *her*.

"And why is that, Lord Stancliff?" the queen asked in acerbic tones as James returned to his seat. Usually the court discourse was conducted solely by women.

"If a man has no need of a woman's illustrious title or dowry, he should love beneath him."

The Court attendees erupted. Ivy felt her jaw go slack. Was he joking? She refused to notice the little thrill that shot through her at his scandalous declaration. Surely his words were part of some plot to catch her off guard?

"What you say is practically treasonous to the

noble way of life, as you no doubt realize," the queen interjected, quieting the rumbling crowd. "Would you care to substantiate your views, or would you like to safeguard your rebellious hide and recant the statement?"

Ivy held her breath. Would he disavow the sentiment that had made her heart race?

"I would support my claim, Your Majesty." He continued despite the wave of muttering in the hall. "A man who has no need of the money or title would be better served wedding a strong woman of a lower class, thereby strengthening his family line."

"You mean a laborer?" Marie sounded horrified.

Ivy envisioned Roger's wife with bulging arms and thighs the size of tree trunks. The notion brought an irreverent grin to her lips.

"Nay, merely an independent woman who is accustomed to doing a few tasks for herself, such as a lower-ranking noblewoman or a refined merchant's daughter."

She clamped a hand over her mouth to hide her gasp. A merchant's daughter. What game did he play? Indignant protests resounded until the timbered rafters fairly trembled with the crowd's outrage.

"As usual, you cause a ruckus, sir," Queen Eleanor interjected, quieting the assembly.

"My apologies." Roger bowed deeply. "It has been my experience that some noblewomen are so gently bred that they falter at life's least obstacle. Unlike Your Majesty, of course, who was raised in the most refined of environments, yet cultivated an inner strength that is exemplary to men and women alike."

Eleanor laughed. "You are wicked indeed, Sir Roger. You effectively insult my entire court, but carefully flatter your queen. Tonight I am amused." She leveled her gaze, all trace of humor fleeing her angular features. "But do not attempt such insurrection again. And, Sir James, I do not think it would be remiss for a man of lower station to attempt to wed above him, but it seems a foolhardy pursuit if the woman's father has any sense."

The Comtesse de Champagne rose to deliver some final remarks, but Ivy scarcely heard. Her poet's mind had embarked on a fanciful journey, imagining all the scenarios that might have made Roger so embittered about the women of his class. His demeanor this eve differed vastly from that of the slick courtier she had glimpsed at his last Court appearance. Which man was real? The resentful speaker who enraged the crowd or the silver-tongued gallant who could charm away any maiden's good sense?

While the rest of the court found their quarters, grumbling all the way about Lord Stancliff's outrageous remarks, Ivy vowed she would find out.

When she plotted her lesson for their next bower meeting, Ivy determined to put that question at the top of her list. The earl would not hide behind his smooth manners any longer.

Chapter Five

❧〜✦〜❧

The vultures were out in force.

Ivy hid in the shadows of a nearby copse as she observed Gertrude and her cronies arrange themselves in comfortable positions around the bower. Although Ivy had schemed to conduct today's lesson early to avoid a crowd, apparently she had not scheduled it early enough.

Ladies Faith and Grace, both of whom suffered under the misguided notion that their virtuous names endowed them with those attributes, blocked the entry to the queen's private arbor. Lady Isabelle, a self-proclaimed expert on love who was rumored to have driven all three of her husbands to the grave, claimed a seat inside the bower and withdrew a distaff to occupy herself. She seemed to give Gertrude's dog a sharp poke in the ribs with her toe whenever the creature ventured too near. Smart woman.

For her part, Gertrude made no pretense of doing anything but waiting for Roger and Ivy as she peered about the grounds, arms folded across the straining seams of a rose-colored silk kirtle.

Ivy's hands fluttered restlessly over her skirts. For a woman who disliked controversy or public attention, she had certainly attracted enough of both since arriving at Poitiers. But she would not renounce her hope of being a celebrated poet. And if playing tutor to a shameless heartbreaker or facing down a bunch of heartless noblewomen were the only ways she could achieve her dream, then by the saints, she would do it.

Backbone steeled, Ivy stepped from the safety of the thicket and strolled toward the bower.

Gertrude straightened at her approach, as if preparing to do battle. "Good day, Mistress Ivy."

Ivy paused to curtsy. "Good day, Lady Gertrude. I hope your presence means you will be joining my discussion with Sir Roger today."

Perhaps drawn by the crackle of a storm brewing, Faith and Grace sidled over to flank their friend. Their nearly matching green kirtles complemented Gertrude's rose one so well the trio almost blended in with the rows of foxgloves behind them.

Grace sniffed her disdain, poking her patrician nose into the floral-scented air. "We could not afford to miss it, mistress. It seems you have already taught poor Lord Stancliff some most heretical notions of social order."

Poor Lord Stancliff? Ivy strained her lips into something she hoped resembled a smile. "On the contrary, it seems I have not been able to teach the earl anything thus far." Ivy still burned inside to think of all *she* had learned at their last lesson. Today, she would make certain he did not catch her off guard again.

Lady Faith waggled a chastising finger in front of Ivy's nose. "Come, mistress. Stancliff's proposal yesterday that a merchant's daughter could be the recipient of a nobleman's affection made it obvious you have been filling his head with an inflated sense of your worth."

Ivy fell back a step, reeling from the accusation as if she had been pushed. Did Lady Faith truly think as much? Or was she simply being cruel? All at once she realized her disadvantage at being born a tradesman's daughter went deeper than she'd ever suspected. No matter how broad her education or how extensive her wardrobe, Ivy did not have the experience to navigate complicated social terrain such as this.

Gertrude's eyes narrowed. "You realize, don't you my dear, that he only hopes to gain your bed—"

"Approval." Roger's voice boomed over Gertrude's. His appearance beside Ivy seemed to give the ladies a start. He grinned broadly. "I seek to gain Mistress Ivy's *approval* and the satisfaction of improving myself by learning the much-touted rules of chivalry."

Ivy's heart hammered in her chest, a pounding combination of anger and nervousness. How on earth would she have responded to Gertrude's crude remark if he hadn't arrived? And was there some truth to Gertrude's suggestion? A wise woman would be on guard for more advances from Stancliff.

Especially when he looked the way he did today, in his dark hauberk and tight braies that outlined muscular thighs. His somber colors provided a stark contrast to the bright gathering in the gardens.

Faith recovered the fastest and proceeded to smooth her fingers over her gown. "Honestly, my lord. 'Tis no wonder you require lessons in manners when you can scarcely remember to bid a lady 'good day.'"

Roger bowed deeply before claiming Ivy's arm. "I am remiss, as always. Good day, ladies. I pray you will join us for today's instruction, which Ivy has promised me will be brief since I have an appointment this afternoon with the queen's hunting party." He pulled Ivy along beside him as he strode toward the bower.

Still shaken by the encounter, Ivy did not care if he ignored her rule about giving a lady some space. She craved his protection from the viragoes that followed them and she clung to his strength like ivy to a rock.

Roger seated her on a sun-warmed bench, giving her fingers a discreet squeeze before releasing her hand. The other ladies joined Lady Isabelle in the partial shade of verdant grapevine that sheathed the rafters.

Gertrude cleared her throat. "Tell us, my lord, what will you be discussing today?" She nodded toward the other ladies. "Perhaps we may be of some assistance."

Roger lounged across from Ivy. His gaze did not leave her as he responded, "I leave that to my teacher's discretion."

Hoping to forestall any protest from Gertrude, Ivy launched into her topic. She knew nothing of Roger's appointment with the queen, but she had no problem being brief, in light of their audience. For all she knew, the man had merely cooked up a ruse so that they would not need to spend too much time in Gertrude's company.

"I thought it would be appropriate for me to explain to Lord Stancliff that a chivalric man chooses only one woman as the object of his affection."

Lady Isabelle paused in her spinning to rest a distaff full of golden thread in her lap. A smile spread over her sharp features, softening her visage into a weathered sort of prettiness. "A noble endeavor, my dear."

Ivy met Lady Isabelle's gaze and sensed she had somehow made an ally, if not a friend. Feeling marginally more confident, Ivy faced Roger and continued the diatribe she had outlined in her mind the previous night. "A man must admire only one woman, my lord."

He nodded, but from his sudden fascination with the mossy bower floor, Ivy presumed his attention wandered.

"One of the most basic tenets of courtly love suggests we pledge ourselves to a single person," Ivy continued. "If you strive to follow the path of a chivalric gentleman, sir, you must see only one woman, hear only one woman and sing the praises of only one woman."

When he looked up at her this time, his silver gaze had taken on the sardonic gleam she recalled from his first formal appearance in the Court of Love. A dimple marred his perfect cheek. "Then I can only assume courtly love honors the sacred institution of marriage with its policy of exclusivity."

Gertrude snorted, drowning out the sound of Lady Grace's giggle. "Do not be obtuse, my lord."

Ivy fought the temptation to brush imaginary dust from her hem—to do anything to avoid his gaze. Roger's comment recalled Ivy's own doubts about the code of courtly love. It seemed immoral to love someone outside of marriage, yet the rules were that in such a relationship, love was never to be physically acted upon. Could such pure love be objectionable?

"Nay, my lord. The recipient of one's affection must not be one's spouse." She could feel the heat burning her neck and cheeks as Roger regarded her. She did not particularly appreciate this aspect of courtly love, having grown up in a household without love between her parents. But then, because Ivy was no noblewoman she wouldn't need to concern herself with such a marriage.

Faith laughed. "Mistress Ivy is quite correct. And not only is it important that the woman not be your wife, she must also be socially above you."

Like a third snake in the Eden of the bower, Grace added her own comment. "But then, you do not seem to approve of admiring a woman above you, do you, my lord?" She raised her chin to stare down her nose at him. "Last night you argued so passionately about the merits of lowly women."

Roger smiled, but Ivy discerned a more fierce expression in his eyes.

"I think a discussion thrives when someone is willing to take an alternate view," he returned, flicking a small beetle from his sleeve. "Do you not agree, Mistress Ivy?"

Thankfully, Lady Isabelle's dramatic sigh broke some of the tension in the bower and prevented Ivy from having to respond. Isabelle lifted her distaff and began to spin once again.

"I vow, it is a fortunate thing none of my husbands knew the dictates of chivalry. They would have been heartbroken to learn they could not love me."

Abruptly, Roger stood and bowed to Isabelle. "As I would have been were I your husband, my lady." He spun on his heel to face Ivy. "With your permission, I shall take my leave early to ponder today's teaching, since I found it especially insightful. Perhaps I will see you at this evening's revel?"

"Of course." From his terse leave-taking, Ivy suspected he was not always so at-ease at court as he pretended.

As soon as Roger sauntered away, Grace swung on Isabelle. "You made yourself sound as if you were born of common parents, Isabelle."

Gertrude's dog howled in protest, along with his mistress.

"Perhaps she meant to entice the earl," Faith

chimed in, "knowing how well he likes women of a lower class."

Gertrude placed her dog on the ground and stood, shaking her hem to free her skirts of wrinkles. Her pet strained to bark more viciously at Isabelle. "Don't be ridiculous. Isabelle's father was as noble as you or I. Just because her mother hails from a diluted bloodline does not mean Isabelle is without some social merit."

Unseen by her companions, Isabelle winked at Ivy.

"Come along, my friends," Gertrude called to Faith and Grace over the racket of her mutt. "Let us enjoy the day with a stroll and you can tell me what you plan to wear to the revel tonight. I think we had best leave Mistress Ivy to ponder strategies for keeping her pupil at his studies in the future." She glared in Ivy's direction before tossing her veils over her shoulder and bustling away.

While the others hurried to follow, Isabelle gathered her golden thread and distaff slowly. "Your upbringing is not that unlike my own, Mistress Ivy," she confided once they were alone. "You must know neither of us would be here now if the queen did not think us possessed of exceptional breeding and talent." She patted Ivy's hand before stepping toward the entry. "Do not allow yourself to forget that."

Feeling marginally better now that the worst of the day was over, Ivy congratulated herself on having survived Gertrude's scrutiny. No doubt Roger was equally pleased to have dispensed with his obligation to attend today's lesson.

Unfortunately, their audience had made it impossible for Ivy to ask him about his comments the previous evening. Why had he made such incendiary statements at court, knowing they would rouse the women's ire?

Telling herself she wanted to know merely because she was curious and not because she felt any lingering attraction to the knave, Ivy vowed she would find a way to ask him at tonight's revel.

After identifying himself to the gatekeeper, Roger left the walls of Poitiers on foot. He tramped down the narrow wooden bridge that crossed the moat, cursing himself with every creak of the dry pine boards.

His mission thus far had been an unmitigated failure, and he had told the king as much in the encoded letter he now handed to a runner hiding in a thicket beyond the bridge. Henry had arranged for a messenger to meet Roger every Wednesday afternoon to carry missives to the Gisors keep in Normandy. Roger sent the runner on his way quickly, then returned to the bridge to lean against the rail to look out over the countryside.

The sight of peasants tending their young crops, coupled with the pungent smell of the moat, gave him some perspective. Inside the gilded walls of Queen Eleanor's magnificent keep, one could almost forget that life existed—coarse and common—outside courtly society. He could not afford to get caught up in the glamour of the court, or the enticement of Ivy, and forget his objective.

Yet in the short time he had been at Poitiers, he had already allowed himself to become distracted— to the point he'd stepped out of his carefully cultivated role today to defend the institution of marriage, of all things. Certainly he wanted to reform his ways, but did he wish to start a riot in polite society with his suggestion that a man might love his wife?

He'd spoken gibberish for reasons he couldn't understand. But he did know that Ivy Rutherford was a wrinkle in this task he had not foreseen. He had not felt such attraction to a woman since Alice had died.

His attraction, however, was the least of his concerns. It was his damned need to defend and protect her that kept getting in his way. Instead of starting conversations with potential sources of information, Roger found himself sitting near Ivy at mealtime so she would not be taken in by James Forrester's charm. Instead of listening to the debates in the Court of Love for some hint of what really went on among the queen's ladies, Roger found himself orating about the value of lower-class women.

How would he gain anyone's trust when he embraced such unpopular views? Although, he reminded himself, he was quickly acquiring Ivy's. Whether she knew it or not, she softened toward him day by day, her natural curiosity getting the better of her good sense as she made a real effort to teach him something. When was the last time anyone had thought him worthy of teaching?

He pinched the cords of tension in the back of his neck and watched the kitchen servants dump spoiled food into the moat below. If only a man's mistakes could be discarded so easily. Every day he spent in Henry's service made him regret his choices in life, and yet at the time of Alice's death, he had not seen any other way out of his grief. His need to defend Ivy surely stemmed from his inability to protect Alice from the corrupt forces at work in a world that appeared so refined on the outside.

But the merchant's daughter needed to discover those things on her own. Her education was not his duty, no matter what Eleanor's words had implied that first night. He would do well to forget about Ivy's allure and focus on using tonight's revel as an opportunity to gain information for the king to earn the trust Henry had placed in him despite Roger's tumultuous last few years.

Breathing in the odor of foul waters one last time, Roger pulled his head from the clouds and back down to earth. No more flights of fancy about playing the gallant for an innocent lady troubadour. From now on, he would concentrate on remedying the mess he'd made of his life.

Digging through a wardrobe stuffed with gowns, Lady Katherine called to Ivy's maid. "Hold one of these, Jeanette, would you, please?" She yanked out a green gown and thrust it toward the harried servant. "Or maybe this one." She pulled out an ivory silk and laid it over Jeanette's shoulder to admire. "How does one woman acquire so many kirtles, Ivy? Your father must spend all his hours ordering garments for you."

Ivy joined her friend at the wardrobe and ran her fingertips over the imported silk.

"He devotes much time to my education, too. During what little time he spends overseeing his trade, he usually spies one bolt of material or another that he thinks I must have. He does not realize I am miserably spoiled already."

"You are hardly spoiled." Katherine tossed the ivory on the bed and shoved the green back into the wardrobe. She flitted about the chamber, choosing shoes to match the kirtle. "Truly, Ivy, you are fortunate to have a father who pays so much attention to you. Many women at court are second-class citizens to their brothers."

Ivy chose not to spoil Katherine's vision of Thomas Rutherford by revealing his true designs for sending his only daughter to Poitiers. While she considered how to compose a letter to her father about her lack of marital prospects, Ivy submitted to her friend's tugging and pulling as they worked her gown carefully around her partially coiffed hair.

Katherine was already garbed for the revel and looked perfect, as always. She chattered more than usual and had hardly sat still since she arrived. "That is why serving Eleanor is so refreshing. She doesn't allow us to be continually silenced."

"Are you nervous this evening?" Ivy prodded.

"Of course not." Katherine laughed a bit too quickly. "I am merely looking forward to the celebration. Are *you* nervous?"

Ivy stood still while Jeanette adorned her with an emerald-covered girdle. "I am perpetually nervous at court."

"Why be nervous now that you have a gallant lord to protect you?" She paused her rifling through the wardrobe to grin at Ivy.

"What?" She tensed.

"Ivy, even you and all your naiveté cannot feign ignorance. Stancliff obviously admires you."

"Do not be ridiculous."

"And I suppose he debated the virtues of women from lower social classes just for the fun of it at court yesterday?"

Ivy shook her head. "There is more to that, and I mean to find out what. Perhaps he has some sort of problem in his past—"

"I'm sure the man has many wicked problems in his past." Katherine laughed, looking truly relaxed for the first time since she had arrived in Ivy's chamber. "But in this case, I think Stancliff simply likes his new teacher."

"Gertrude tried to say he argued the merits of lower-class women in an attempt to gain my bed." Ivy felt the blush on her cheeks but refused to keep the pronouncement to herself any longer. The idea had upset her all day.

And, if she were honest with herself, perhaps it had unsettled her all the more because she had once—briefly—dreamed of welcoming him into her arms.

Katherine gasped. "She would not dare. She actually said that to you?"

Embarrassment fading in the face of her friend's indignation, Ivy smiled.

"She tried to, but Stancliff literally shouted to muffle her words."

Katherine fell back on the bed in a gale of laughter. "What I would give to have seen Gertrude's face." She placed a hand over her mouth. "You see? You are well-protected."

"For once, I am going to take an unsentimental view and agree with Gertrude. If Stancliff is trying to gain my notice, then it can certainly be for no noble purpose." Ivy extended a hand and tugged her friend to a standing position. "Besides, it is my duty as his tutor to discourage any sort of unseemly behavior on his part."

Sighing, Katherine smoothed her skirts. "Fie on duty, Ivy. I thought you were a romantic."

"Only in my dreams." Ivy strode toward the door, a wistful smile hitching at her lips.

Linking arms, they stepped into the corridor and made their way toward the courtyard for the night's revel. Ivy prayed she could be as stalwart against Roger's charm as she had pretended to Katherine. Be-

cause as romantic as it might seem to be wooed by a
charming knight, Ivy knew the man's admiration was
as thin as her parchment and far less durable.

Chapter Six

Roger accepted a drink from a roving cupbearer as he entered the terraced pleasance that hosted the evening's revel. He sipped the Bordeaux appreciatively. Aquitaine boasted incomparable vineyards, and Eleanor's storerooms overflowed with their yield.

Roger saw the queen's hand in all he surveyed. Poitiers was no smoke-filled demesne full of hounds and dirty rushes, but a refined keep where the deft reign of women encouraged art and music, debate and oratory. Tonight, jongleurs and acrobats practiced their arts just outside the ring of torchlight. A pipe and tabor minstrel strolled through the crowd, providing a pleasing backdrop to the conversations that became more relaxed with each pass of the cupbearer.

Budding yellow flowers of laburnum branches decorated the terrace, while chestnut trees adorned with white candles provided a leafy canopy for the fete. The women's brightly colored kirtles and glittering jewels completed the perfect, living tapestry.

In his year of dissolution, Roger had traveled England and Europe and had been entertained in the most lavish residences. To assuage his guilt he had journeyed continually, preying upon the hospitality of any keep that was not home. He knew well that nowhere on the continent rivaled Eleanor's court at Poitiers for beauty and elegance.

As he finished his wine, he noted Ivy entering the gathering with her lively friend at her side. An interesting pair they made. Roger had encountered Lady Katherine before, but his memory of their meetings was dim. By contrast, he knew he would never forget his first encounter with Ivy.

And damn it, he would not spend the whole evening thinking about her like some pathetic hero in her poetry. With an effort, he yanked his gaze from her long enough to spot James Forrester working his way through the crowd. Roger had not discovered Eleanor's purpose in placing the man in an adjoining chamber, thus forcing them to share a solar, but at least the man kept to himself.

"This is heaven on earth for a man of simple tastes like me," James remarked as he reached him, crossing his arms over his chest.

"It is heaven on earth for anyone." Especially when one could feast his eyes on the allure of Ivy Rutherford with her long, elegant neck and soft pale skin.

"But you were born to this grandeur. My background may be marginally noble, but I assure you, we lived far more humbly than this."

"No one lives quite like the queen."

"Those who live with her do. Her court seems well accustomed to royal extravagance."

"Fortunately, the queen is somewhat impartial about who can join her court. She seems to rank talent and intelligence above the accident of a person's birth."

"My presence attests to as much. As does Mistress Ivy's."

Roger bristled. The man was staring in the direction of Lady Katherine and Ivy. Did James still seek Ivy's attention?

Turning from his scrutiny of the women, James added, "I only wish the rest of the queen's court were as unbiased as their sovereign." He gave Roger a shallow bow before striding toward Ivy Rutherford.

A direction Roger would not allow him to take for long.

If comfort in extravagant clothes was the measure of a woman's nobility, Ivy decided it was clear she'd been born of a lower class. Her jeweled girdle cinched her hips so tightly she practically feared for her future ability to bear children. But then, Roger Stancliff's brooding gaze had made her more twitchy than usual and her restless movement didn't ease the girdle's pinch.

She had not spoken to him since their lesson that day and she half feared another encounter now that she'd discovered they had something in common: a belief that love and marriage need not always be mutually exclusive. She did not appreciate the realization that the man had redeeming qualities. Honorable qualities. Yet she could not deny seeing hints of both, the more time she spent in his company.

As she set down her empty drinking horn on a cupbearer's serving tray, she heard a sharp intake of breath. Glancing to her right, she saw Katherine stiffen so much she looked like one of Eleanor's garden statues.

"Are you all right?" Ivy whispered.

She had barely uttered the words when Sir James joined them.

"Good evening, ladies." He bowed.

He looked dashing in his usual somber colors. His grin graced his person with as much decoration as a man needed, as far as Ivy was concerned. She had thought much the same about Roger when she first met him, she recalled.

"Good evening, Sir James," Ivy greeted him, wondering why Katherine did not do the same. Her friend nodded in acknowledgment instead, looking every bit the spoiled heiress.

Did she disapprove of James because of his station? Ivy could scarcely credit such a notion, given how fond Katherine seemed to be of her. She had noted the tension between the two before but had not remarked upon it in an attempt to be polite.

Undaunted, James bowed before Katherine once

again. "I noticed they are lining up to dance, my lady. Would you do me the honor of partnering me for the round?"

Katherine, usually so sure of herself, so bold, bit her lip.

"No, thank you, sir," she finally managed, offering him naught but the slightest curtsy Ivy had ever seen.

How could anyone refuse such a polite request from a man as nice as James? Perhaps in an attempt to salvage his dignity, he turned to Ivy and bowed again.

"Mistress Ivy? Would you consider gracing me with your hand?" His blue eyes held hers in a plea that resonated with the sting of Katherine's spurn.

"Of course." She glared at Katherine as James drew Ivy away by the hand.

Once they reached the area reserved for dancing, Ivy forgot to be annoyed with her friend. Ladies lined up on one side, men on the other. Partners faced each other across a space of several feet while the minstrels argued how they would collaborate on their music.

James shouted to a cupbearer. "A few more jugs for the minstrels, mayhap?"

Ivy laughed, along with the other dancers, and soon the lilting music began. Carefully, she counted out the measured steps as her dancing instructor, Mistress Drusilla, had taught her.

As she turned to meet James in the center, he smiled. "You count very well, Lady Ivy."

They parted to dance around the person next to them, then met again in the center.

"I'm better at counting then dancing, I fear," she whispered back, amazed how relaxed he made her feel even when she paraded before the most glamorous court in the world.

James lifted his arm so that Ivy could lay one hand upon his sleeve. "Nonsense. I am extremely grateful for your capable dancing skills."

Ivy wondered why she couldn't fall in love with Sir James. Heaven knew, he was perfect for her. A gallant knight favored by his queen, he should be all she ever hoped for in a man.

Yet she felt nothing more than fond affection for the affable James Forrester. After having experienced the profound effect Roger Stancliff could have on a woman, how could her idealistic nature ever be satisfied with anything less?

Ivy dragged her thoughts from Roger and counted her way back to the center of the dancing area. She held out her hand to place it upon Sir James's elbow and watched it land, not upon staid black linen, but upon scarlet silk.

"Good evening, Lady Ivy." Roger grinned down at her, no doubt enjoying the confusion that must be scrawled across her face.

She peered around the pleasance for James and saw him heading back toward Katherine.

"Do not get too distracted, my lady," her partner whispered. "You might lose count."

Ivy glowered, and then, as if he had scripted her performance, she turned the wrong way to dance with a partner who was not there.

Hastening to turn herself about and revisit their starting places, Ivy scrambled to recapture the rhythmic count in her head.

She faked her way through the steps that followed until the ladies moved to the middle. Before she could lay her hand upon Roger's sleeve, he grabbed her about the waist and guided her through the steps with his hand.

Heat burned through her thin silk gown. His eyes seemed to sizzle through her with the same intensity, commanding her thoughts along with her body.

With her girdle constricting blood flow to her belly and Roger's touch robbing her of her breath, Ivy swayed on her feet, suddenly light-headed. Scarlet silk blurred before her eyes, giving Ivy the brief impression of a fire eager to consume her.

"Are you all right, Ivy?" Roger's rich, masculine voice rumbled through her, shaking her from the faint that had threatened to claim her.

She blinked, struggling to focus on his face.

"Ivy?" He pulled her away from the dancing and music, away from the torchlight and scented trees.

The night air seemed cooler, more abundant, once they left the gathering. The trees did not crowd them after they stepped away from the pleasance. Slowly, she regained her senses, though they continued to swim a bit whenever he touched her.

"I am fine, my lord," she managed finally, wondering if she could loosen her girdle without his noticing. His tunic did not seem so vibrant in the dark, nor his visage so dazzling. They moved further from the group, however, which made her a little nervous. "Perhaps I only need a drink."

He paused in the moonlight then, having maneuvered them away from any trees and onto a clear patch of lawn. Staring down at her, he tipped her face up to his.

A quiver shook her to her toes. Did he mean to kiss her?

"Your eyes are still dilated. Do you feel any better?" He studied her face, her eyes, apparently entertaining no roguish thoughts.

Ivy cursed her foolish fancy along with the damp grass that now soaked her best slippers. She should be delighted the western world's most renowned scoundrel had no desire to kiss her.

"I feel fine." She swiped his hands away from her cheek. "Perhaps we should return to the revel. Katherine will wonder where I am."

Roger laughed, the harsh sound grating the silky night air. "You mean Forrester will wonder where you are."

Had he been any other man, Ivy might have thought him jealous. But this was Roger Stancliff, who could seduce any woman he chose with naught but a lingering gaze. "Nay, my lord, I mean Katherine will wonder where I am. I did not even rank as Sir James's first choice as a dance partner, so I do not think he will waste time bemoaning my disappearance."

"You are as naive as ever, are you not?" he scoffed, pacing the tiny patch of lawn. "Even after the lesson I gave you that first day in the bower, you believe the men and women here seek only to converse about poetry and art and idle away their days." He turned her to face the glittering gathering on Eleanor's garden.

Some thirty feet away, the revel went on as if nothing were amiss. As if Ivy did not reside in Roger's arms, hidden by the cover of darkness.

"But they are not." His voice scraped along her senses from over her shoulder. "They are here to advance political agendas and to have love affairs. They seek to win coin and the queen's favor. And in the process, they seek to earn more tangible favors from her ladies in waiting." He spun her to him. "Do you understand?"

Ivy could not stifle the impulse to lay her hand across his heart, to touch the scarlet silk that cloaked a man whose character was not as careless as he wanted her to believe. "Is that why you debated the merits of lower-class women last night, my lord? Because the ladies of your own class have made you unbearably jaded?"

His jaw dropped. Ivy guessed he would have been less surprised had she slapped him for his impertinence. Had he, in fact, hoped to incite that sort of violent reaction?

She smoothed the quilted scarlet with her fingers,

startled at the boldness of her actions, but strangely comfortable with them. She sensed, somehow, that this man needed a simple kindness he would never ask for.

He clutched her fingers. "Haven't you heard the rumors regarding that, Ivy? Or are you such a paragon of virtue that your virginal ears do not hear the idle chatter around the keep?"

She tried to free her hand from his, but he only squeezed it tighter. Why was he being deliberately cruel? "I assure you, I hear very well, even with my inexperienced ears."

"Then you must know my remarks have set rumors churning all over Poitiers."

Ivy stilled.

"They say I spoke out as a way of declaring my preference for you, Ivy."

She gasped.

He smiled. "They say it was a rather bold move on my part, proclaiming my affection for a merchant's daughter in front of the entire court in that manner." He lifted her imprisoned fingers to his lips.

Wrenching them away from a mouth that threatened to truly make her faint this time, Ivy crossed her arms across her chest. "Don't be foolish. We both know you meant to do no such thing."

Having lost her hand, he settled for smoothing a stray curl behind her ear. "Do we? I cannot imagine how you would know my intentions, Ivy."

She stiffened at his second use of her Christian

name. Even "*Lady* Ivy" seemed preferable to the painful intimacy of just Ivy.

"Please, my lord. It is no wonder your behavior makes tongues wag, when you refuse to call a woman by her proper title. This may be something we need to tackle as a lesson. If you are really that negligent with your manners, I can see where we might have to ask Lady Gertrude for some extra—"

He bent a bit closer, startling her into silence. His lips loomed near hers, making it difficult to sustain a train of thought.

"Maybe I intended to alert the whole keep to my interest in you." His words were so soft, they seemed to fan over her lips like a breath until he scowled. "Although James Forrester apparently has not caught on," he muttered.

The pipe and tabor paused their lively music while the queen's guests applauded. Nearer to Ivy and Roger, a nightingale sang a tune no mortal instrument could match.

This really was too much. Ivy did not know what kind of game he played, but he had taken it much too far. She stepped back, eager to put distance between them and return to the safety of the revel. She would be loath to leave the beauty of the nightingale's refrain, but at this point it seemed wiser to embrace a simpler song.

"Enough, sir. I will not tolerate being trifled with. The queen specifically told you…" *Not to debauch me*. She could not bring herself to say as much, however.

"What?" His grin returned, dissipating any threat Ivy might have felt from his presence. "I don't seem to recall."

The knave. Wouldn't he just love to embarrass her even more? She lifted her chin, arming herself with the imperiousness the queen used so effectively. "She told you that you were not trifle with me, my lord. So please cease your foolishness before I have to report your behavior to her."

"I certainly wouldn't want you to do that." He lifted his eyebrows in mock surprise.

Why did he look so damn unrepentant if he did not want her to go to the queen? Did he think her devoid of backbone? She nodded, preparing to return to the fete. "Very well, my lord."

She had taken two steps toward the revel when his loud musings halted her.

"But I don't see how the queen could object when I am only following the edict of my very strict teacher regarding the rules of courtly love."

She stood in the dew-damp grass, torn between returning to the revel, where she could remain quietly anonymous, and hearing whatever absurdity Roger Stancliff would spout next.

The knave won.

Ivy turned to face him, lifting her hem slightly to avoid getting grass stains on the delicate silk. She mustered all the patience she could, her Eleanor guise failing her when she needed it most. "Whatever do you mean?"

He scrubbed his hand over his jaw in pretended thought. Despite the increased distance between them, the movements of that scarlet silk were still visible in the wan illumination of the moon.

"I mean I cannot see why the queen would protest when I am merely doing my best to implement your rules, my lady teacher."

Her brain screamed out a warning. She had seen this affable demeanor before. Right before he had tricked her into allowing him to kiss her hand. Once again, he was leading her toward a conclusion she couldn't quite see.

But she knew it was trouble.

"How can you say you are following my rules by dragging me away from the revel when I made it quite clear that a chivalrous gentleman allows a lady some space?" She did not think he could argue that sound point.

A wicked grin revealed a flash of perfect white teeth. "I believe I am executing another rule, Mademoiselle Teacher. The one in which I am to pledge myself to a single person."

Ivy's fingers itched to loosen the girdle that cinched her waist and hips. In cutting off her circulation, perhaps it also thwarted her hearing. "Pardon me, my lord?"

The scarlet silk drew nearer, bringing Roger into sharper focus once again.

"Did you not tell me to pledge myself to a single person?" He slid his hands down her arms to her elbows, bringing his palms within achingly close reach of her breasts. "That I must see only one woman, hear only one woman and sing the praises of only one woman?"

"Yes, but—" Her heart began to thrum in her chest like a lyre being played by a child. The jerky rhythm stole the last shreds of her patience.

He placed her hand against his chest. Ivy remained too dumbfounded to protest. The nightingale's melody resounded in her ears, its dark beauty as hypnotic as Roger's logic.

"I have chosen that woman, Ivy. The woman who will be the center of my cosmos. The woman whose praises I will sing above all others."

Too late, she saw the imminent conclusion of his tangled reasoning. Too late, she realized he was about to make her life both heaven and hell.

"And that woman is you, Ivy Rutherford."

Chapter Seven

Perhaps he had been unwise to announce his intention to stick close to Ivy.

Roger's feet trod warily over a graveled pathway toward the bower two days after informing the lady troubadour he would make a point of singing her praises above all others. She had departed the revel shortly following his declaration and he'd half regretted scaring her off from an event she would have no doubt enjoyed. He'd assumed he would make peace with her the next day, but she'd shown an excellent talent for avoiding him and he'd been forced to wait until this afternoon.

Her sense of honor would not allow her to miss today's lesson, despite how uncomfortable he'd made her. He knew that even as he also knew she would find a way to brush aside his confession as if it mattered not to her.

Spying her approaching the garden sanctuary from the opposite direction, he wondered where she'd been and what she'd been doing outside the keep. He knew better than most that dangerous doings were afoot in Poitiers this spring. That awareness had been half the reason he'd decided to declare for her at the revel. Any woman who was the center of his universe should never stray far from his side.

In theory, at least.

"Good day, lady," he called out to her as she crossed the warm, sunlit gardens.

She wore a blue kirtle of voluminous silk, her sleeves embroidered with rich gold thread and pearls. Its simple neckline drew attention to her perfectly proportioned features. She was an uncommon beauty, a woman of such elegant bone structure and creamy skin that she would be a sight to behold in ten years and twenty years and—God willing—fifty years.

At the moment, she did not appear pleased as she charged toward him through a meticulously trimmed hedgerow.

"I would hardly call this a good day when you have single-handedly besmirched my reputation with your antics." She peered around the gardens, looking relieved to see their relative privacy. "I'd like a word with you, please."

"About the other night—"

"I will not speak of it here, where anyone might come along. Either we sit down to the task at hand

and not speak of it, or—" Once again she studied the handful of guests strolling the winding pathways and labyrinths between flowerbeds and fountains. "Or we walk somewhere where our privacy will be ensured if others enter the gardens."

Only now, as they stood closer, did he notice the slight smudge of purple beneath her eyes. Had she not slept well?

"We'll walk." Unwilling to let her retract the offer, he took her arm and looped it through his own as he struck off to the west. "I know a quiet path this way."

"Not so quiet that there will be more whispers about us, I hope?" She did her best to match her stride to his as they strolled between two rows of pear trees beneath a leafy canopy.

He breathed deeply to catch the scent of her skin and her bath soap, more enticing than the creeping honeysuckle flower clinging to the decorative fence lining their path. She fit so well beside him, he could almost imagine—but that was foolishness. He would be the biggest villain Queen Eleanor had ever known once he uncovered the truth of the rebellious royal's political plots. None of the queen's followers would ever see him again.

"I will make it my duty to ensure no unflattering gossip troubles you." He slowed their pace to take advantage of the seclusion.

"Stop it." She halted on the path, her slipper kicking a loose stone over his shoe. "Just stop. We both know you are not concerned about gossip or you wouldn't have provoked the court with your comment about admiring women beneath your station or your insistence on making me the center of your attentions."

"You think I am not sincere?" He had not seen this forthright side of her before and did not know what to make of her direct manner.

"I *know* you are not sincere." She yanked her arm back from where he'd twined it through his own. "Remember, I heard your petition to the Court of Love. I was there when you antagonized the queen with your admission that you came here because her court is known for its wealth of women."

He winced even as he struggled to explain himself. The burden of his secret weighed heavily upon him, his duty very much at odds with his personal preference.

"Have you ever feared you were caught between two worlds, Ivy?" He drew her deeper down the path, behind the safety of a fat pear tree. "You of all people must know what it is like to have one foot in one society and another foot lodged in a different one."

"Yes. But I do not see a parallel." Her lips puckered in a worried frown.

"I am caught like that. But instead of straddling the worlds of merchant class and nobility, I stand awkwardly between my past and my future, not fully belonging to either one." It was true enough, but not the full truth, of course. He would toss off the chains of his past quickly enough if not for the demands of Henry and Montcalm. If not for his own lingering guilt.

"Your past as a knave with no claim to any one woman." She folded her arms, her shoulders straight with tension. He could not help but notice the way her arms lifted her breasts into tempting view. "And your future as—what? What do you hope to gain from your guise as a chivalric gentleman, my lord, aside from a laugh at my expense?"

"That's not what I want." Damn it, he'd never meant to hurt her in all this. "I truly want to be a better man, Ivy. The revels of a man's youth do not provide the sustenance necessary for real happiness later in life. But it is equally true that I do not believe your ideals of courtly love will provide that meaning or value, either."

She leaned back into the stalwart strength of the gnarled tree trunk. Roger found himself wishing she would trust him enough to lean on him that way.

"You said something like that in the bower the other day with Gertrude—something about disagreeing with the way courtly love prohibits true affection within marriage." Unfolding her arms, she stared up at him with genuine interest. "Would you have me believe you honestly think a husband and wife should hope to find romantic love in a union of lands and alliances?"

"Yes." He said it as fiercely as he believed it. He could not be honest with her about so many things, but this much he could share with her at his most unguarded. "I think it is reprehensible that the laws of love being established here dictate that a man needs some kind of worshipful fascination with a woman who is not his wife."

"She is his lady." Ivy ducked as a fat partridge swooped from its nest in the tree overhead. "His savior. The woman who inspires him to lofty ideals and a nobler purpose."

She spoke like a disciple of these new ideals, yet her tone did not strike him as defensive. She seemed to honestly want to understand his views. Perhaps she did not subscribe completely to the theories she voiced at court. Did a part of her long for a legitimate union that was passionate too?

Her intriguing contradictions fueled his passion almost as much as her slender figure and soft, full lips hovering so close to his.

"In an ideal world, maybe." Unable to stop himself, he stepped closer. "But men and women do not relate to one another on an ideal level, Ivy, much as we might wish we could."

She blinked up at him as he loomed nearer. He reached for her hands where they dangled at her sides. Linking their fingers to align their palms, he let his actions speak more eloquently than his words ever could.

"A man cannot worship a woman from afar because she is no cold holy statue, any more than he is." Although one part of him fully realized the meaning of being hard as stone, he thought. "They are living, breathing, feeling creatures with endless capacity for passion. And what starts as an innocent admiration can't help but ignite hotter desires because, after all, we are only human."

She moved her lips in silent argument, or perhaps she merely echoed his sentiment with the round *O* of her mouth. Either way, Roger did not hesitate to take advantage of her parted lips, slanting his mouth across hers for a taste of the woman he'd dreamed about every time he closed his eyes since the first time he spied her.

Ivy had both feared and longed for this moment. Now that she felt Roger's kiss on her lips—the first kiss of her life—she found she could not scavenge up fear if she tried. Her pulse raged in her ears, beating in hasty time with her ragged breath. Her lips accepted the kiss with soft welcoming, her mouth molding to his with all the hungry longing she desperately hadn't wanted to feel over the past week.

The silky heat of his tongue seduced her senses, awakening her body to scandalous sensations even though he touched her with naught but his mouth. A moment of blinding clarity made her realize the exact nature of passion her fellow poets described with such fervor. The experience was so much more than she could have guessed, so decadent and indulgent, so satisfying and unfulfilling at the same time. The more he kissed her, the more she wanted to explore every facet of his hard, masculine body.

Abruptly, he broke away, a hoarse oath upon his lips as she swayed on her feet at the loss of his heat. His taste.

"I'm sorry." His terse apology recalled her from

the sensual reverie in which she'd already been pulling his hauberk from his shoulders to run her fingers across his bare chest....

"Do not be." With a sigh, she forced her sweet imaginings from her mind and knew she'd never be able to write such sweet—naive—love poetry again. "You've actually done me a great favor."

She took small comfort from the perspiration on his forehead that couldn't have resulted from the mild warmth of a day when a light spring breeze blew through the trees. Surely she had unsettled him as much as he'd excited her.

She would be mature about this. Reasonable. And sweet, merciful heaven, it would be easier if she wouldn't continually envision him half-naked. She considered it a blessing that she could not quite visualize a man's *complete* nakedness, else she would have thoroughly undressed him in her fanciful musings.

"What favor?" He speared an impatient hand through his silky dark hair and scowled. "I have failed in my promise to the queen not to touch you. I have kissed you with the familiarity of a lover even while I spout idealistic visions of passion existing only between husband and wife. Furthermore, I've practically proven every cynical rumor about my character to be true with one moment of—"

She waited, surprised at his outburst. No matter what courtly guise he wore, she realized that Roger Stancliff was a man of some propriety. Conscience. Why else would a kiss upset him to this degree?

Every poet in residence at Poitiers wrote about the exuberant joys, the devastating allure, of kissing. Surely she and Roger had done no wrong.

"Still, it was but a kiss. Nothing more." She would simply pretend she didn't notice the irresistible urge to touch her lips where his had been just a moment ago. "And you've helped unveil the mystery of kissing for me. I'd been feeling like a fraud these last few weeks in residence as a court poet, a minstrel of love lyrics, when I'd never experienced any of the passionate encounters I tried to describe on parchment."

"Dear God." Roger paced away from her and then back again, his stride tense as he scowled. "You were sitting in judgment of the kiss for the sake of your art?"

"I suppose many women would throw themselves in your arms at such an event, wouldn't they?" She could understand the temptation. But even if she had begun to see Roger was not such the rake his reputation suggested, she knew this man far out-ranked her. To care for him would be foolish. "But I am content to translate the emotions behind kissing into poetry. I believe I can imagine well enough what a moving experience it would be for a couple who held one another in the highest regard."

"Hell's breath, woman. You cannot critique my lovemaking without warning me." He reached for her, drawing her close. His hands rested on her waist, the heat of his skin penetrating her delicate silk kirtle. "I demand a rematch."

The elegant gardens seemed to grow more still in

the wake of his statement, as if all of nature awaited her reply. She swayed like the low branches in the breeze, her body pulled to him even as her mind hauled her back.

"That's quite unnecessary." Her voice escaped her before she'd had time to collect herself, so the sound squeaked into the garden as little more than a whisper. "Really."

"Don't worry, Ivy." He gazed into her eyes with the familiarity of a lover, just long enough to make her forget the game they played. "This one is strictly for research purposes."

She could not take her eyes from his as he bent over her, his body powerful and commanding even as his silver eyes seemed endlessly gentle. Patient. Knowing.

Helpless in the face of his approach, she gave herself over to the sensation of being the center of Roger Stancliff's world, if only for a few stolen moments. Her eyelids fluttered closed, her hands clutching his shoulders for support in a world rapidly tipping sideways.

And then his mouth slid over hers with slow deliberation, his tongue flicking leisurely along her lower lip before venturing deeper for a more thorough taste. This was no fumbling encounter of untried youth. Roger Stancliff kissed like a god, like he'd been created just for kissing, and he took his time to execute every movement with perfection.

Ivy dug her fingers into the soft fabric of his hauberk so she might feel the heavy masculine muscles beneath. A mewling sound emanated from her throat—a soft, needy cry that articulated wants she couldn't begin to understand.

She would back away in a moment. Just one more moment to deceive herself that she wasn't just a merchant's daughter, an imposter or Roger's unwanted tutor. Just one more moment to imagine this kiss meant something real, something special.

He shifted her against him, pulling her body to meet his in undiluted contact. His hard strength pressed her, silently demanding more from her as her breasts molded to the sculpted solidity of his chest.

Heat blasted through her veins like a brushfire with new fuel, singeing her insides with a depth of passion she had not expected lurked inside her.

She was about to break away, truly she was, when Roger edged back first. He moved his finger to seal her lips shut, gesturing for her to be quiet.

Confused, she wriggled against him, ready to back away. But he held her fast and tightened his grip.

A couple strolled down the garden path behind them, their voices carrying on the breeze as they spoke in hushed tones.

"…and Richard does not always bend to her will the way she wishes, so she may be in for a surprise when Poitiers is no longer a safe refuge."

When the man stopped speaking, the woman with him gasped.

"You don't think Richard would side against her, do you?" She lowered her voice even further. "He has been so loyal…"

Their conversation faded as they moved away. Ivy wanted to speak, to question Roger about the incident, but his expression had shifted in such a way that she wondered how well she knew him. All traces of the scoundrel courtier had been replaced by a dark intensity she scarcely recognized.

He moved with utter stealth around the tree to peer in the direction the speakers had wandered. Satisfied, he rejoined her, guiding her in the opposite direction.

She followed his lead, navigating through a low row of hedges and under a rose-covered archway into the more formal portion of the gardens, where a few ladies of the court strolled in the afternoon sunlight.

"Roger—" she began, but he whipped around and halted in his tracks.

"We will speak of this, but when the setting is private."

"At court?" Ivy plucked a foxglove and smoothed the soft petals along her cheek in a wasted effort to calm her overexcited nerves. Between the kiss and Roger's unusual behavior now, Ivy found herself wary and tense. "Surely you know better than to expect any privacy in a royal residence, my lord. If you'll remember, the whole reason we embarked down the wooded path was to find privacy, and look what happened."

"I cannot bring myself to regret what happened as much as I probably should. But I see your point. We are never alone here, because someone's always watching." He gave her a rueful grin as some of the dangerous brooding look fled from his gaze.

"Or listening." She would wait for her private moment with Roger to ask him the questions chasing each other around her brain, but she already knew that being alone with him could tempt her to make mistakes she could not undo.

She had hoped to chastise him today for his rash declaration at the revel, and instead, she'd fallen into his arms as easily as any other woman.

"So it would seem." He pivoted to take note of who was around them in the gardens and then leaned closer. "Tell me, Ivy, how much longer do you plan to be at court?"

The abrupt change in conversation surprised her. Her suspicion that more intriguing layers lurked beneath his slick exterior increased. He was not the man he first appeared.

"Until All Saints', perhaps. Why do you ask?" She would mourn every moment spent away from Eleanor's idyllic haven now that she'd seen the creative possibilities for a community of artists and poets, writers and minstrels.

She'd been inspired in so many ways. And now she had Roger's kiss ingrained in her memory, an event that would surely inspire a new creative burst. The sweetly seductive mating deserved to be committed to parchment.

"I recommend you look into returning sooner. Does the political situation at Poitiers not concern you?"

She recalled the hushed words they'd heard on the walking path.

"I do not think Eleanor is in residence here because of politics. What she has accomplished with this court will have a more lasting effect on our society than any movement of troops or armies."

"You believe that because you are a poet, but I assure you, Eleanor is not here solely because she's a patron of the arts." Reaching for her elbow, he steered her through one of the low labyrinths, where hedgerows flourished with tiny white blooms. "She has wed two kings and has mothered a new generation of kings. Believe me, Ivy, she cares very much about politics, particularly Henry's politics. How long do you think she can preside over this court when her husband lives in another country? He is bound to retrieve her soon."

"He has done naught to call her back home these last four years. Why now?" Ivy wished he would dismiss the question with an airy wave of his hand, but he only bent his head closer.

"Why not now? The more women who populate the court, the more men who languish at home, resentful that their wives are not under their roofs where they belong."

Her feet slowed on the grassy walkway as his meaning sank into her head.

"You think this makes the men unhappy?" She knew her father would not have missed his lady wife if her duty as a noblewoman had called her from home. Then again, their marriage had not been a peaceful union of houses, but a tumultuous and often bitter exchange of status for money.

She remembered her mother, Rosamunde Burkshire Rutherford, telling her scarce friends that she had received the better end of the bargain because her family had secured the money up front, while Thomas Rutherford's status remained negligible once he took a fallen noblewoman to wife.

"Forget happiness. This situation rankles a man's pride. Among other things."

"Male pride. Always a delicate matter, I gather." The longer she resided at court, the more she learned about human nature and men in particular. Men were, after all, a favorite topic of the mostly feminine guests. "But tell me, will you be leaving Poitiers soon?"

The question seemed like an intimate one, and yet he had had no qualms about asking her.

"I have no choice but to stay, or I would offer to see you safely home." Behind him, Ivy could see a throng of garden visitors headed their way with Gertrude at the lead, her demonic dog already yapping excitedly as if it sensed an upcoming battle.

"But if you will be here, I am certain to be safe. Am I not the center of your cosmos, my lord?"

"That's why I think so highly of your safety." He bowed slightly, likely to hide the gritting of his teeth, Ivy guessed.

"A pretty notion, but I think you would rather exercise your great devotion to me only when it suits you." She took his arm in a gesture she could tell surprised him, but she had no wish to be cornered by

Gertrude. "You have not explained why you chose to…honor me with that declaration the other night."

Peering over his shoulder, Roger apparently spotted the flock of noblewomen descending on them and put his feet to good use.

"I would have thought my reasons would be obvious." He walked quickly, but Ivy couldn't complain about the pace since she wished to avoid another Gertrude encounter at all costs. "I am overwhelmed by your ease with the rituals of courtly love. It's a classic case of the student falling in love with his teacher."

"I may be an innocent, but I am not that naive." She savored the warm strength of his forearm beneath her fingers and tried not to remember what it had felt like to taste his kiss. "Keep your secrets to yourself, if you like. I think the day will come soon enough when you won't want to carry the burden of hidden intrigues, and you may discover I am not as blind to the world around me as you think."

Having reached the keep in record time, Ivy excused herself before the lesson had been given, her feelings too overwrought to play teacher today. She prayed the queen could understand as Ivy sought her chamber to remember their kiss in private and pour the wealth of emotion it had inspired onto parchment. Stancliff might not be willing to share his secrets with her, yet he had imparted a gift of sensual wisdom she would not squander.

And despite the clamoring in her heart for something more from him than the dalliance he'd probably shared with dozens of other women, Ivy thought a kiss was probably more than enough.

Chapter Eight

I have proof of the queen's sedition and I advance toward Poitiers with all haste. Your only mission is to keep the court in residence long enough to answer for their crimes and you will be rewarded with your father's lands.

The note was not signed, but Roger knew who'd penned the missive. Henry advanced on Eleanor's court and would arrive before Pentecost if he did not tarry.

Crumpling the parchment in his fist, Roger tossed it into the hearth, where a blaze had been set at dusk. The king commanded him to stay here and be a silent witness to Henry's subjugation of his wife's household. There had been a time in his life when Roger could have done so, but the loyal and idealistic subject he'd once been had died along with his betrothed. He could no longer abide an un-blinking acceptance of duty at the expense of those he cared about. He should have released his future bride from her promise to him, but he had been too unbending, too sure that she would grow to accept their arrangement.

The ache of guilt and remorse had lessened some in the last year, but not enough to allow him to re-peat old mistakes. He could enforce Henry's will without allowing Ivy to be hurt. There would be res-idents at Eleanor's court when the king arrived, but an innocent troubadour who only wanted to pen her poems would not be one of them.

The decision settled comfortably enough on his shoulders, but his plan created a whole new set of concerns. Most notably, he wondered why he would risk his lands, his future and possibly even his title for a woman he might never be able to claim as his own. Because no matter how enticing Ivy's kisses might be, he would have nothing to offer her if his king discovered he had spirited her away before Hen-ry's arrival. The king could view the act as traitor-ous, strip Roger of his lands. His title.

Unless, perhaps, he wed Ivy and extended the ben-efit of his rank to her before the king could accuse her of any wrongdoing. The idea troubled him, for he feared he had little trust when it came to women, even a woman as honorable as Ivy. But if the moment arose where Ivy's honor was called into question by any of the cynical old hens who savored scandal more than good wine, he would not hesitate to provide Ivy with every scrap of protection he could offer.

His years at court had taught him that a romantic heart was a rarer commodity than any precious gem, and for a man who had been burnt by the sharp tongues of a cynical world, Roger understood that goodness and honesty were treasures to be guarded.

Ivy felt as if a mask had been lifted from her eyes as she moved through the wide corridors of the keep toward her private chamber, after the evening meal.

Whereas just yesterday she would have viewed the art, the people and the architecture with a wistful longing for a world she would never completely join, tonight she spied darker significance in everything she observed. Couples walking in quiet conversation were no longer exchanging courtly confidences but plotting political intrigue. Eleanor's sophisticated collection of art from around the world no longer seemed like an assortment of riches that had struck a wealthy woman's fancy, but proof of the queen's allies across the map.

Even now, as Ivy turned down her hallway to seek her room, she noticed Katherine in intense conversation with James Forrester. Considering that Katherine didn't even like James much, that kind of intimacy struck Ivy as peculiar. It made her think of the encounters she'd shared with Stancliff in which they were continually circling each other, both wary and attracted.

James pivoted on his heel abruptly and stalked away from her friend. He bowed politely to Ivy, but his bearing seemed strained. Tense.

Remembering conversations with Roger when she had walked away taut as a new bow, Ivy realized her friend might be able to help her understand her confused feelings. If nothing else, they could closet themselves away from the older women of the court and share a laugh and a cup of wine, the way they used to before Poitiers had hosted a certain knave.

"Katherine." Looping her arm through her friend's, she dragged Katherine toward her chamber. "We are friends, are we not?"

"The best. You have endeared yourself to me as much as any sister." Katherine stole a final glance down the hall where Sir James had departed before allowing herself to be drawn into Ivy's small chamber crammed full of books. "More in fact, since my eldest sister is questionable company sometimes."

She shuddered, even as she unfurled a mischievous grin.

"If we are such dear friends—" Ivy paused while she locked the door behind her and then lowered her voice, "—why have you not confided your affection for Sir James to me?"

Katherine blanched, her mouth working to form a response. "Who told you such nonsense?"

"No one." She shoved aside a leather-bound collection of ancient Roman poetry and cleared a space for them to sit on her bed. "But if I had any doubts about the matter, they were just confirmed by your guilty expression."

"Perhaps I was merely horrified at the thought of a liaison with a man." Katherine dropped to the mattress with a pouf of her full skirts.

"I think not. I seem to recall conversations about men in the past where you have not been remotely horrified at the thought." She retrieved a few more precious books off her bed and packed them into the wooden chest at their feet. She had not accumulated such an extensive collection of reading material by being careless with her volumes. In truth, she cared far more for the integrity of her books than her abundance of gowns.

"Perhaps the thought of James Forrester *is* the tiniest bit appealing. I had hoped no one noticed."

"My eyes have grown more acutely attuned to signs of romance, I think." Ivy would not say why just yet, not until she understood more about Katherine's opinions on romantic attraction. Would Katherine have allowed a kiss in the gardens the way Ivy had? "It seems as if you are intrigued and yet you rebuff him at every opportunity."

She desperately wished to know why, to gain some more insight into the complicated relations between men and women, but she hesitated to push her friend if Katherine did not choose to share more.

"I cannot bear to get close to him again since *he* rejected *me* the last time we met, last spring at a mutual friend's keep, for a fortnight of hawking and revelry." Leaning back onto a clump of misplaced pillows in the center of the bed, Katherine twirled a lock of artfully fashioned hair about one finger while her shoulders slumped. "After sharing much pleasant conversation, he told me we were ill-suited because of our disparate stations in life. He did not even try to speak to my father or ask my view on the matter."

"He did not want to mislead you, apparently." Ivy frowned, drawing one of the extra velvet-covered pillows beneath her as she sank down beside her friend. "But what did he mean—disparate stations? He is the son of a knight, isn't he?"

"He is a fourth son of a knight with few holdings, not that I have researched his lineage in any great depth, mind you. And my father has no need to make a political match through me, with all my sisters to solidify his alliances, so what would it have hurt if I had—" She trailed off and then pounded her fist against a small golden pillow covered with tassels and needlework. "But what does it matter? James is not interested and neither am I."

"Maybe you will be James's liege lady one day, and he will sing your praises and pine for you for all his days."

"Let's hope he suffers mightily from all that pining." Katherine folded her arms and turned her lip into a formidable pout for all of two seconds before she sighed. "But while a chivalric knight dying of love for his lady fair is all very romantic, that sort of love—well, it does not warm the bed or the heart."

Visions of Roger warming a woman's bed rose to Ivy's mind. Heaven help her, she could only see herself in that bed with him.

Heat rushed to her cheeks as she remembered their kisses and the sharp ache for more that had accompanied them. She needed to be careful where he was concerned.

"Ivy?"

"Hmm?" She shook off the wanderings of her imagination with an effort.

"Have I embarrassed you? I do tend to speak my mind more than I should—"

"Absolutely not." Ivy clutched her telltale cheeks and smiled, knowing it wouldn't be fair to prod around Katherine's heart without sharing some of her own fanciful thoughts. "I'm afraid my thoughts took an unseemly turn regarding another gentleman."

Bolting upright, Katherine swatted her arm and squealed with delight. "Ivy Rutherford admits to unseemly thoughts? Be still my heart. I thought you were far too perfect to ever consider the facets of love that weren't all noble and pure thoughts of the mind."

"I'm not perfect." She weighed Katherine's gentle accusation in her mind. "I just never had any inspiration for those kinds of thoughts, but truly, we digress. We were going to speak about James's obvious affection for you."

"You see? It is not so comfortable to be the topic of such personal conversation, is it?"

"I promise we can revisit that topic in a moment. In the meantime, do I overstep my bounds to ask you about such a private matter?" Ivy had learned to be cautious with the nobility, but she had thought her friendship with Katherine made it possible to overstep her customary boundaries.

"Of course not. You care about my happiness and I appreciate that, but there is nothing to be done about my situation with James. We are not meant to be, apparently, whereas you might still find happiness with the man who has been an *inspiration* to your normally lofty thoughts of late."

"Oh, no." Ivy half wished she hadn't started the discussion about her wayward daydreams, but there was no one else at Poitiers she could ask about Roger's past. "I do not have any designs on the man and he is certainly unattainable even if I did, but I have wondered—"

"Yes?" Katherine slid off her slippers to tuck her feet beneath her.

"Do you know anything of the earl's past? He has implied that much gossip exists—"

"Stancliff?" Katherine's teasing smiles disappeared as a furrow deepened between her brows. "Ivy, you know better than to—"

"Of course I know better." She wasn't sure if Katherine had been about to lecture her on the obstacles of social standing or the futility of admiring a known heartbreaker, but Ivy believed she was well-versed on both those subjects. "I have spent a great deal of time with him this past sennight and I've learned how careless he can be with his endless flattery."

Although his impassioned defense of the sanctity of marriage charmed her. And his urging her to leave the court for her own safety…if he'd truly been concerned, that swayed her vulnerable heart as well.

"Good. Because he is a scoundrel of the first order." Katherine toyed with the red ribbons tying back the bed hangings. "In fact, that is where the gossip originates."

"He is an indiscriminate lover, then?" A wave of jealousy surged through her, surprising her with its force.

"Actually, his numerous liaisons came after the bigger transgression of driving his betrothed to despair. The rumors say she jumped from the tower of her father's keep rather than wed him."

Ivy blinked, scarcely able to credit such a story. Roger had seemed dismissive of the gossip about him. Was there a chance the story had been a falsehood?

"Perhaps the tale has been embellished?" She knew wicked things had been said of her mother when Rosamunde had deigned to wed a merchant for the sake of her family's debts.

"Perhaps," Katherine agreed. "But it is true enough that his betrothed flung herself from a tower. My sister's husband holds a keep near the Montcalm lands. Near Stancliff's, too, I hear."

With a troubled mind, Ivy could not contribute much to the rest of the discussion, although she urged Katherine to follow her heart where James Forrester was concerned. Perhaps the man had realized the error of his ways in bowing out of a courtship the previous spring, since he certainly seemed to maintain an interest in the youngest de Blois heiress.

But most of Ivy's thoughts remained with her new fears of political unrest at Poitiers and the turmoil in her relationship with Roger. Something had shifted between them in the gardens today. A sensual transaction she couldn't take back. Ivy had thought she spied something honorable in him, something noble beneath his slick exterior. Had she been deceiving herself to justify her desire to kiss him?

But she'd been correct in at least one assumption about him. If his betrothed had died, he certainly possessed depths she had not begun to understand.

Ivy found herself scribbling Roger's name on her parchment in the great hall the next afternoon instead of revising the poem she'd been drafting. Surprised to see the letters there in bold ink, she peered around the room, in which the queen's ladies were gathering to hear the latest petitions before the Court of Love.

Clearly, Ivy needed to correct her mistake before someone spied the damning name that could only lead to trouble for them both. Sketching the first two letters into the beginnings of a flower, she worked with quick efficiency until a masculine voice sounded behind her.

"I need to speak with you."

She started at Roger's resonant tone, skidding her quill across a length of vellum in an untidy scrawl.

"For pity's sake." She frowned at the mark and blotted away the color with a scrap of cloth at her side, her cheeks heating at his proximity. "I am working. Can it not wait?"

Roger stared at Ivy's bent head, uncertain why she seemed so agitated but unable to spare time to find out. As soon as she had dried the excess ink, she shoved aside the vellum with an abrupt movement. While the gesture made him curious, he could not inquire about her activities when trouble brewed so close to the keep.

"It cannot." He gripped her wrist and motioned for her to follow him. They needed to leave before the queen arrived. "Have you not heard? The king marches on Poitiers, burning villages in his path in his quest to—"

"Ladies and gentlemen." Eleanor's voice suddenly filled the hall, her steps quick and purposeful as she entered the vast chamber full of brightly garbed women, exotic furnishings of a Moorish style, and enough colorful tapestries to adorn almost every inch of the surrounding walls.

One of Eleanor's retainers shut the door to the great hall behind her.

"We must attend the queen," Ivy whispered, yanking her wrist from his grip. "I have duties to fulfill."

Roger saw no chance to escape unnoticed, so he settled beside Ivy while the hall rumbled with the queen's abrupt appearance and terse manner. He had hoped to take Ivy away from the court the moment he heard of Henry's approach, but he could not afford to make an enemy of the queen by defying her openly.

He would bide his time.

"My dear ladies, you have brought me great comfort these last years that I have lived apart from my husband." Eleanor paced past the chair where she normally sat for the court's proceedings, her restless energy evident in her long strides. "The discussions we have initiated at Poitiers have already begun to spread throughout Europe and all the way to England. It is my fondest wish that our rules of love will inform the world and provide new understanding to men and women the world over."

Roger ground his teeth to prevent himself from speaking out against a code that made a mockery of marriage by championing love outside that holy union.

"Even as our laws govern our social behavior," Eleanor continued, "so shall our code of love govern romantic behavior in ways that will edify our relationships and provide men and women with grounds for new respect for one another."

Roger watched Ivy as she gazed up at the queen

with obvious admiration. Indeed, even the cagiest of Eleanor's women seemed enthralled by her words. Her ideas. No doubt Eleanor of Aquitaine was a formidable orator. But to instill that kind of rapt attention even while encouraging her ladies to defy their husbands and their king? Perhaps the ideas born at Poitiers these last few years were truly as revolutionary as Eleanor made them sound. Certainly Henry must think the women's dogma of love had critical momentum, or he would not be wasting so much manpower to disband the court.

True, Henry resented Eleanor's efforts to encourage her sons to rebel against him, but if that were her only crime, the king would not wage war on the whole court. And by all accounts, taking Poitiers by storm was exactly what he planned.

"But today," the queen continued, "it is with both regret and gratitude that I must release you all to your homes or whatever safe haven you can find. My sources tell me Henry approaches, and I fear our time together has reached an end."

The hall erupted in a chorus of gasps and cries. Eleanor spoke to a handful of women closest to her. Roger saw an opportunity to help Ivy leave as quickly as possible, before Henry and his men arrived to wreak whatever punishment they had in mind for a keep filled mainly with women.

Standing, he held a hand out to help her, but she stared blankly toward her sovereign until he reached to lever her upward.

"You knew." Her accusation was not a rebuke, but rather a soft sound of surprise. She turned sharp green eyes on him that did not seem as innocent as they had the first time he'd seen her.

"I have many friends close to the king." He did not see the point of subterfuge, but now wasn't the time to discuss his convoluted relationship with his overlord. "Henry's household has come under scrutiny lately due to the unrest here, the queen's refusal to come home and Henry's dispute with the archbishop. Perhaps he seeks to solidify whatever support he can garner by settling the matter with Eleanor. Whatever his motives, we need to make haste."

"We?" She shook her head, although she gathered up her vellum and quill as the hall hummed with activity. "I will dispatch a messenger to my father, but once that is done, I have no choice but to wait for his instruction."

Ladies Faith and Grace raced by with Gertrude close at their heels, the women forsaking all pretense of grace in favor of speed. He only wished Ivy would follow suit. Still, he felt compelled to shout out above the chaos that the court would be better protected within the walls. At least he could honestly tell Henry that he'd tried to contain the exodus. And he'd have witnesses.

"Have you no eyes for what takes place all around you?" He propelled her through the pandemonium quickly taking over the hall as women departed in every direction. "The queen has released you. That's her way of saying 'get thee hence as fast as your mount will carry you.' Trust me, lady, you do not wish to be here when Henry arrives. He has threatened to arrest everyone in residence."

"Arrest us? Can he do that?" She bit her lip as she hastened her step. "Don't answer that. I suppose he can do whatever he chooses. I just never thought—"

"The shield of nobility only protects a person so far, Ivy. The queen herself is not safe."

As they reached the corridor to Ivy's chamber, Roger noted James Forrester in heated conversation with Lady Katherine outside her apartments, across the hall from Ivy's.

"Perhaps I can accompany Katherine for part of the way." Ivy seemed to speak to herself as she navigated through the busy corridor full of young maids falling over one another, their arms full of their mistresses' belongings. Hastily packed trunks littered the hallway while the air crackled with tension, teary goodbyes and shouted orders from the women to their servants.

"You will both need escorts." Roger had no doubt from the body language between James and the youngest de Blois that they were having essentially the same argument as Roger anticipated with Ivy. "The roads are dangerous and Henry is wreaking devastation on the villages between here and the coast."

Ivy missed a step at the news, causing him to reach out and steady her. Although he regretted the need to frighten her, he could not afford to mince words when they needed to leave. Roger had weighed the cost of not being in residence when Henry arrived, and found it worth the risk. His orders had been to watch the queen, which he had done. In good conscience, he could not extend his obligation beyond that, even if Henry now expected him to keep the court in residence. He had, at least, publicly declared that the court would be safer within the walls than encountering the king's army outside Poitiers.

"I will speak to Katherine about the matter." Ivy slowed her step as she reached her chamber door, and Roger noticed James had cajoled his way inside Katherine's room.

"Hellfire, woman, you don't have time to consult your father or your friends. You need to leave now." Tension knotted in his neck, straining his shoulders, his head. "Do you realize what could happen to you if you cannot clear the grounds by the time the king's men arrive?"

"Eleanor is his lady wife. I am a guest of a royal household." The uncomprehending look in her eyes did not stem from stubbornness, Roger guessed, so much as from disbelief that her world could fall apart so quickly, so completely. He, at least, had some warning of what would unfold here, while Ivy had been focusing solely on her art.

"You cannot cling to your romantic notions now, not when your future is at stake." He opened her chamber door for her and nudged her across the threshold. "I swear to you by all that is holy, your queen is riding hard and fast from Poitiers even as we speak. You will not see that fierce lady waiting around for her husband to try her for sedition."

"I cannot think that the Queen would leave. Tomorrow is Pentecost."

"Damn it, Ivy, Henry won't be joining us for a feast and I will not allow you to wait around here until he hauls you back to London under armed guard." Unwilling to wait for her to act, he yanked open her trunk. "Now pack whatever you need for the journey, because we're leaving."

"You really think it would be foolish to remain here? Even though you told the others it would be safer to stay?"

He could see the fear in her eyes and knew he'd finally succeeded in communicating his message. Outside Ivy's apartments, footsteps raced back and forth as the mass exodus continued.

"I know damn well it is." Rifling through her belongings he sifted past the most luxurious fabrics in hope of something more functional. Durable.

"You are the most notorious idle knave in all of Christendom." Fear threaded her voice despite her attempts to cover it with outrage. "How do you propose to know the political maneuvers of our sovereign?"

Tossing two of her gowns into a lightweight sack, he steered her toward the door, all attempts at playing the chivalrous knight abandoned.

"Because I've spent the last fortnight in Henry's employ, gathering information to convict the queen of crimes against the crown. And before you ask, let me assure you she is guilty as sin."

Chapter Nine

Her father would disown her, her best friend had abandoned her and she was now in the safekeeping of a traitor to her beloved queen.

Ivy scanned the lush, idyllic grounds at Poitiers, now filled with noblewomen in all stages of harried retreat from the keep that had been their home and intellectual haven just the day before. She saw no sign of Katherine as Stancliff dragged her through the crowds toward the stables. Her chamber had been vacant. And when they reached the stables, Ivy saw that Katherine's prized mare was absent from its stall.

"Hurry." His terse command gave her no comfort as he secured a saddle to a horse she did not recognize. One of *his* horses, she realized. The metal clasp on the mount's bridle had been inscribed with the Stancliff crest.

So was the bridle on a second mount he coaxed

from its stall, suggesting he must have brought a servant, or a second animal to carry trunks. As he worked, he soothed the skittish animal with crooning words, his methods smooth, efficient and marked with a calmness that irritated her to no end.

"I could decry you for a traitor here and now," she threatened, her hands clutching a sack stuffed with limited supplies for the journey. A sack that contained one lone volume of her poems, which she'd filched from her bed on the way out her chamber.

"I'm sure your news will be of great interest to people scrambling to save their own necks," he replied dryly as he hefted her onto her horse's back. "Please, feel free to make your announcement in verse while you're at it. A poem would probably be welcome entertainment now."

Deflated, she sagged into her saddle as Roger swung a muscular leg over his mount's back. She had come to the same conclusion about the unwelcome news of Roger's loyalties to Henry. No one would care *who* had helped their king find proof of Eleanor's plotting when they themselves might come under royal wrath at any hour. Any moment.

Ivy took up the reins as Roger urged the horses into motion. Leaving with a man she did not trust— a man whose presence beside her could irreparably compromise her worth and reputation—was still preferable to being sent home in shame under the king's guards. That threat seemed all too real. Poitiers had emptied out like a ripe harvest field at sunset. She would be a fool to wait for Henry to arrive.

But she would be an even bigger fool to believe Roger Stancliff had her best interests at heart as he raced beside her, out of the keep and across the green spring grass. The Poitiers gate yawned wide behind them. Ivy looked back at the grand keep as it became smaller in the distance, knowing she would never see the inside of those glorious walls again. The greatest adventure of her life had come to an end too soon, too abruptly, giving her no time to say goodbye to the people and places that had forced her to rethink so many of her old beliefs.

Now, she had no choice but to look forward to the life of a merchant's daughter that awaited her, full of riches and small indulgences but lacking the intellectual stimulation she craved. If she escaped the king's wrath, she had her father's fury still to anticipate. She did not deceive herself that he would be anything but angry with her lack of progress in finding a husband at court, even though her time had been cut short. The only reason Thomas Rutherford had funded Ivy's trip was to give her a chance to obtain a titled suitor.

But her failure on that count, at least, was one she refused to regret.

"You can't be serious." Ivy slid off her mount in weak-kneed relief, knowing her companion must have a better plan for the night than the one he'd shared with her.

"Deadly serious, I'm afraid." He allowed the horses to drink their fill at a nearby stream as he approached an abandoned wooden keep that appeared no more than a ruin to Ivy's eyes.

"My father provides weaponry for noble houses throughout the region," she argued. Calmly. Logically. "If you know no one in the area, then we might use his name to obtain entry to far more appropriate lodgings for the night."

She stumbled on a rock from the crumbling foundation as she ambled up the hill behind him. No doubt the fortress had been abandoned because of its antiquated defenses, the high perch of the keep inadequate against sophisticated invaders who could burn down wooden walls like so much dry hay.

"While your preference for something appropriate is amusing in its maidenliness, I don't imagine the locals whose villages have been razed by Henry would find your predicament all that distasteful. Those who remain alive after the king's carnage, that is."

Ivy shuddered at the vision his words created. As she followed him through a low archway to a great hall now open to the stars above.

Her soaked slippers chilled her toes, the beaded velvet doing little to protect her feet on the harsh terrain. She'd packed heavier shoes, but had not actually put them on her feet in haste. The night air was not cold yet, but she did not doubt the temperature would drop further before daybreak, and the shelter provided little protection from possible rain. She wondered how Roger could hasten his step so easily, his long legs covering the landscape with a flex of taut thighs while she felt ready to collapse at the next strong gust of wind.

"How can you abide your actions, knowing you've cost innocent people their lives?" She had not meant to voice the comment, but the thought seemed to settle on the cooling breeze without her permission. She had harbored such romantic thoughts of him. Not once, but twice, and twice she'd been made a fool for her imaginings. She'd seen him first as a chivalrous courtier and then learned he was a renowned knave. Then, despite her hardened heart, she'd thought she had made some small impression upon him to reform his scandalous ways.

Again, she'd been wrong. He'd only suffered her tutoring to cover a political agenda at the court.

"I cannot control my king's sword arm any more than you can control your queen's tongue. Their actions are their own, lady, and you would be wise to remember where your loyalties lie before we return to a land where you can be sent to the gallows for treason to a king."

He halted in front of her, pivoting on his heel to confront her in the shadowy remains of the old keep.

"And do you think I need to apologize for being loyal to my art? For seizing an opportunity to let my poems flow? I have done nothing wrong." Anger forced her to flex her tense fingers. She could scarcely credit that she had once kissed him. "You, on the other hand, could have prevented needless harm by warning the court of Henry's approach. You have put all of Poitou in jeopardy."

She mourned the violence in the lands that had brought her only joy until now. Her fanciful attraction to Roger seemed all the more frivolous alongside the frightening events that had been taking place all over of Poitou without her knowledge.

"I can't deny my guilt, even if I earned it through loyalty to my king. I will do everything in my power to persuade Henry to deal fairly with the court. That much I promise you."

She wanted to believe him and the warm sincerity she spied in his eyes, yet Katherine's words about his past resurfaced just then, cautioning her against placing too much trust in a man she'd been attracted to from the moment they'd met. She could not soften toward him for a third time. How could she face her conscience if she allowed herself to be so naive?

"I hope that is true." She became aware of his nearness in the shadowy ruins, surrounded by naught but a few hills dotted with sheep and the purple rays of a setting sun in the distance. They were utterly alone in the remote countryside. "But I am too unsettled this day to think through the consequences of Eleanor's return to England or my potential status as an enemy of the crown." She shuddered.

"You are frightened."

"This surprises you?" He didn't need to comprehend *all* the fears that worried her. Her doubts about him—about his character—weren't a topic she wished to examine here.

Alone.

Ivy never thought she would have missed Lady Gertrude and her yapping dog, but any chaperone would have been welcome right now. Even one who had a demonic viper for a pet.

"It should not, I suppose." He brushed past her to return the way they'd just come, his tall, lean frame somehow appearing all the more male without the trappings of court to detract from his strength.

Curious, she followed him.

"But it does," she said. "You thought I would be secure in the decision to leave court and race headlong across unfamiliar terrain in the company of a man whose reputation as a heartbreaker is nearly as great as his well-known preference for—"

She halted herself before she went too far, but perhaps her companion filled in the blank, since his pace slowed. Stopped.

"For what, Ivy? A troubadour should know better than to prolong the suspense overmuch when her audience is hanging on her every word." He turned to consider her, his narrowed eyes glittering. "What is it that you think I have a preference for?"

Her mouth went dry at the question. If her brain could have produced a plausible lie, she would have gladly used it. But with the weight of his stare seeing clear through her, she could not make any answer but the truth.

"Innocents." Her whispered admission echoed in her ears more loudly than a clap of thunder breaking over a spring rainstorm.

"Forgive me, lady." He bowed to her with the lazy grace and polished manner that had marked his first appearance at the Court of Love. But his silver gaze held none of the self-deprecating gleam that had been there then. All she saw in his eyes now was anger. "I thought that because you know me better than does any other woman at court, you might choose to let my actions shape your opinion of me, rather than tired rumors and well-told gossip."

Guilt pinched her conscience as she recalled that he had never given her reason to doubt him. Had he wished to steal more from her than a kiss that day near the pear tree, she would have granted him all he wished, and yet he hadn't pressed his advantage. He'd even chastised himself for the lapse.

"I—"

"I do not know what to say to ease your fears this night. It is unsafe to risk riding any farther. However, I assure you I will do all within my power to provide you with more circumspect surroundings tomorrow night, so that you will have no cause to worry about your—" he paused for a moment and bit off a curse before leaning forward to emphasize the point "—innocence."

The full impact of his words settled around her. She had not only angered him; she had hurt him, too. He'd trusted her enough to let her see the man behind the courtier's mask, and she had repaid him by flinging his past in his face. A past that might or might not be true.

He turned from her then to descend the mound on which the old keep had been built. As she stared after him, she realized the sun had fully set, leaving her in utter darkness to make sense of the day's events. Her life as a troubadour to Queen Eleanor was over, making her feel almost as bereft as the sight of Roger Stancliff walking away from her with all due haste.

A wise man would still be sitting at Poitiers waiting for his king to arrive. If Roger had ignored the plight of those around him—one green-eyed poet in particular—he could have been present to accept Henry's thanks and make sure the king honored his bargain to return the Stancliff lands to Roger's control.

But, as Roger readjusted his bedroll and yanked yet another rock from underneath the linens so it wouldn't jab his shoulder blade, he had to admit he had nothing in common with a wise man, or he wouldn't be escorting an ungrateful merchant's daughter halfway across the country just so he could prolong their time together while he told himself he was ensuring her safety.

Saints deliver him from his own idiocy. He did not think Henry would clap him in irons for not seeing his assignment through to completion. However, there was a chance the king would view consorting with Ivy as traitorous, since all of the troubadours would be suspected of supporting Eleanor in conspiring against the crown. Roger needed to remain watchful for troops sent to find those who had escaped Poitiers.

Pitching the rock across the decaying great hall, Roger stared up though the mostly missing roof at the abundance of stars in the sky and tried not to think about Ivy sleeping a mere few feet away. Soft. Warm. And scared out of her wits that he would take unfair advantage of her.

The injustices of his past had never given him cause for so much regret. He'd been livid with his betrothed. Enraged at the choices she'd made without giving any thought to him. Of course, he had been deeply sorry at her death, but he had mourned more for her parents than for himself.

And he had mourned her unborn child above all.

With an effort, he wrenched his thoughts out of the past and into a present that seemed continuously tainted by a short period of his life he had no power to fix. He had thought his time at Poitiers would be a chance for a new start, but if anything, the court had only shown him how deeply engrained his reputation had become among his peers. And among watchful young innocents like Ivy Rutherford.

She sighed in her sleep, her throaty hum inciting a physical response and forcing him to admit she was one innocent who appealed to him on every conceivable level. Not that he would ever do a damn thing about it.

Except kiss her, his conscience reminded him.

Staring up at the stars dotting the sky, he relived that kiss just long enough to ensure he'd never find a peaceful night's sleep with her lying so near. Well, not that near. She'd carefully chosen a resting spot well away from him until she'd heard the feet of a rodent skittering across the crumbling stone floor.

Ah, the comfort of knowing he ranked higher than common vermin on her list of preferences.

He forced his eyes closed and timed his breath to hers in the hope that he could follow her into sleep. In. Out. In.

In again. Sharply.

Ivy pulled up to a sitting position beside him, her movements sharp. She sat utterly still for a long moment before her hands reached out alongside her. In the pale illumination of a partly clouded moon, he could not discern what she might be searching for on the hard rock floor. A loose stone that caused her discomfort? A sip of wine to soothe herself back to slumber?

Or, perhaps, did she reach for him?

The thought tantalized him even as he knew that could not be the case. She'd fit so perfectly against him the one time he'd thrown off all caution and tasted her. He dreamed of her even while waking, his thoughts never far from imagining what it would be like to take another small sampling of her lips. And more…

His heated thoughts vanished as she rose to her feet. What did she think she was about?

Instantly alert, he said nothing as she stole closer to the sack containing her garments. Did she think to depart like some stealthy thief? Perhaps she regretted her hasty decision to let him accompany her away from Poitiers, but she must know that to make a journey on her own would be foolishly lack-witted.

Incensed that she would consider something so dangerous rather than accept his protection, he began conjuring a chastisement to blister her ears when she tugged something from her bag—something thin and long—and smuggled the item back to the pile of linens she'd thrown over some cut tall grasses for a bed.

What mischief was this?

"If you've hidden a dagger in your bag, you'd better have a bloody good reason."

She yelped in surprise, dropping the item with a soft thunk onto the bed linens. Already he was on his knees, leaning over her to see for himself what she'd stowed away from him.

"It is nothing." She scrambled back, but he held her fast, his hand closing around her arm to keep her from running. Possibly to keep her from reaching for a weapon.

Alice had had so many secrets from him. A side to her character he'd known nothing about. How could he be fooled continually by women who wore the guise of innocence?

"I would prefer to decide for myself if it is nothing. Generally when someone chooses the route of subterfuge, that person has guilty secrets they do not wish to share."

His hand felt along the linens in the dark, his frustration urging him to ignore the softness of Ivy's kirtle and her arm beneath it. The scent of her clean hair and of clothing that must have been stored in a wardrobe packed with dried flowers. So great was his anger that he could almost ignore the bolt of desire that shot through him when his searching hand grazed her thigh as he patted the linens to find the item she'd hidden.

Almost.

"You are mistaken," she protested, her hand now feeling along the ground beside his even as she folded her legs beneath her. No doubt to keep them out of the way of his roaming fingers.

His hand found what he sought a short distance away, where it had rolled off the linens onto the ground. The item was not a knife, but a lightweight tube.

"What in the name of—?"

He tried to pull it away to examine whatever he'd found, but her hand joined his on the object at the same moment.

Night birds called a lonely song in the silence between them. The moon edged from behind a cloud to light their encounter a little more thoroughly.

She'd been hiding a parchment scroll.

"Poetry." She made the declaration with a passionate sense of importance that even Queen Eleanor couldn't have topped.

Poetry? Heaven help him, it probably was. And yet...

"What manner of poetry requires you to read in the dark?" He released her arm in the hope of thinking more clearly. Now that he had her scroll for leverage, he didn't fear that she would try to escape him. The contents of the parchment were obviously important. What if she had hidden messages from the queen? She had Eleanor's ear and the wit to carry off such a plot.

"Private poetry." Ivy released the scroll slowly. "No artist wishes to have her words displayed for public consumption until they have been retooled and refined."

"And you work on this in the dark?" He wanted to believe her.

"When the subject matter is sensitive and I do not have the luxury of sitting in my solar beside a warm fire to chase off a spring night's chill, yes." She straightened in a movement he could detect even among the shadows cast by the overgrown trees surrounding the ruins.

He extracted the parchment from the tube.

"I cannot come close to making it out." He strained his eyes, but even with the parchment lifted nearly to his nose, he could discern none of the letters on the page.

"It is difficult to see, but then I was not in the act of reading." Her voice contained a hint of soft vulnerability that made him suspect she told the truth.

An Important Message from the Editors

Dear Reader,

Because you've chosen to read one of our fine romance novels, we'd like to say "thank you!" And, as a **special** way to thank you, we've selected <u>two more</u> of the books you love so well **plus** two exciting Mystery Gifts to send you — absolutely <u>FREE</u>!

Please enjoy them with our compliments...

Pam Powers

Peel off seal and place inside...

lift here

How to validate your Editor's
"Thank You"
FREE GIFTS

1. Peel off gift seal from front cover. Place it in space provided at right. This automatically entitles you to receive 2 FREE BOOKS and 2 FREE mystery gifts.

2. Send back this card and you'll get 2 new Harlequin® *Historical* novels. These books have a cover price of $5.50 or more each in the U.S. and $6.50 or more each in Canada, but they are yours to keep absolutely free.

3. There's no catch. You're under no obligation to buy anything. We charge nothing—ZERO—for your first shipment. And you don't have to make any minimum number of purchases— not even one!

4. The fact is, thousands of readers enjoy receiving their books by mail from The Harlequin Reader Service®. They enjoy the convenience of home delivery...they like getting the best new novels at discount prices BEFORE they're available in stores... and they love their Reader to Reader subscriber newsletter featuring author news, special book offers, book reviews and much more!

5. We hope that after receiving your free books you'll want to remain a subscriber. But the choice is yours— to continue or cancel, any time at all! So why not take us up on our invitation, with no risk of any kind. You'll be glad you did!

GET TWO *Free* MYSTERY GIFTS...

*SURPRISE MYSTERY GIFTS COULD BE YOURS **FREE** AS A SPECIAL "THANK YOU" FROM THE EDITORS*

The Editor's "Thank You" Free Gifts Include:

- *Two NEW Romance novels!*
- *Two exciting mystery gifts!*

▲ DETACH AND MAIL CARD TODAY! ▼

Yes!

I have placed my Editor's "Thank You" seal in the space provided at right. Please send me 2 free books and 2 free mystery gifts. I understand I am under no obligation to purchase any books, as explained on the back and on the opposite page.

PLACE
FREE GIFTS
SEAL
HERE

349 HDL EFV4

246 HDL EFZ4

FIRST NAME

LAST NAME

ADDRESS

APT.#

CITY

STATE/PROV.

ZIP/POSTAL CODE

(H-H-08/06)

Thank You!

Offer limited to one per household and not valid to current Harlequin® Historical subscribers.

Your Privacy — Harlequin Books is committed to protecting your privacy. Our Privacy Polic is available online at www.eharlequin.com or upon request from the Harlequin Reader Service. From time to time we make our lists of customers available to reputable firms who may have a product or service of interest to you. If you would prefer for us not to share your name and address, please check here. ☐

© 2003 HARLEQUIN ENTERPRISES LTD.
® and ™ are trademarks owned and used by the trademark owner and/or its licensee

The Harlequin Reader Service — Here's how it works:

Accepting your 2 free books and 2 free mystery gifts places you under no obligation to buy anything. You may keep the books and gifts and return the shipping statement marked "cancel." If you do not cancel, about a month later we'll send you 6 additional books and bill you just $4.69 each in the U.S., or $5.24 each in Canada, plus 25¢ shipping & handling per book and applicable taxes if any.* That's the complete price and — compared to cover prices starting from $5.50 each in the U.S. and $6.50 each in Canada — it's quite a bargain! You may cancel at any time, but if you choose to continue, every month we'll send you 6 more books, which you may either purchase or return to us and cancel your subscription.

*Terms and prices subject to change without notice. Sales tax applicable in N.Y. Canadian residents will be charged applicable provincial taxes and GST. All orders subject to approval. Credit or debit balances in a customer's account(s) may be offset by any other outstanding balance owed by or to the customer. Please allow 4 to 6 weeks for delivery.

If offer card is missing write to: The Harlequin Reader Service, 3010 Walden Ave., P.O. Box 1867, Buffalo, NY 14240-9952

BUSINESS REPLY MAIL
FIRST-CLASS MAIL   PERMIT NO. 717-003   BUFFALO, NY

POSTAGE WILL BE PAID BY ADDRESSEE

HARLEQUIN READER SERVICE
3010 WALDEN AVE
PO BOX 1867
BUFFALO NY 14240-9952

NO POSTAGE
NECESSARY
IF MAILED
IN THE
UNITED STATES

Lowering the scroll, he mulled over the meaning of her words.

"You woke from sleep to write in the privacy of darkness." He had heard stories of jongleurs and minstrels who composed songs while drunk. Perhaps her preference for nighttime writing was merely a creative eccentricity.

"When the right words come to me, I must capture them in ink no matter the hour."

"Very well." He eased away from her, giving her room to collect herself after he'd touched her arm. Her thigh. Dear God, he'd never sleep again, now that he possessed yet another memory of her body beneath his hands. "I will make a deal with you."

"A deal?"

"A bargain of sorts."

She blew out a frustrated breath and sat back on her heels.

"I'm listening."

"If you tell me what bit of poetry you planned to pen tonight, I will take you at your word about what's contained on this parchment and spare you the embarrassment of having me walk to the fire to retrieve a glowing coal by which to read for myself."

Her sharp intake of breath followed by a long pause did not bode well for her honesty. His jaw tightened along with his fists as he wondered what dark intrigue her writings might contain.

But then, she lifted her voice in the clear, high lilt of a stage performer and began to recite.

"I place my heart in jeopardy,
To look upon his face.
But still I wish most fervently
To lie in his embrace."

The silence that followed her words might have stretched out for hours, since Roger could find no answer to her blatantly sensual poetry. *This* is what she wrote? This unashamedly corporeal celebration?

His breathing became labored. But before he allowed himself to be swept away on a tide of answering lust, he had to ask just one question.

"I'm not going to sleep until I know to whom this poem is addressed." His blood pulsed through his veins with all the brutal force of a spring river full of melting snow. "So tell me, Lady Ivy. Whose embrace do you covet so keenly it keeps you awake at night?"

Chapter Ten

Ivy waited for her heart to slow its galloping beat, praying she could draw a full breath before she needed to make her answer. While the stars winked above them, she thanked the saints for the cover of darkness that hid her fiery cheeks. Could she help it if Roger was providing as much of a romantic education for her as she had once planned for him?

Except that while Ivy had tried to teach him about the ennobling power of love and the way pure love could enrich a man's life, Roger had taught her that the relationship between a man and woman could be far more complicated, because it wasn't just a mental commitment. The physical component was so powerful it could make a woman's pulse race and her mouth go dry.

A heated condition with which she'd become much too familiar, despite the cool temperature of the spring night.

Finally, pulling her temporary bed linens back over her legs in a laughable attempt to shield herself and her vulnerabilities, Ivy forced herself to push words past her lips.

"What makes you think I am the speaker in the poem?" She had hoped to deliver the question with a certain amount of cool disdain, but she could not quite manage the task when she could scarcely catch her breath.

Curse the man for putting her in an untenable position, when she'd only sought to jot a few lines of her poem. But she could not risk him reading the full text of the piece she'd been writing, or he would see too much between the lines.

"Isn't that the convention in your art?" His voice wound around her with silky warmth, the rich timbre humming through her agitated nerves, soothing and exciting at the same time. "I seem to remember many of Comtesse Marie's poems starting with a reference to herself as 'I' before she revealed her topic and transferred her attention to a 'he' or 'she.'"

"I am bound by no rules other than to create meaningful works of poetry that will move my listeners." She had been striving for authentic subject matter. Little had she known she only had to crack open her heart for all the world to see to succeed in creating something beautiful.

"And yet you have obviously crafted a piece full of passionate meaning. Perhaps it would be more to the point to inquire where you found your inspiration for such a…powerful piece of verse."

Her embarrassment at the sexual nature of her poem lessened a small amount at his admission that he found it powerful.

"It has always been my goal to write moving pieces." She savored the compliment even while she stalled for time to answer his question.

"I believe you mentioned that when we first met." His crisp tone struck her as abrupt, or perhaps annoyed. "I think you've achieved your desire, since I find myself moved indeed."

"Then perhaps in acknowledgement of my increasing poetic prowess, you could return the scroll to me and we could put the whole matter behind us." She reached out, seeing the shadowy outline of her parchment still his hands.

And while she wanted her poem back very much, she had to admit the outline of *him* was no less enticing. His squared shoulders were as stalwart as those of any workman who made a living by his strength. And although she had complained he was too bold in his speech—a true enough observation—he still possessed far more refinement than the coarse men who moved in her father's world.

"I will admit the unexpectedly lustful snippet you've shared with me has made me all the more eager to read the rest." He maintained his grip on her work, his soft threat unleashing a wave of panic inside her.

The scroll loomed within tantalizing reach. And it was hers, after all.

She lunged for the parchment.

Her fingers brushed hard male instead of delicate vellum, however, her nails scratching lightly along his braies as she extended herself onto his bedroll. Off balance, she steadied herself on him as she fell even further forward, her depth perception skewed in the darkness that swallowed them. But her fingers did not sink into his solid, unforgiving strength. She would have fallen neatly into his lap if his arms had not reached out to steady her. Embrace her.

Oh.

The heat of him surrounded her. Enveloped her. He gripped her upper arm with one hand while his other slipped past her shoulder to rest on her spine. She had not removed her clothes to sleep, so she was not completely without protection, but his touch penetrated silks and velvets to enflame the skin beneath.

She remained there, for an endless moment. Even when they kissed they had not been so close. And now that she remembered the scent of him, the feel of him, she found herself recalling the taste of him.

"You must release me." Her words were more a plea than a command, but heaven help her, she was not sure if she could extricate herself without his help. He wore a tunic but no surcoat, and the strength of his muscles beneath the thin linen was all too apparent. Just the suggestion of his chiseled form made her body sink ever so slightly toward him, as if to test how they would fit together.

"You are free to go whenever you wish." His words emanated from a place too near her own lips, his breath warm on her cheek in the chilly night air.

Any moment now she would pry herself away from him and return to her own blanket. She only needed a little resolve, and a lot more control of her wayward impulses. But then the hand that had been on her arm slid up and along her shoulder to skim her neck, her jaw.

Her whole body remained motionless, spellbound by his touch, waiting to see what he would do next. She sensed him come nearer in the darkness, leaning, seeking, coaxing her forward.

"But if you would like to stay," he murmured into her ear, "you are more than welcome to sleep beside me."

The suggestion echoed the lament in her poem, and her hunger for physical connection was as potent as any need she'd ever experienced. But somehow, hearing him speak the words aloud gave her the impetus she needed to draw away. She remembered how forbidden intimate contact remained.

"Do not speak of such things." She retreated from him the way one might leap from a balefire fueled by a sharp wind.

"Why? We can only think about them?" He leaned close again and she edged back. "Or write about them?"

When something scraped against her knee, she realized that he'd only been handing her the scroll that had precipitated the whole tangle of limbs.

"Thank you." She didn't know what more to say at this point. Her thoughts were too scrambled where he was concerned.

"I would have given you the damn parchment, you know." He lowered himself back to his bed on the hard stone floor and yanked the blankets back in place. "I am a man of my word, despite what you may believe."

"I see a man who has betrayed his queen." Her attraction to him would not erase that fact.

"I know you do. But since we will soon return to the land where you may viewed as the betrayer instead of me, perhaps having a loyal subject by your side will not be such a bad thing."

Tucking her poem into her bed linens beside her, Ivy settled deeper in the blankets and thought about what he'd been trying to tell her. Soon she would not be able to voice her support for the queen without fear of censure. Or worse.

By the time they returned to England, she might need Roger's assistance to vouch for her loyalty to the king, if she wanted to avoid whatever fate Henry had in mind for Eleanor's court members. Then again, Ivy might escape everyone's notice, because of her lowly position and lack of noble ties since her mother's death.

For the first time in her life, she thought that kind of anonymity would prove beneficial, because under no circumstances would she wish to be beholden to a man whose touch left her defenseless.

* * *

Luck rode with Roger the next week when he encountered men from an English keep in Normandy on the main road north shortly before noon. He and Ivy had traveled far enough north and west to put themselves well away from Henry's troops marching on Poitiers, but their horses were weary.

As was he.

Leaning low against his mare's neck, he urged her faster. This was no warhorse bred for battle, but a fleet-footed mount that thrived on speed. After the torment of the days and nights alone with Ivy, he found himself ready to run from the solitude that put them in such close quarters. Tonight, he would install them safely at Beauvais Keep so that he did not have to risk another night under the stars with a woman he had no right to touch.

A shout from behind him forced him to rein in his mare, reminding him he needed to be vigilant about Ivy's safety. Thieves abounded in the wooded stretches of the road.

"Do you seek to outrun me?" She caught up to him and slowed to a walk, her breathless words recalling to mind how remiss he'd been in his duty to watch over her.

"Hardly. But since it is usually me who is in pursuit of you, I thought you might appreciate a moment of freedom from being the center of my cosmos." He patted his mare on the neck, grateful for her effort and speed, even if he had not used them wisely.

"You have no audience here, my lord." She peered around the forest road, the woodlands vacant except for an occasional roe in the distance and a few birds overhead. "There is no need for pretense that I am any more to you than a means for maintaining your court residence."

Settling her long skirts over the horse's flank, she plucked at the embroidered fabric with a gaze that seemed too intent.

Too practiced.

Realization slammed home.

"And you think my attention to you was all part of an act." No wonder she didn't trust him. Bad enough he'd turned traitor to her beloved queen. He'd compounded his sins by appearing false on every count in her eyes.

He gathered the reins of her mount to draw them out of sight of the road. He did not think they'd been followed, but he could not risk discovery by the wrong people—not now, when they'd made it this far.

"I always knew it to be a façade." She peered down her nose at him with wise green eyes that looked too old and knowing for an innocent romantic. "As did everyone else at court, since I was hand-picked to be an undesirable tutor for you. But I can understand your need to play the charmer to me in front of everyone else, since your incorrigible ways make you the ideal candidate for love lessons."

Her phrasing called forth a primal image in his mind as he considered how he would like to repay her with a few love lessons of his own. It seemed to him they had not covered the most intriguing aspects.

"What I fail to see is why you feel the need to continue the pretense of impassioned lover when we are alone."

"I do not think our shrewd queen chose you as an undesirable tutor so much as a harmless companion for a knight she probably suspected to be a spy. And trust me, lady, you have not experienced my impassioned lover aspect." Although the thought brought a smile to his lips.

And a pretty blush to her cheek.

"You're right. I would allow no lover of mine to speak to me so boldly."

"You mean so intimately?"

"Yes," she snapped, chin tilted high as she refused to look at him.

He studied her as they guided their horses through the undergrowth alongside the road, the fluttering hem of her gown occasionally brushing his leg in a way that made him think of all the things he shouldn't. The caress was light, fleeting.

Memorable.

She looked so at home here, hidden from view from anyone save him, her guileless beauty more in keeping with the natural surroundings than with the sophisticated glamour of the court. Her blue kirtle and surcoat were made of fabric an expensive shade of blue that few women could afford. The garments hugged in a way that did not reflect the very latest fashion but suited her much better than the current exaggerated silhouettes.

"You will see one day that you cannot dictate behavior to a lover." He only wanted to impart a bit of hard-won wisdom to her, but as soon as he spoke the words, he realized how personal they were. "That is the blessing and the curse of it all. No matter how carefully you devise a vision of what love is supposed to be like, you will find your own relationship unique and unable to conform to your ideals."

"You make it sound disappointing." She was looking at him now, her green eyes curious and catlike in their unblinking assessment. "Do you think perhaps you create part of the problem in your liaisons because you always expect to be disappointed?"

He listened to the steady drone of their horses' rhythmic steps through the thicket as they made their way steadily toward Beauvais. Toward safety.

At least for a night or two.

"I cannot say, lady, but I do know that expecting disappointment is far better than expecting too much and falling short."

He would never forget that sense of failing to make Alice happy. Most men wouldn't care about a wife's contentment as long as she provided the right amount of political influence or money, but Roger had seen himself as a more considerate man.

How much easier it would have been for everyone if he'd simply set Alice free.

"At least those are honest words." She steered her

horse around a fallen branch, as competent at riding as she seemed to be at every other activity normally mastered only by the nobility. But then, he had heard somewhere that her mother had been the daughter of a high-ranking lord.

"I have been honest with you," he protested. "Aside from my work with the king, I have been nothing less than forthright from the moment we met."

"Your attention to me is not honest." She turned to meet his gaze, her expression serious. "And since I find it unsettling, I wish you would desist in the pretense now that you no longer need to fulfill a role at court."

Her simple, understandable request make him regret his aggressive pursuit of her more than any outraged accusation she might have made. Despite her birth, Ivy ranked as the most noble of women in his mind because of her high principles and uncompromising dedication to lofty ideals he'd once scoffed at as naive.

His life had simply conspired to make him more cynical then Ivy.

"Not for all the world would I wish to make you unhappy." He sounded like one of the lovesick suitors the troubadours praised in their poems, but he knew the words to be true. "Your friendship has been an unexpected treasure to me in a difficult time, and I promise I will not risk losing what regard of yours I might still hold."

He could promise no more than that, since Ivy

would be much more unsettled if she knew how she had dominated his thoughts of late.

"Thank you." She replied haltingly, perhaps realizing he had not truly offered the pledge that she'd requested. Still, she seemed determined to maintain peace and civility—and perhaps a certain amount of distance—between them.

"And while I have enjoyed our conversation— only moderately, of course, in deference to our new agreement—I think we have tarried long enough if you wish to rest in a real chamber this night. Beauvais is still many leagues from here."

They were better off racing over the countryside than making conversation in which he found more to admire about her. Besides, he needed to quiz his old friend Beauvais about the intrigue at Henry's court and what was to become of the deposed women of Poitiers.

"In a moment." She peered ahead down the winding road that had given way to rolling hills and open meadows of new green grass. The scent of wildflowers rode the breeze while the sun warmed their backs. "First you must tell me why you chose to accompany me from Poitiers and did not extend that offer of protection to anyone else."

When had the woman found such boldness? The more he knew her, the more he realized her quiet, reserved exterior hid a backbone of pure steel.

And—perhaps—some very torrid dreams, judging by her poetry.

"Can you imagine me with Gertrude for a sennight, or however long it would take to accompany a troupe of women to their homes?" He shuddered at the thought. "Half the women at the queen's court wanted to run me through for showing my arrogant face in their precious domain."

"Aye. While the other half wanted to seduce you."

He whipped his head around to look at her.

"Who the hell are you and what did you do with my sweet and innocent tutor?" Holy hell, he feared she'd made *him* blush.

And she sat there grinning unrepentantly upon her mount, her blue veils lifted by the breeze to reveal more of her long neck.

"I seem to have left her behind, along with my dream of finding fame as the queen's troubadour. I told you I expected no pretense from you. I hope you will allow me the same courtesy to speak freely, now that we are not living in the confines of a household where gossip spreads faster than pestilence." She swatted a dragonfly that hovered near her shoulder. "And it is plain to see you are more pursued by women than they are pursued by you, so I just wondered if this was why you chose not to offer your protection to anyone else at court. Have women become too much trouble for you in the past?"

Her words struck closer to home than she could possibly realize.

"Most of the women at Poitiers have husbands to attend them." He changed topics swiftly, more than ready to pick up their pace again to escape the conversation.

"Many of their husbands may side with Henry against their wives."

"Nevertheless, I would overstep my bounds to assist a married woman. You and Katherine de Blois were in the minority of unwed women, and I saw that your friend had already received an escort who seems to know her better than I. Since you had extended your help to me at court, I thought it only fair I repay you with safe passage home to your father."

He wasn't sure which part of his speech caused her to go quiet, but she retreated to her own thoughts then, as if the idea of returning home caused her worry. Did she regret the loss of her court position so much?

Or did it pain her to think of leaving behind the luxury of the queen's residence for her far less exalted familial home?

Whatever had caused her to turn quiet, Roger was grateful for a reprieve from her picking around his head. He had shared more of himself with Ivy than he had ever given to any woman and yet his tenuous position with the king—with his homeland— prohibited him from offering her any more than his friendship.

Truly, after the hell his betrothed had put him through, he feared he would never trust any woman to be faithful. And romantic Ivy was a woman who deserved more from a man than doubts and jealousy. She should settle for nothing less than the simpering courtly lover she dreamed about and wrote poems about.

Roger hated him already.

Chapter Eleven

Beauvais Keep bore little resemblance to the queen's residence, but Ivy looked forward to spending the night in a structure with the roof intact, especially since the gathering clouds suggested a storm brewed nearby. And the political storm brewing...she did not claim to understand the complex relationship between Henry and Eleanor, but she knew their maneuverings had little to do with courtly love and everything to do with power.

No matter that Eleanor revered the arts and made a place for them in her court, at heart she was as strong and ambitious as her political husband. The falling out between London and Poitiers would shake foundations all over Europe. Beauvais Keep might be loyal to the king, but Roger knew the family and knew the king was not in residence.

They would be safe here.

Ivy and Roger arrived at Beauvais shortly before sunset, the sky streaked with purple still illuminating the courtyard in front of the massive stone tower that housed the living area for the Beauvais family. Men at arms roamed the courtyard instead of gently bred ladies, the presence of swords and hounds and an active practice yard reminding Ivy that she might have witnessed the most elegant court ever known in her time at Poitiers.

"I will explain our situation to our host," Roger warned as he helped her off her horse to stand beside him on the smooth stones of the well-worn floor. "The Beauvais have been loyal to our throne for generations, so we dare not glorify Eleanor's court while we remain here."

She nodded, intimidated by Roger's serious manner and the looming, male-dominated keep. Would she be welcome as a guest with her tradesman heritage? Or would she be asked to sleep with the servants?

She did not fit anywhere in a keep that ignored the arts. She was a poet, not a servant. Not a noblewoman. And while her modest sense of pride would not balk at sleeping on the floor of a great hall with twenty other strangers, she would feel awkward doing so while Roger remained a guest.

Taking his arm while they walked across the courtyard to the main doors swung open wide to the mild weather, Ivy considered she would have been better off sleeping under the stars again.

At least in nature, class boundaries did not matter.

They were escorted into the keep by two armed guards, a frightening indication of the uneasy times. Since begging Roger to take her back into the anonymity of the forest for the night was no longer an option, Ivy simply clung to his arm for as long as he would let her. She realized now that she'd been too hasty in questioning the propriety of their sleeping quarters the night before. She should have been more concerned about the complicated politics of the kingdom and how they could hurt her than about her attraction to Roger and what the world would think of her if she spent the night close to him.

Would it matter what anyone thought of her if she were clamped in irons by Henry's supporters before she made it home?

"You are safe," Roger whispered in her ear as they wound through a passageway toward the great hall, where the voices of men in angry conversation could already be heard. "Do not worry."

Apparently she hadn't disguised her fears well. She had probably dug a hole in the back of his hand with her nails.

They had scarcely rounded the corner where the great hall came in view when a familiar feminine voice assailed her ears.

"Ivy!" From the dark recesses of the smoke-filled chamber, Katherine de Blois suddenly appeared before her, still wearing the same kirtle and surcoat she'd had on when Ivy had last seen her at Poitiers, her garments a little worse for wear but her face flushed with pleasure.

"Katherine." Ivy hugged her friend despite the wealth of male eyes upon them, their reunion distracting the men from their heated discussion of Henry's rebellious sons.

The men at arms announced Roger, although the noble in the center of the dais table had already risen to greet him as if they were friends. Ivy noted James Forrester sat at the high table as well, making Katherine's presence in the back of the hall all the more strange.

"Stancliff." The big, bluff nobleman who greeted him wore heavy chain mail even in his own hall. His long, dark hair matched a beard that fell to the middle of his chest. "You and your lady are well met."

She tensed, wondering if Roger would be honor bound to identify her properly. After all, she had told him earlier that day to keep things honest between them. What a poor time to realize a small amount of subterfuge on occasion wouldn't offend her in the least.

"We are weary from the journey and would be most grateful for a night's shelter on our way back to London, if you have room." He neatly avoided introducing her at all, but then their host didn't look interested in her presence.

"There is always room for a friend, as I told Forrester here." The nobleman, who could only be Edward Beauvais, gestured to James and drew Roger closer to the high table as he waved over a cupbearer. "You are both king's men, so perhaps the two of you can talk sense into these young loggerheaded miscreants who sympathize with Henry's whelps, who vie for his seat before their father's in the grave."

Ivy might have felt more bereft at Roger's defection if not for Katherine tugging on her arm.

"Let us retire," she whispered as the men took up their argument, drawing Roger and James into the debate. "I have already been given a chamber for the night. You can share with me."

Grateful for the chance to escape a hall that didn't seem to observe normal protocol anyhow, Ivy nodded, picking up her traveling bag and allowing Katherine to lead her away from the smoke and dirty rushes toward a narrow staircase.

"I've been worried about you," Ivy confided as they traversed the stairs. A gray-striped cat sprinted past them, no doubt chasing vermin the scant torchlight hid from view.

"You needn't have been." Katherine's hushed voice couldn't disguise her excitement. "This has been the most wonderful adventure of my life."

"Having the Court of Love disbanded? Probably forever?" Ivy halted in the shadowy corridor that emitted a musty odor, even on the second floor. She still couldn't bear to think about the life she'd lost. Her art. Her inspiration. "Did James not inform you we may all be enemies of the king for our loyalty to Eleanor?"

"Well, that aspect is worrisome, I'll admit. Although that is where my family's ties to Henry will smooth the way for me. If anything, it is I who should worry about you. What will happen to you now?" Katherine opened a chamber door and brought a torch from the corridor inside the room with her, since no fire had been laid to cut the chill. Or the mustiness.

Ivy shook her head helplessly.

"I cannot say. My father will expect me home." To marry a wealthy merchant with all haste, since she'd failed to obtain the noble lord he would have preferred.

She could not think about it.

Ivy laid more wood in the hearth to help her start a blaze with the torch. There were piles of bark in place already—maybe for years, judging by the dust on the hearth—and the fire caught quickly.

"So what has been a wonderful adventure for you?" Eager to dismiss her somber thoughts, Ivy peered around the chamber, seeing few of Katherine's possessions except for a brush and a fresh surcoat. "Oh, wait. I know."

Realization made her smile.

"James." Katherine confirmed Ivy's guess as they worked together to beat the linens on the bed. "I refused to leave Poitiers with him unless he admitted he cared for me."

"You wicked woman." Ivy pulled her own sheet from her traveling bag to lay over the linens, just to be safe. "Are you not afraid he would have said anything to protect you from the descent of Henry's men?"

"Ivy Rutherford, what happened to your romantic streak?" Katherine withdrew a blanket from her bag to add to their improvised bedding. "You've been spending too much time with Stancliff if you would take such a dark view. And, no, I am not worried that James lied to me, because I have known all along that he cares for me. He simply could not admit it to himself."

"Does he plan to speak to your father?" Ivy wondered if a marriage based on love was possible despite everything the women at court had told her.

"I do not know. I told him I'm more than willing to let him steal me away so he can avoid talking to my father altogether." She untied the laces at her waist before presenting her back to Ivy to silently request help with the remaining fasteners. "What choice would my family have but to give their blessing if I decided to run off with James?"

"What if your father disowned you?" Ivy unhooked the jeweled girdle around her friend's waist, unwilling to let Katherine make a rash decision without thinking through the consequences. "My mother's family accepted a small fortune from my father for their daughter's hand, but they refused to have anything to do with any of us after the wedding."

Not even when Ivy's mother lay dying in a difficult childbirth ten years after Ivy had been born. The Burkshires had wanted no contact with a merchant family, even if they'd sold their own daughter into a life she'd never wanted. Ivy had lost her mother and her baby sister the same year she realized how deeply her grandparents regretted their association with Ivy's family.

"How sad for her." Katherine held her fallen girdle in one hand and squeezed Ivy's arm with the other. "How sad for you all. But my family is not counting on me to make an overly profitable marriage, and I do not think my father would take issue with a knight for his daughter, since our ancestors built the family legacy through recognition gained in battle."

"In other words, James Forrester is no merchant." There seemed to be no polite way around the obvious. "I understand this. I just want to be sure you are prepared for how grave the consequences could be if you deny your family the right to choose your husband."

Katherine slipped off her surcoat and left her kirtle on for sleeping. The evening was still young, but the bed seemed the only clean place to sit if they were to make themselves comfortable. Settling between the clean sheets, Katherine bit her lip and seemed to consider the notion.

"And I do not know that James wishes to act upon my regard for him." She lay back on the pillows with a thump, and Ivy imagined that if they could see the room more clearly, a cloud of dust would be visible wafting up from the existing linens on the bed. "He is noble to a fault about not wanting me to settle for a marriage that is beneath me."

"He wants what is best for you." Relieved that James would not resort to bride-stealing at Katherine's request, Ivy tugged off her surcoat and hose for the night. "The mark of a worthy man."

"Too worthy." Katherine did not sound all that pleased about the fact. "He is impossible to corrupt, although I'm trying my best."

A knock sounded at the chamber entrance and Ivy answered in only her night rail, hiding behind the door while a surly maid dragged in a small bucket of water without a word and then left just as quietly, taking with her the torch that Katherine and Ivy had filched from the wall outside the chamber. In the brief time the door had been open, Ivy heard the shouts of dissension in the great hall as the men argued about the future of the kingdom and which of Henry's sons was the most capable.

"I don't suppose it's hot?" Katherine called from where she'd buried herself in blankets after the maid shut the door behind her.

"Of course not." Ivy knew the answer even before she dipped a finger in to test it. "I think we should celebrate that anyone even remembered us. Do you suppose our hosts are at least feeding the men?"

Rinsing her teeth before using the rest of the water to wash, Ivy dripped dry and then claimed the other half of the bed.

"Perhaps they are too immersed in their talk of battle and politics to notice the lack of sustenance. I, for one, will be grateful to leave as soon as possible." Katherine levered up on her elbow, perhaps too restless to sleep. "Not that I don't enjoy your company, because I'm thrilled to see you. I just hope to make some headway with James before he returns me to my home and breaks my heart for two summers in a row."

"You mentioned you were trying to corrupt him?" Ivy had not forgotten that startling revelation. She peered around the chamber, noting the faded tapestries and an expanse of leaded glass in a high window, and decided the keep must have been cared for at one time.

"I'm working diligently toward that end, but since I am unfamiliar with seduction, I do not know how effective my methods have been." She plaited her hair while she spoke, the firelight casting a golden glow around her dark hair. Her exotic beauty gave her a look that had been at home in Poitiers with its Spanish and Italian influences, but Katherine must stand out among English noblewomen.

"You cannot be serious." Scandalized, Ivy wondered if other unwed women practiced such techniques. She'd seen the married women of the court throw themselves at other men—Roger in particular—but she hadn't thought the practice used by younger women.

"Maybe not." She paused in her plaiting, her hair wound around her fingers. "Do you think me an unwholesome hussy, that I would consider such a scheme?"

"Of course not." But since she couldn't hide her discomfort with the idea, she confided the truth. "My own father once suggested I do the same to win the attention of some dashing young noble so that I might raise myself up in the world, but—in that sense—the notion made me quite ill. What you are doing is entirely different because you like James and he returns your affection."

"Your father wanted you to seduce a man at court?" Her eyes grew round and her fingers picked up speed on the braid again. "I cannot picture any one making such a suggestion to you, Ivy, let alone your own sire."

"He is ruthless and shrewd, just as you would envision a clever tradesman. And while I don't begrudge him his wily assertiveness in trade, I wish he would not foist his methods on me when they are clearly not well-suited to my character."

"You could seduce Roger Stancliff in a trice."

Ivy's thoughts stilled like a mental hiccough, and then raced forward with unseemly visions.

"Do not be ridiculous." Although, her pride argued, he had kissed her readily enough in the Poitiers gardens just a few days ago. "Every woman at Eleanor's court agreed that I was in danger of being seduced by him, not the other way around."

The fire leaping in the grate at the foot of the bed echoed the heat that rose inside her at the thought of such intimacy.

"Granted, I am no expert, but from what I can tell, seduction works both ways." As Katherine leaned forward, her silky dark braid fell over her shoulder to curl on the bed beside her. "No man entices a woman he does not covet, right? So it stands to reason he is susceptible to you if he himself has entertained the thought of luring you to his bed."

"You've given this far too much thought." And now, no doubt, so would Ivy. She'd be fortunate to find any rest with the image of mutual seduction tantalizing her every time she closed her eyes. "And it makes no difference since I would never try to persuade a man of Lord Stancliff's station in life to compromise himself by…"

"You're the one who would be compromised, Ivy. With Roger Stancliff's reputation, he will be fortunate to make a marriage to anyone of consequence. What conscientious father would give his daughter to a man who drove his last intended wife to take her own life?" Closing her eyes, Katherine settled deeper into her pillow. "He would be fortunate to have you."

Ivy didn't know about that, having already decided Roger's reputation couldn't be all that bad if women threw themselves at him with regularity. Although perhaps flirting with a man was a far cry from marriage.

If anything, her heart ached for Roger, who might never find an appropriate spouse with such a dark past hanging over his head. He deserved more than an unwilling wife whose family was so desperate for gold they would sell her off to a man who could obtain no one else.

If only she possessed the noble credentials to help him, she could declare him reformed by the standards of the Court of Love. But who would accept her word, now that she was returning to her life as a merchant's daughter?

As she forced her own eyes closed, Ivy wondered if there could be any greater punishment for a poet than knowing her words carried no value. All too quickly, another voice inside her head spoke up. As a love poet, perhaps it would be a greater punishment to know her only chance at romance—if only for a brief time—was ending before she'd had the chance to explore the feeling for more than a few fleeting moments.

Roger did not wait for the sun to rise the next morning to knock on Ivy's door. He regretted waking her early when they'd ridden long and hard the last two days, but his discussion with Edward Beauvais last night had brought news that required urgent action.

Immediate departure.

"Ivy." He called to her through the door as he knocked, hoping she was not a heavy sleeper.

And, despite his haste to leave the keep, he could not stave off a physical response to the idea of her slumbering on the other side of the door, her body clad in naught but a night rail.

"Who is it?" She responded softly on the other side of the door, her words hesitatant.

"Roger." Who in Hades else would knock on her door in the middle of the night?

His grip tightened on the torch he carried. "I'm sorry to disturb your rest, but we must ride before sunrise. I will explain to you when we are safely away."

"Is something amiss? I will wake Katherine."

"Nay," he whispered, not wishing anyone to know of their defection. "She is safer here, but I need you to come with me."

"I will need a moment," she returned, her voice very close to the door now, as if she leaned against the barrier. "Our fire is out and it is difficult to see my way around a strange chamber."

He thought about offering to bring her a torch, but guessed she would not appreciate his presence while she dressed. Besides, he would rather Ivy's outspoken young roommate did not catch him in their bedchamber. Especially since Katherine's protector was more dangerous than Roger had ever guessed.

Not to Katherine, but certainly to Roger. And more importantly, James Forrester could be very dangerous to Ivy.

"I am ready." Ivy appeared before him suddenly, handing him her traveling bag as she closed the chamber door quietly behind her. Her jerky movements betrayed her nervousness. "But I pray you are right that Katherine is safe."

"I would not ask you to leave her if she was not." He took her arm to guide her through the dark corridors. "I would commend you on your swiftness, lady."

His mother had always taken excessive time with her appearance and he'd thought such inordinate attention to beauty was a trait many females shared, but Ivy's hair remained unbound around her shoulders with no veil in sight to restrain it. Her surcoat had not even been properly laced up one side while her girdle lay over her arm instead of around her waist.

"If I could have seen anything in that pitch-blackness I would have taken more time to dress, but it seems I could not find my own laces in the dark." Her flushed cheeks and tousled hair were an enticing combination. Her left cheek retained a tiny crease from a pillow or blanket, perhaps, the sleep line a delicate flaw that made his finger itch to trace its path and soothe away the exhaustion.

"I'm sorry." The longer he stared at her in the flickering torchlight, the more he regarded her with growing tenderness. "I wanted to stop here so that you could rest more peacefully, but instead I've only robbed you of more sleep."

"It is no matter." Her fingers worked quickly on the ties at her side, cinching her gown around her rounded curves.

Roger's mouth dried at the sight of her breasts molded against the soft velvet of a clean surcoat, the fabric cupping the mounds as gently as a lover's touch.

When she finished her task, he told himself now would be a good time to wrench his gaze away, but he was powerless for a long moment despite the knowledge of Forrester asleep in the keep. Roger remembered too well how she'd tasted when he'd kissed her, how she'd felt in his arms when he'd caught her the night she somehow landed in his lap.

When at last he met her gaze, her cheeks were bright pink while her eyes chastised him for his impertinence.

"You, sir, are an incorrigible lout to stir me out of bed with whispers of urgency and then linger in the corridors with bawdy thoughts."

Conceding her point, he urged her down the passageway, his torch raised high to light their way out of the keep.

"And just how do you propose to know my thoughts?" He'd rather keep her distracted with incidentals than have her question him about what was wrong. "I thought you were too innocent to suspect such things."

"You give me far too little credit, sir."

"At least my thoughts were honest." He hid his smile, surprised to discover Ivy's presence somehow made his worries lessen to a small degree. "I seem to recall you touted the merits of honesty between us yesterday."

Scoffing with obvious indignation, she followed him down the staircase, past the great hall and out the main entrance. Roger had given his thanks to their host the night before when he'd informed him their departure would be early.

Very early, judging by the position of the moon. But then, Roger had not slept at all after he lay down. Rest would elude any man while he resided under the same roof as a man who'd undermined and betrayed him.

"Roger?"

Her use of his first name made his step falter. He halted, surprised.

"Yes?"

"Sorry." She shook her head. "My tiredness is no excuse for poor manners."

"Of course it is." He wondered if he'd ever hear his Christian name spoken so simply, so intimately, from her lips again. "Besides, we have formed a rather close...friendship. I am glad you think of me that way."

"Truly, it is only that I am still half-asleep." She shrugged and he noticed her girdle now hugged her waist. She must have slipped it around herself as they walked. "I just wanted to mention that I haven't eaten and I hate the idea of leaving a keep with a larder—"

"I packed food for the road." He patted his bag and nudged her forward again, eager to ride out of Beauvais Keep—and, perhaps, eager to have Ivy all to himself again for at least a little while longer, before the rest of the world intruded on their tenuous connection. "We will stop a short distance from here and break our fast once the sun rises."

Once he could be certain they had not been followed.

Damn.

After learning the real reason behind James Forrester's presence at Poitiers, Roger knew his status with the king must have fallen in the time he'd been in Aquitaine. If Roger didn't return to London quickly, he might not have any lands left to his name, let alone any political weight to protect Ivy from Henry's anger with his wife and anyone he perceived to be her supporter.

Roger and Ivy each had their own reasons to fear royal repercussions in London, but together, they would present an even more visible target for the king. They needed to part ways as soon as possible to protect themselves, but saying goodbye to Ivy could prove to be a bigger challenge than any battlefield maneuver Roger had ever undertaken.

Chapter Twelve

Picking a deserted clearing for her request, Ivy shouted her words over the steady drum of their horses' hooves.

"I would know the truth of your reason for leaving Beauvais under cover of darkness." She had waited for some discussion to commence, but after riding for hours with no conversation, she could keep her silence no longer.

The coast surely loomed near. The scent of water teased her nose whenever a hard wind blew out of the north. The day had dawned gray, but not even the threat of rain had made Roger slow their fierce pace. He'd scarcely nodded at a band of pilgrims traveling toward the Holy Land, not even slowing down to receive a blessing from the priest or to make a donation to their noble cause. Whatever had chased him out of his friend's keep had surely been of dire consequence to inspire such a relentless ride.

Slowing his horse, he peered around the landscape as if debating whether or not the place provided adequate privacy.

"If we ride hard, we can be at the coast within two hours. Are you sure you would not rather speak of this then? The skies look ready to open at any moment." His mount sidestepped beneath him, still ready to run. Judging by Roger's scowl, Ivy suspected he echoed the sentiment.

"The skies have appeared thus all day. Unlike you, I do not return home to vast holdings. Reaching London signifies the end of my dreams as a court poet and the beginning of my father's quest for a suitable husband, which I shall despise at every turn." She had tried to thrust the matter from her mind, but the farther north they rode, the more the truth preyed upon her. "So whether or not the rains come, it would please me greatly to dawdle about this clearing until the moon rises. Or the next ten moons, for that matter."

Both horse and man seemed to relax a bit at her words.

"A husband hunt." Roger seemed to mull over the idea as he hauled one long leg over the animal's back and slid to the ground. "You have been promised to no man already?"

"Nay." She followed suit, dropping to the ground before he could help her, since the thought of his hands upon her made her anticipate the sensation far too much. "But let us not speak of that. I am more interested in our hasty departure from Beauvais.

Even if I was offered no bread or wine during our stay, I found the accommodation pleasant enough with my friend in residence."

His jaw tightened at the mention of Katherine. Or perhaps he merely reacted to the rumble of thunder in the distance.

"Beauvais told me there is a fair in progress some leagues distant. Not far from the channel where we will make our crossing." His words were punctuated by another roll of thunder that sent the horses dancing nervously. "We could find shelter there at least. I fear the rains will not accommodate a conversation."

"A fair?" She did not know which she feared more—a bolt of lightning or a meeting with her tradesman father, who often traveled to such markets to sell his armor and weaponry. Chances were slim he would be at this fair at this time, but still…

"An international gathering of peddlers and performers, lords and vassals alike." He drew her horse closer and hefted her up before she could argue.

The heat from his hands warmed her despite the drop in temperature. She wondered how well she knew this pragmatic man who bore so little resemblance to the charming scoundrel she'd met in Aquitaine.

"I do not care for fairs," she replied, but her answer was lost in the onset of a thunderstorm.

Raindrops pelted her back as the sky darkened. The wind gusted through the clearing, snapping off leaves and branches from nearby trees.

Without any further discussion, Roger prodded

both their horses forward toward the merchant haven that surely housed some of her father's friends, if not her sire himself. And while her time as a poet dwindled, Ivy's priorities crystallized in her mind.

She might not delay a marriage much longer now that her days at Eleanor's court were over, but she still had time for once last taste of romance. Roger might never be the epitome of knightly chivalry, but his kiss could enflame the most innocent of women. Perhaps if she discovered the truth of his betrothed's death, she could trust him enough to make one final request before they parted company. Ivy might have taught Roger the principles of courtly love, but when it came to true passion, she regretted her lack of education.

And she was certain Roger could teach her all that any woman wanted to know.

The fair near the Norman coast was not as big as those near Paris or Champagne, but the gathering attracted foreign traders and local commerce alike. Roger surveyed the throng of tents and temporary animal pens as he and Ivy rode closer through the driving rain. Sometimes bad weather discouraged trading at such marketplaces, but judging by the hum of voices, music and laughter from within the enclave, the rain had merely driven more travelers to linger. Here, shelter could be found in the colorful canopies of lesser merchants or the permanent halls housing the primary transactions of wool and cloth, spices and precious stones.

Horses and other animals congregated on the eastern side of the assembly and Roger tugged on the reins to guide his mount there. Perhaps Ivy would lose her taste for conversation in the excitement of a marketplace that left little room for private discussion. He had no wish to confide revelations that would only disturb her.

Slowing his pace as they reached the grounds, Roger secured their horses and helped Ivy down, her mud-spattered hem and rain-soaked garments filling him with guilt for dragging her from the warm safety of Beauvais.

His own lands—or at least a fortified house and a small fief—were not far from here and would provide both privacy and safety, but he had no idea if Henry had parceled off some of the Stancliff holdings or if Montcalm had helped himself in Roger's absence. The Norman fiefdom was small compared to the vast lands he held north of London, but his Norman retainers were charged with the important strategic function of alerting Henry to approaching armies.

But even if Roger knew his lands were safe, he would not take Ivy there because of the private nature of the household. There was no court to vouch for his good behavior where she was concerned, no witnesses to attest to the innocent nature of their visit. And since they were spending unchaperoned days together, Ivy would require that kind of supervision to vouch for her purity in light of his unfortunate reputation.

She stumbled slightly as he helped her to her feet, her knees no doubt weak from the hours of riding.

"Are you all right?" He peeled back the hood of her cloak to study her face, relieved to find her hair and shoulders dry even if the rest of her clothes were soaked.

"I am fine." She nodded, steadying herself on the packed earth beneath a large canopy leading into the small tent city. The ground remained damp but not muddy thanks to the presence of stone trenches for run-off water around the fair.

The scent of pastries and fresh bread from the cookshops mingled with the odor of damp earth and wet animals. Roger nudged Ivy to the left, toward the bakers and spice merchants, but she pointed in the other direction.

"I would prefer to visit the cloth merchants first." She hesitated a moment before smiling brightly. "Perhaps I can find a dry cloak."

"You have visited this fair before?" He led her toward the hall full of wool and fur traders at the back of the fair that couldn't be seen from the eastern entrance.

"My father used to let me travel with him before he decided I should have an education." She cast furtive glances over her shoulder. All at once, Roger understood her desire to set their course around the marketplace.

"You hope to avoid seeing someone you know, perhaps?" He wondered if her heritage embarrassed her somehow.

"I would rather not see any of my father's colleagues." She stepped onto the stone walkway that separated the permanent buildings from the tents full of more transient tradesmen.

On either side of them, workmen of all sorts could be seen plying their crafts. Tanners and shoemakers showed their wares near an old monk selling rosaries. The silk merchant and linen weavers came next, their bright displays set up around a large loom that never stopped pumping.

"You are concerned for your reputation if you are seen with me?" He guided her around a small flock of geese roaming the narrow street.

"I would be more concerned for yours," she observed dryly, pausing beside a withered old nun's table full of parchment, scrolls and quills.

"I assure you, my reputation is already tarnished enough." He had done her no social favor by spiriting her away from Poitiers, but he remained certain he'd protected her from possible persecution at the king's hands. "I know you've heard the rumors."

"One hears many rumors in a court full of women with considerable idle time." Ivy's gaze roamed the parchment tables with a longing eye, but she began walking once more. "I do not give credence to everything I hear."

She peered up at him, her expression open and—by the saints—trusting. He had done nothing to deserve such trust. Indeed, he'd kissed and touched her in ways that should put her on guard with him at all times.

"You would be wise to heed such warnings." He threaded her arm through his to speed their pace, knowing he could not withstand her sweet, compassionate nature for much longer without caving to the temptation to hold her again. Kiss her. Make her his own. "In the future, when you hear rumors of a man's sordid reputation, you will run with all haste in the opposite direction."

Two small children with grubby faces stuffed fruit pies in their mouths in front of the building housing the wool merchants, but Ivy seemed to have forgotten her desire for a new cloak. She strode past, frowning.

"I would speak of this in private." She peered around the small fair, green eyes seeking some retreat, he suspected.

"Our last private conversation is a vivid reminder to me why we should avoid such intimate situations at all costs." He hauled her around the perimeter of the assembly with considerable speed, dodging roving minstrels, beggars and almsmen. He told himself he'd double his donation at the next Mass to atone for his haste.

"Then you will not mind explaining to me in front of all the world why we left Beauvais with such secrecy this morning." She arched a delicate brow as he halted in front of the cookshop, from which all manner of delicious aromas emanated.

They'd taken the long way here, no doubt just to avoid whomever Ivy did not wish to see. Roger ordered extra meat pies, bread, sweets and ale for the journey home and then took the bundle of food to the back of a brewer's shop, where a handful of merchants were drinking themselves into raucous good humor. A troupe of players entertained passersby, but Roger found an empty table in the back with scant view of the play where he and Ivy could eat and—heaven help him—talk.

Dousing his frustrations in a long swig of ale, he assured himself they were better off speaking here than in his nearby fief, where he could have Ivy all to himself. A dangerous thought.

"We left Beauvais early because I discovered James Forrester is a spy in the king's employ." He thought it better to put the matter bluntly so they could end the discussion as quickly as possible.

"So are you." She set her bread aside before a morsel had even reached her mouth. "I don't understand the problem."

"Henry didn't inform me of Forrester's presence and let me assume I would be watching the queen on my own." He should not have been surprised at Henry's stealthy political maneuvering, yet he could not deny the sting of the blow. Roger had fought alongside the king in his Welsh campaign. He'd made mistakes since then, but did he deserve such lack of confidence? "I can only surmise that he sent Forrester to watch me as well as Eleanor."

Allowing his gaze to linger on a group of women now dancing for the fat merchants, Roger could not shake the sense of foreboding the news had given him. And how could he ever make peace with his past when everyone around him insisted on reminding him of it?

Everyone but Ivy.

His glance slid back to her as she sipped her ale. She, too, watched the dancing women peddle their wares to the merchants, their salesmanship as sharp as any crusty old trader's. The prostitutes lived off their fair earnings for months if they were efficient.

"Perhaps the happenings at Poitiers were too important for the king to leave the matter to any one man. Even one he trusted a great deal."

She reached beneath the trestle table to wring out a corner of her skirts that were still soaked from their ride through the rain.

"You must be cold." He should have taken her to his holding. "Shall we move closer to the fire?"

With her sparkling green eyes and long, gleaming hair, Ivy had always been the picture of good health. So full of life. But she would not flourish in these conditions if he did not seek out ways to take better care of her.

A huge hearth dominated one side of the brewer's hall, and the merchants had claimed that section for their own. But Roger would gladly scatter the company to the four corners of the chamber if Ivy wished a better seat.

"Nay." Closing her eyes, she sipped her ale and released her wet garb. "Just a bit damp."

He could not remove his gaze from her face, relaxed into sleepy lines, her dark eyelashes fanning over her high, pink cheeks.

"Ivy Rutherford?" A man's voice from the other side of the hall boomed through the brewery, jarring her eyes open in startled surprise.

A squat man in a fur-trimmed cloak stalked closer, his florid face wreathed in a smile as he squinted at her. "Thomas the silversmith's own daughter, how fine ye look!"

The eyes of all the merchants turned toward Ivy, who paled at the recognition before she forced a smile.

"Good day, sir." She nodded and then studied her ale in an obvious attempt to dismiss the man.

Unfortunately, her acquaintance didn't seem to recognize the obvious.

"As I live and breathe," he continued moving closer. The other merchants behind him rose to their feet as well. "You could almost pass for a fine noble lady with yer fine clothes and yer—"

Roger stood, uncertain what threat the merchant men posed, but understanding Ivy's wish to avoid them. They'd all had too much to drink, for one thing. And for another—damn, but Roger did not appreciate the way they looked at her.

"Excuse us, won't you? Ivy is under my care and she isn't feeling well." He drew her to her feet, leaving their cups of ale behind but gathering up the rest of their food. "Good day, sirs."

He ignored their protests and one man's shouted oath that her father would hear of her poor manners.

Roger guided her toward the door and back onto the thoroughfare around the perimeter of the marketplace, carefully avoiding the side of the gathering where the smiths and metal workers congregated.

"We should not have stopped here." He knew that now. His arm tightened around her as they passed a woman shrilly accusing a spice merchant of cheating her of her rightful portion of pepper.

"You see why I am in no hurry to return home." She smiled wanly, and Roger could not help a pang of empathy for this woman of high ideals and romantic notions who'd been raised among such practical and materialistic folk.

"Do not worry." He had no intention of making her cross the channel in the driving rain. He would do what he should have done earlier today. "I have a holding nearby. We will spend the night under my own roof."

Chapter Thirteen

❧❧❧

"Is no one in residence?" Ivy struggled to make out the shape of Roger's holding in the heavy shadows of half a waning moon.

They were southwest of Calais and close enough to the water that she could hear waves lapping a nearby shore, but she could discern no more than the outline of a simple tower and a low-lying roofline surrounding it. Her legs ached from the long day of riding and her nerves had been stretched thin by the persistent fear that her presence at the fair would be relayed to her father and that he would come to collect her.

Once she returned to her father's keeping, she would be displayed for sale like one of his finest swords, her worth measured in gold and haggled over endlessly. The longer Ivy waited to face her fate, the better.

"There are a handful of retainers who oversee the lands and ensure the defenses are maintained." His words were underscored by the approach of horses through the thicket. "With any luck, these are my men."

Ivy recognized the Stancliff standard at once as the riders trampled the hedgerow to greet them, but part of her remained uneasy as she wondered who else Roger thought might be lurking about his lands.

"Good eve, my lord," the foremost knight called. "We did not expect you."

"We will not stay long. Just for a night or two at most." Roger exchanged pleasantries with one of the men while the other rode back to the shadowy fortification ahead of them.

Apparently, the other rider had made an attempt to make the house more welcoming, for there were torches lit within by the time she reached the small gate. They rode into the courtyard, where an entrance to the living quarters was situated across from a small garrison within the tower she'd seen earlier. For a house and not a true keep, the holding seemed extremely well-defended.

But then, she knew little of such matters. Her eye for silver- and metalwork could discern excellent armor and weaponry upon the retainers she greeted in passing, however.

Roger had spared no expense to arm his men. Because he was cautious by nature? Or because he had enemies to fear? She could not ask now, when her legs wobbled with her own weight, but she would not leave this place without the answers she sought. Perhaps she could even buy herself a small reprieve from her return to London with a short stay as Roger's guest here. An unorthodox request from an unwed woman, but then nothing about her departure from Poitiers had been anticipated.

She had amends to make with Roger Stancliff, whom she'd judged too quickly in the past. And she had a fair idea how to compensate him for her lack of faith in him.

But before she could accomplish her plan, she had a certain poem that needed completing. Unfortunately, she had no idea how "The Lai of the Dark Knight" ended.

Roger awoke in the middle of the night to absolute silence and an unshakable sense that something was wrong. He had been asleep for naught but a few hours, judging by the position of the moon through a wide window looking out on the water of the English Channel below. What had awoken him? A noise? A dream?

He pulled on a tunic as he slid out of bed, the silence echoing in his ears. He had Ivy under his roof, so he could not allow himself the luxury of letting his men handle whatever unrest was at work in the house. With Montcalm still clamoring for Roger's head in England and now the king showing little faith in him as well, he had plenty of reason to fear for his security. And while Roger held more lucrative properties in England, this house on the Norman coast made for the easiest target from a military perspective.

He fastened his braies at his waist and stepped into shoes with a soft leather sole so that he could steal about the walls while the rest of the household slept. He wouldn't wake additional men unless he found reason to suspect action outside the walls.

Lighting a torch from the hearth in his room, he explored the corridor on the upper gallery before descending the stairs to the second floor, where Ivy slept.

He'd installed her in the chamber directly below his since it possessed a hearth as well, the house having been built with the grates all located on one wall. The garrison boasted numerous fireplaces, but in the living quarters, only the hall and two sleeping chambers had access to a grate.

He paused outside Ivy's chamber, waiting. Listening. When he could discern no movement within he crept onward through the second floor, peering out windows as he went to take the measure of the lands outside. Still, no marauding troops seemed to approach the household and his men looked to be at their posts on the other side of the courtyard near the gate.

He had almost made a full circle of the second floor gallery when a light appeared ahead of him in the shadowy corridor. A taper burned low to the floor and off to one side, close to an open archway that overlooked cliffs falling off to the seawater below. Reaching for the dagger at his waist, he hastened his step.

A hint of feminine shoulder made him slow down

again. In the moonlight spilling in through the window he could see a portion of a familiar silhouette seated in the archway, her back against the wall and her slipper-covered feet stretched out in front of her. A thick, dark fur covered the floor, he realized, warming the cold stone for the graceful lady who sat upon it.

Ivy.

His chest expanded at the sight of her, his breath lodging in his throat as he soaked up the picture she made in her white night rail with a creamy bed linen tucked around her as she bent over a piece of parchment in her lap. Her quill moved furiously over the page, the feather dancing gently with the movement of her hand. Her fair hair spilled down her shoulders unbound by veils or any other adornments. Indeed, she provided a seductive picture of innocence and allure except that she was perched in an open casement high above a rocky cliff face.

If she moved suddenly, or if he frightened her, she could tumble off the ledge.

Memories of his betrothed fogged his brain, blurring past and present. His slow steps faltered to a halt while his heart kicked up speed, his forehead breaking into a cold sweat.

Holy hell.

Desperate to reach her, to save her, he threw aside his torch on the stone floor and yanked her backward into the safety of the hall, falling on top of her in the darkness as he did. She yelped in surprise, but he did not realize she also cried out in fear until his brain registered that she'd kicked him in the shin and still struggled beneath him.

Damn.

Slowly, his mind cleared enough to speak to her, to gentle his hold.

"Ivy." His voice was ragged and deep, not at all like his own. With an effort, he sucked in a deeper breath and tried again. "Ivy."

She stilled, staring up at him in the now dim hallway. Her taper had gone out when he'd dragged her across the floor, and his torch lay extinguished farther down the corridor.

"Roger?" The tentative note in her voice assured him she had no idea who had grabbed her. Let alone why.

"I'm sorry." He remained on top of her, their breath mingling as their eyes adjusted to the lack of light.

Her hips grazed his although they didn't meet squarely. But her breasts pressed fully against him, the shape of her all too evident with no barrier between them save her night rail and his tunic. The softness teased him, but the tight points at the tips sent a flash fire of heat to his groin.

He might have stood a chance at pushing himself away from her if memories of his Alice hadn't weakened him just before he grabbed Ivy. But he'd been floored by the thought of anything happening to a woman in his protection. A woman—God help him—he wanted.

His reserves to fight off this desire were down to absolutely nothing. And so, with the heat of Ivy's perfect curves beneath him, he did the only thing he could.

He slanted his mouth across hers and kissed her.

Ivy had heard the expression "to tumble a maid" but until now she had had no idea how literal and apt a phrase it proved. In fact, despite the scare of being thrown to her back and dragged along the pelt-covered floor, she decided she would rather like to be tumbled. Often.

Her arms wound around Roger's neck. Now that she knew who held her, she savored the feel of his body against hers, a sensation she'd been dreaming about as she penned poetry that should be for her eyes alone. Writing words of longing entertained her, but not nearly so much as fulfilling that longing.

Her back cradled by the warm fur she'd carted from her bedchamber, she arched up against the even warmer man stretched on top of her. To kiss him in the garden the first time had sparked sensual dreams she couldn't escape. But to kiss him now, clad in the thinnest of linens, her mind still reeling with provocative visions from her poem...*this* was pure madness.

And yet she did not think about letting go. Not when she was finally receiving the education she needed as a love poet. Her idealistic fantasies would only delight a reader for so long unless she possessed a keen understanding of the physical hunger, the carnal craving and sweet torment of real passion.

Her hands gripped his back through his tunic, testing the ripple of male sinew and strong shoulders as she discovered him. He held himself just above her—his chest touching hers without giving her all his weight. His hands bracketed her shoulders as he dipped to kiss her. Her lips parted for his, welcoming the swipe of his tongue against hers. The slick heat of him tantalized her. Her whole body trembled at the sensation of him tasting her, his head turning this way and that as he searched for the best angle to savor the kiss.

With a soft whimper she arched closer, increasing the pressure of his chest on hers. His low growl of pleasure emanated through him, the vibration a delicious sensation against her full breasts. As if sensing her need, he stroked her back with one hand and released her mouth to trail kisses down her neck, down into the open *V* of her night rail. A tie fastened the garment together, a tie he tugged loose with his teeth.

Heat blossomed inside her at the sight. Her skin looked unnaturally pale in the moonlight spilling through the archway. And as his dark head bent to kiss the curve of her exposed breast, she closed her eyes for a moment to implant the view upon her memory, to memorize the raw beauty of the night.

His tongue played wanton games with her skin, fanning the heat that threatened to incinerate her from the inside out. But each moment that she thought she could not tolerate any more desire, he proved her wrong by nudging her hunger higher.

Stronger.

When his mouth finally closed on her nipple, she cried out with the exquisite pleasure of it. He drew hard, suckling her, and then released her to lick and nip the taut tip.

And now, the heat that built in her did not center on her breasts, but grew deep in her womb, settling between her thighs. Dark and complex, the ache unfurled within, stretching and extending even as it concentrated in one deliciously humming spot.

"Bloody—" He wrenched away from her breast, biting off an oath as he tipped his forehead to hers, his breathing harsh and ragged. "I could devour you whole and you make not a single sound to turn me away."

She hadn't wanted to turn him away. But since she assumed that was obvious, she didn't say anything.

"Where are all your rules now, Ivy?" He pulled his hand from beneath her back and used it to lever more of his body off of hers. "Why can't you make me give you space, the way you did in the bower that first day? I'm not supposed to crowd you, remember?"

"Somewhere along the way I became more intrigued by your rules than mine." She did not move her hands from his back, her fingers craving some connection with him after the rest of him had pulled away. Her body still sang from his kisses and while she suspected she would not be able to solve completely the mystery of physical love this night, she intended to experience all that she could for as long as he remained beside her.

"Do not." He covered her lips with his thumb while his other fingers cradled her jaw, shutting her mouth with gentle force. "Never say that you admire any part of me, Ivy. Your rules are full of romantic ideals, while mine are dark and unseemly—"

"They are earthly and *real*." She lifted his thumb from her lips while imprisoning the rest of his hand against her cheek. "And I have learned that you cannot idealize love until you understand all its facets. How can anyone appreciate the sacrifice of courtly love, of holding dear that which you can never possess, unless you understand the full extent of what you are denying yourself?"

She hadn't understood her reasons for wanting him until then, but surely that was part of it. The idea sounded logical, after all.

"Noble Lady Ivy. Sacrificing herself for her art." He pulled away from her, wrapping her in the fallen bed linen that she'd tucked about herself when she left her chamber earlier.

"I do not equate pleasure with sacrifice." She would not allow him to turn this into something sordid when his touch took her breath away. "I would hope that's not how you view it, either."

He sat back on his heels, staring at her as if he'd never seen her before.

"You're serious."

He looked so incredulous that a flutter of embarrassment wafted through her, tying her tongue. She nodded.

"Do not make more of this than it was." His eyebrows swooped downward in a fierce expression. "We suffered from too much privacy and too much damn moonlight here. I will take you home as soon as you are rested and we will both forget this ever happened."

With tense movements, he collected her parchment, quill and ink, then threw the pelt over his shoulder. He waited to escort her back to her chamber in the dark. She stood, but she didn't think she was ready to move just yet. Not until she'd explained a few points of her own.

The sting of his words—his warning that what they'd shared meant nothing—threatened to bring her to her knees. The rebuff shouldn't hurt so much, but on the heels of the kissing, the touching, the unrestrained *emotion* of their encounter, Ivy found every feeling heightened to a fever pitch.

"Perhaps *you* suffered from too much moonlight, sir, but I hail from practical folk who do not need to call a kiss an accident in order to disguise what they feel." She gathered up the bed linen. "Furthermore, I don't think I will feel rested enough to leave anytime soon after the endless day we've shared. If you find the call of the moon too much to bear, perhaps tomorrow night, you can remain safely in your chamber."

Turning on her heel, she spun away from him and hoped she could find her way down the corridor in the dark, because she wouldn't let Roger Stancliff anywhere near her.

* * *

The next day, Roger began to think Ivy truly meant to install herself at the small holding for as long as she pleased. As he finished a talk with his men about increasing the defenses against possible usurpers, he peered up at the living quarters toward the chamber where Ivy had remained all day. The sun had not yet set, but it had turned mellow and golden as it neared the horizon, casting a burnished glow over the limestone walls.

He could not put off a visit to her chamber any longer. The import of what had happened last night had kept him away until now, guilt pummeling him for not finding more restraint with one so young. So innocent. Hadn't he promised the queen that he would respect her and keep his distance?

He could not help but recall that Alice had been innocent like Ivy at one time, before loyalties to love and to family had divided her heart and ended her life too soon. He would not let Ivy embroil herself in those complicated, messy emotions, no matter how much she thought she wanted to experience real life for the sake of a cursed poem.

"My lord?" The voice of one of his men shouted down from the tower as Roger stalked across the courtyard toward the living area.

"Aye?" Shading his eyes, he called up to the sentry on watch duty.

"Three riders approach from the south."

Roger raced to a narrow set of stone steps up the

tower wall, and climbed the stairs, muscles tense. Who the hell would look for him here?

Unless…did they think to stride right into a vacant holding to claim the property for their own? The fiefdom was not a true fortress, but the holding boasted many subtle defenses an attacker would not suspect. And Roger had no intention of relinquishing any of his lands without a fight, no matter what his king might dictate.

He'd been steering the course of dutiful subject all spring and just look where it had gotten him. Henry had supplanted him with another spy he trusted more.

Feet reaching the narrow walkway on the low battlements, Roger stared out at the landscape and saw William Montcalm's family banner floating on a flag just above the older man's shoulder. Alice's father rode with two other men. One he recognized as Stephen Weymouth, Alice's quiet and brooding older stepbrother, but he couldn't be certain about the identity of the other man. The trio slowed as they reached the walls of the holding, their gazes turned upward to where Roger stood flanked by his sentries.

"We just happen to be riding back from business with the king," Montcalm shouted, his voice clear and strong despite his advanced years. The man had a ruthless reputation on the battlefield and he had been as canny as a horse trader during negotiations for his daughter's marriage.

Roger had liked him immediately. Respected him. He regretted that her death had made them enemies.

Roger had heard rumors that Alice's beloved step-brother had sought to hunt Roger down in a vengeance quest in the weeks of raw rage following her death, but at least the elder Montcalm had too much sense to allow Stephen to carry out something so public.

"As am I," Roger returned, tensing from teeth to toes at the confrontation. He would not allow Montcalm to think he had no standing with Henry.

"We thought we would view this property since it will not be yours much longer, Stancliff." Montcalm reached behind him to retrieve the flag with his family crest. Lofting the banner and the pole high, he speared the end of the pole into the soil at his horse's hooves, in front of Roger's front door. "Today I claim the holding in the Montcalm name."

Even from the considerable distance of the tower's peak, Roger discerned the anger in the gesture, the fury that had not cooled in the year since his daughter's death. And while Roger empathized with his loss, he refused to duck his head and bear a blame he didn't deserve any longer.

"You have no claim on my lands." He would have gone down to talk to the older man face-to-face if he hadn't been certain Montcalm would thrust a dagger between his shoulders without the least qualm.

"And you had no right to my daughter." The hurt in Montcalm's voice brought back the guilt that had driven Roger to personal depths he could not afford to revisit.

Meeting Ivy—more than any threat of losing lands—had made him see how he could not compound his past mistakes by hurting more people. And his year of drunken, churlish behavior had done just that.

No more.

"I would give anything to have her back, William, but handing over the life's work of my ancestors to you will not make that happen." He shouted the words so the growing crowd in the courtyard behind him would not miss the exchange. His time to proclaim his stance on the matter was well overdue. He'd been hiding from the past for too long.

A moment of silence followed. The wind whipped off the water, snapping his tunic against his skin.

"You will bloody well pay the debt to me one way or another." The old man yanked his horse sideways as if to leave, but he spat on the ground first. "And God help you if you have a daughter of your own one day."

Biting off an oath as he watched Montcalm ride away with the two younger knights, the stepbrother glaring over his shoulder, Roger pivoted to find Ivy perched at the top of the steps to the battlement. Her cheeks were pale, her unbound hair blowing wildly about her shoulders in the wind.

The day darkened even more as he realized she must have heard his conversation. Montcalm's curse on future Stancliff generations. And the man's insistence that Roger had committed a foul deed.

"I see you chose a fine time to leave your chamber, lady." Anger coursed through Roger's blood and he refused to care that a watch guard remained atop the tower now, surely capable of overhearing every word of their exchange.

"On the contrary, it seems I left just in time." She folded her arms across herself in a gesture that looked protective.

Was she thinking about his betrothed falling from a high precipice like this one? The rumors had been sordid and unkind.

"You are unwise to linger with me on a high ledge." He didn't know why he felt the need to goad her now, when his mood was already dangerous. "Perhaps Montcalm didn't make it clear enough what happened to the last woman who made the same mistake when she was alone with me."

The pain of the memory ripped through him all over again. He had dulled it for months on end by false revelry that had scarcely masked the raw sting of a wound that would probably never heal.

"Apparently your memory has failed *you*, my lord, for I'm quite certain *I* was the last woman to share a high ledge with you." Her voice held a cold note he had never heard from her before. "Or was last night that forgettable for you?"

Only then did he realize she wasn't scared.

Ivy Rutherford, the starry-eyed romantic whose innocence was as well known as her idealistic dreams, stood quietly seething before him. And if he didn't miss his guess, she folded her arms across her chest not as a protective gesture, but as a way to avoid launching herself at him, claws unsheathed for battle.

Chapter Fourteen

⟨⟨⟨⟳⟩⟩⟩

The moon would rise before she moved, Ivy told herself as she stared him down on the battlement of the holding's lone tower. But she would not allow Roger to pass until he shared some small piece of himself with her. He had dismissed their night together as some passing fancy that did not affect him, but he would not dismiss her or the heated words he'd exchanged with the rider at his gate so lightly.

"Ivy." He stepped toward her, a warning note in his voice, while the young sentry on duty moved to the far end of the battlement to give them privacy.

"Yes?" She did not back up, positioning herself in the middle of the stairway to obscure his path as much as possible.

"Perhaps we should take our discussion some place more private."

"If I thought you wouldn't disappear with all due

haste, I would be glad to do so. But given what I know of our past conversations, you'll have to forgive me if I don't trust you to make time to discuss anything with me." How many times had he delayed speaking with her about his work for the king? Or about James Forrester?

"While I acknowledge your point, you must realize a man reluctant to speak will hardly pour out his heart on a battlement for his man-at-arms to overhear."

Acknowledging that it was a logical point, she nodded.

"Where would we speak?" Grudgingly, she moved aside to allow him to pass, but he merely gestured for her to lead the way down the steps.

"The hall will be empty." His hand snaked beneath her elbow to steady her on her way down the open stairway along one side of the tower. The wind was calm, but the stone steps were worn smooth and could prove treacherous. "And, fortunately for you, there is a decided lack of moonlight within the walls."

Memories of the previous night sent a shiver through her. No doubt he could feel the small response where he touched her arm.

"You will not distract me from my purpose with provocative reminders." At least she hoped he would not. What she had to say ranked as far more important than indulging an admitted desire for more kisses.

"Are you suggesting you could be distracted?" As they reached the end of the tower stairs, he slid her arm through his, his silver-gray eyes alight with teasing mischief.

"No," she lied, savoring the familiar feel of him even as she understood she'd allowed him to mean too much to her. "I'm suggesting you conserve your efforts to save your strength."

"Pity." He made all the usual noises to tease and flatter her, but Ivy knew him well enough to realize this slick façade of worldly charmer was his least personal way of speaking to a woman.

He remained tense and uneasy after what had taken place with Montcalm, but he continued to toss out suggestive banter as easily as most people discussed the weather.

They crossed the courtyard in almost full darkness. The sun had set completely, leaving naught but a few purple rays in a splash on the horizon to light their way. Ivy used the veil of darkness to compose her thoughts for whatever time she might have with Roger.

But as soon as they entered the keep and wound through the corridor to the great hall, he surprised her by turning to face her, drawing up a trestle bench to share near the hearth.

"You arrived on the battlement with surprising swiftness tonight," he noted, seating himself the designated length of space away from her.

Now that they knew one another better, she had to confess she wouldn't have minded him sitting much nearer.

"I glimpsed the riders' approach as I walked through the second-floor gallery." She had not expected this turn in the conversation. She should have initiated the discussion so she might have chosen the topic.

"A rather dangerous response to spying unknown visitors, don't you think?" He reached down to a basket near the hearth and pulled out a wax taper. "You make yourself a target on the battlement."

After lighting the candle from the great hall blaze, he placed it on a pewter holder in the middle of the slab wood table.

"I did not think of that." She hoped the fiery glow of light from the flame would hide her embarrassment. "I only wanted a better view of the newcomers."

He waited, his unasked question very obvious.

"I thought I might know the riders in question." Understanding there would be no way around the discussion, she suddenly empathized with his frequent reluctance to talk. "You remember the merchants we met at the fair?"

"The ones who recognized you?"

Nodding, she ran her finger around the rim of pewter at the base of the candle. It seemed easier somehow to study the pooling wax than to look him in the eye.

"I feared they might have relayed word to my father of my presence."

"I thought your father was in London?" The medallion he wore about his neck clanked against the trestle table as he leaned forward.

"He travels widely to sell his wares. I know him to frequent fairs such as the one we visited." She breathed in the scent of hickory wood and hearth flames along with *his* scent. They were so close she could feel the heat from his body more readily than any warmth from the hearth.

"You are not on good terms with your family?"

"I am on fine terms with my father." How to explain? "But this summer was to have been a reprieve for me from certain pressures to perform...obligations that I am not enthusiastic about."

"You did not wish your father to find you." He stilled, his voice taking on a serious note. "Just what kind of obligations are you unhappy about?"

She'd told him about her father's hunt for a husband for her, but she had not made it clear how urgent a matter her father considered the business.

She hoped her confession would not make him too wary to escort her the rest of the way home. No man of his station would wish to be considered as a potential husband for a woman of her background. And— no matter how outlandish such a proposition might sound—her father would most certainly shove the idea out into the open with all the subtlety of a peddler hawking his trinkets. She could not bear to see Roger recoil from her, or worse, to hear him put into words all the reasons he would never consider such a union.

Seeing no way around the truth, however, she had no choice but to admit her father's all-too-immediate plans.

"When I left for Eleanor's court, my father assured me I would marry as soon as I returned. I expect I will be wed to one of his tradesmen friends within a sennight."

A damned good thing he'd been seated.

Ivy would belong to another man that soon? Roger closed his eyes for a long moment, pondering how he could bear the knowledge. How would sweet, refined Ivy find happiness with a coarse man who cared nothing for her, or her hopes and dreams? Clearly, she was opposed to marrying. He'd heard that same desperation in a woman's voice once before, except that the unfortunate groom in question had been him.

"And you find the idea of marriage so hateful?" He would talk her out of this reluctance as if his life depended upon it. For all he knew, perhaps *her* life depended on it. He'd known with Alice that her frustrations were important, but he hadn't realized he faced a life-or-death situation until too late. His hands fisted on the table, his nails digging into his palms. Surely Ivy was stronger than Alice had been.

"It's not that I think it will be hateful, it's just that I'm not ready to—"

He scarcely heard her reply as her pink cheeks and bright eyes merged with Alice's distraught expression and then, the absolute desolateness…

"Hellfire, Ivy." He turned her toward him, wrenching her away from the candle she toyed with so that she might look at him. Understand him. "No husband is as bad as all that, and if he is, your father will step in to rectify whatever problem you might have."

Although, now that Roger thought it over, he acknowledged the rich merchant's money couldn't buy back his daughter if Ivy's marriage went too far awry.

"How can any man truly understand the anguish of chaining yourself to a man who is—"

She stopped midthought, her expression stricken for an instant before her features flooded with sympathy.

Her pity steeled him to interrupt before she spoke words he couldn't stand to hear. Not from her.

"I see you are remembering that I do indeed understand how deeply some women resent marriage." He would do anything to chase the compassion from her gaze and bring back the anger. But he did not have it in him to hurt this woman any more. He had not been able to sleep the night before, taunted by visions of her bewildered expression when he'd walked away from her.

Damn.

"Whatever happened between you and your betrothed, I am sorry for it, and sorry for her father that he blames you when my every instinct tells me you are not at fault in this." Her fingers grazed his shoulder with such gentleness that he realized, by contrast, that he squeezed her arms too forcefully.

"How can you suggest such a thing?" No one but he knew the angst of Alice's final hours. "Who could blame him for despising me when his daughter killed herself rather than marry me?"

She did not flinch at his harsh words and he knew in that moment her delicate beauty belied a strength and intelligence that transcended any social class.

"Perhaps he did not fully understand his daughter the way you did. I can't help but think some demons lurked inside this woman that her father never recognized. What upset her so deeply she felt called to take such rash action?"

Her insight humbled him, for he'd done nothing to warrant such trust. He'd befriended her to discover secrets of the court and he'd flirted with her to unnerve her. He'd kissed her and then denied the obvious connection between them, yet she repaid him by seeing beyond his wastrel years to the most haunted parts of his soul.

How could he add more falsehoods to the untruths he'd already told her?

Releasing her arms, he skimmed his fingers down her sleeves, accepting her softness. Her giving nature, which he did not deserve. Still, he did not allow himself to touch her as he confided the truth.

"Alice was with child."

The memory had not lost its power to hurt him, but he had expected the sting. Accepted the ache. Ivy, however, had not.

"She took the life of your child?" The anguish in her eyes was evident even in the long shadows that fell across the hall.

His chest ached at her compassionate response.

Alice's father would surely not take the news with such kindness. Nor would the rest of the world.

"No. Because her child was not mine." That had not stopped him from mourning her loss twice as much.

She gasped, a sharp intake of air that she clapped into her mouth with one hand, as if sealing in her response. But then, slowly, her hand drifted back down to her lap. The wood in the hearth cracked and popped in the silence.

"But how do you know this?"

"That she was with child or that I was not the father?"

Her cheeks colored, so he saved her the embarrassment of choosing.

"I only had her word on her condition, but it seemed a fitting cause of her immense distress. And I know I was not the father since I was once a more idealistic man who thought it best not to visit a woman's bed before I took her to wife."

He had visited many other beds since then, but always with the utmost caution. Now that more time had passed he understood what a contemptible reaction that had been, no matter what precautions he'd taken.

"Was she upset you wouldn't marry her?" Somehow during the course of their discussion, she'd taken hold of his hands instead of the other way around, a peculiar feeling that he could not indulge once he'd become aware of the change.

As he propped his elbows on the trestle table, his mind's eye fled to another time.

"Of course not." He scrubbed a hand through his hair, weary with secrets kept too long. "Alice and I had been friends since our youth. I would have gladly wed her no matter that she'd taken a lover at some point, but I demanded she—"

A wave of pain cut through him, slashing at wounds he'd hoped never to remember.

"I think you were entitled to make some demands," Ivy assured him, as she smoothed careful fingers over the cuff of his sleeve where it lay on the table. "She must have known you well enough to understand you only wanted to improve the situation."

"I asked that she give up her lover and it was then that she became too distraught." She fled right past him on the way to the ledge, God help him. He'd never expected her to jump. "Apparently my request was more than she could bear."

"And you've let her father believe all this time that she jumped because she did not wish to wed?"

"She didn't wish to wed. I told him no less than the truth." Alice had cried for hours during the argument that had seemed endless at the time, and afterward had seemed so fleeting. Her heart had appeared so divided that Roger suspected she'd probably wept for days before he answered her summons to speak with him.

"But her reasons went so much deeper," Ivy pressed, her gentle nature unwilling to believe there were no temperate answers to problems that were so harsh. So fueled by passion. "Don't you think knowing the truth would give her father some sort of peace?"

"You would have me announce her infidelity to the world? I'm not sure her father would believe it, and I sure as hell wouldn't want anyone outside her family to think she had compromised herself in that way." His throat burned with the image of Alice begging him—God, he hated that memory—not to share her shame with anyone. "She requested my silence."

"She did not expect you to remain silent now, not when her family is in such anguish."

"Montcalm will find peace in his own time." Roger did not mean the man ill, but he could see no point in spoiling his memories of a much-beloved daughter with allegations of faithlessness. Surely that would only hurt him further.

"Aye, when you are at the end of his sword, from what I gather." She whistled softly to a cat stalking past the hearth in search of a morsel. "Do not forget, I heard him threaten you today."

"That was no threat. He is an old man with a good heart and he seeks ways to make my life painful in an effort to avenge his daughter." Roger would not give up his lands to him, but he considered Montcalm well within his rights to rail at Roger and shake his fist for all eternity.

The simple truth remained that if he'd put out his arms to stop Alice from rushing past him, she would have probably been alive today and her son or daughter would be a beautiful, laughing babe growing up strong and healthy at Stancliff Keep. The month that her babe should have been born had been the darkest for him, filled with childish cries and laughter that he heard in his head, if not his ears.

He slammed his fist into the table when he really wished to throw something. Anything. The pain radiating through his hand provided little comfort.

"You do not serve her memory this way," Ivy admonished him, pulling him from the depths and back into the present.

"I did not serve *her,* either, and I do bear some of the blame for that, no matter how much you'd like to think otherwise." Knuckles throbbing, he rose to his feet and backed away from the table, having endured more than his share of dark memories for the night.

He had a new concern to unsettle his thoughts now. A fear that shouldn't bother him, and yet the worry lingered.

"Thank you for telling me the truth." She peered up at him through long lashes, her appeal stronger and more undeniable the longer he spent beside her.

He would walk away from her soon enough. But for tonight, he would have his curiosity appeased.

"Perhaps you will repay me with a truth of your own." He stalked back toward the table, releasing his aching hand to cup Ivy's chin.

At her puzzled look, he elaborated.

"Who is it your father will have you wed when you return home?"

* * *

Ivy stood. She did not wish to appear rude, but the impulse to flee from his question was strong. She could not allow the familiar touches that inspired too much longing, and she surely could not have this conversation with him.

"The hour grows late and your household has become quiet as we've spoken." Few people shared the living quarters of Roger's house, but what few servants he retained had all found their beds by now. Quiet dominated the hall until the only sound she could hear was the wind grown more fierce outside and her own uneasy breaths.

Wordlessly, he offered her his arm as if to escort her out of the hall. A simple enough gesture. A mere matter of courtesy. And yet touching him had become so much more complicated now that she understood how quickly a touch could turn heated.

He lifted a lazy eyebrow in silent question at her hesitation. Did he suspect her reasons for reluctance? Unwilling to risk him thinking she'd become too attached, she took his arm, his skin warm beneath the sleeve of his tunic. The play of muscle beneath her fingers reminded her of how they'd moved together the night before, their bodies learning each other—

"Ivy?"

Drawing herself out of seductive thoughts, she followed him out of the hall toward the stairs to the second-floor gallery.

"Yes? I'm—um—sorry. We've talked about so

much tonight I fear my thoughts are unsettled and scattered." They were also darkly wicked, but she didn't think she could voice that part aloud. Although if ever she wanted to understand the sensual side of love, the time to do so would be here, in this house with the only man who had ever spurred her curiosity about the physical connection between a man and a woman.

"I think perhaps you are only hedging my query."

By now she was indeed distracted enough that she struggled to recall their conversation. She'd been so engaged in conjuring up memories of heated kisses that remembering anything else required great effort.

"You were about to give me the name of the man your father would bind you to against your will," he prompted, his voice as tense as his arm where she touched him.

"Oh." Her gaze refocused on her surroundings as they reached the second floor, the corridor dark except for a torch burning beside her chamber door. A red tapestry hanging across from her room glowed dully in the reflected light. "My father has not determined the man I am to wed, but I do know he plans to proceed with a marriage immediately upon my return. He mentioned next spring if I had spent the whole season in Eleanor's court this year, but now that I am to return early..."

She could not continue as a wave of dread filled her, the stone wall at her back not chilling her half so much as the well of cold thoughts within her. She would be wed to some wealthy spice merchant within the year and her she would be known as the fattest larder in all of Christendom, rather than the celebrated love poet who touched people's hearts. Or perhaps she would marry into a mining family so her father could obtain his precious metals more cheaply. What was she to the world besides a bargaining tool for her sire?

"It is already past Pentecost," Roger reminded her as he halted outside her chamber. "Your father has little time to clinch a suitable arrangement before Midsummer."

"My father will not care what time of year I wed. He had not amassed a fortune by being slow to seal a bargain. He needs but a few days to accomplish the deed."

She reached for her chamber door, ready to end this discussion the more she thought about the bleakness of a future without poetry and brilliance. A future without Eleanor or Katherine or the thoughtful musings of the Court of Love. A future without Roger or any real understanding of the way fiery passion could fuse two souls, forging separate lives into a stronger whole.

"You may find contentment in marriage, Ivy." He covered her hand with his own, preventing her from opening the door. "Your father must care about your happiness or else he would not have paid to send you to court. Surely he will allow you some say in his choice of mate."

Twisting the handle in spite of him, Ivy swallowed back the anger that rose in her throat at his false impression of Thomas Rutherford. She shoved the door open and stepped inside her solar, where two tapers had been thoughtfully lit on a sideboard.

"My father paid for me to attend the queen because he hoped I would wrest some unsuspecting nobleman into marriage with his wealthy but lowborn daughter, so please don't ascribe any lofty ideals to my father. He is as canny in trade as ever a military strategist was on the battlefield, and his concern for me is directly tied to furthering himself and his own fortunes." She approached the sideboard to pour herself a cup of wine, which she needed quite desperately if she wanted to find the strength to keep herself from touching Roger any more this night.

Their talk of the future had darkened her thoughts, and it would be all she could do to resign herself to her fate without begging him for one taste of true passion first.

"You're serious." He entered the room, his expression shadowed, although his eyes glimmered back at her in the glow of candlelight.

His presence in her chamber implied an intimacy she both wanted and feared.

"Exceedingly." Her hands wobbled only slightly on the cup as she brought the wine to her lips. Sweet and strong, the libation did not begin to quench her thirst.

Especially not with Roger stalking across the floor

toward her. Taking a slow sip of the wine, she kept the silver goblet between the two of them as a barrier to remind her she could not take a taste of that which she wanted most.

"What men did you set your sights on at Poitiers, Ivy?" He stopped a mere hand span in front of her, his voice low and silky in the intimacy of her chamber. "Did our love lessons intrude on your other agenda of finding a husband to your liking?"

She realized that he believed her party to her father's schemes. The dawning understanding should have doused any arousal she felt for this man, but instead her desire and frustration rose.

"I have no wish to marry a nobleman." Her grip tightened on her cup as she observed he had closed the door behind him, ensconcing them in complete privacy. "I saw the misery my parents endured because of their disparate upbringings and I would not wish that kind of unhappiness upon myself or my children."

"So you were not hunting for a spouse at Eleanor's court?" He pried her cup from her fingers and returned the chalice to the sideboard.

"I planned to achieve such greatness with my poems that the queen would never release me." She'd been as naive as anyone at court had ever suspected. As was her idle wish she might one day be recognized, with some small title or acknowledgement. "A foolish plan, I see now, but I could not envision any other future for myself."

"The thought of a man in your bed was too unappealing?"

The answering leap of her pulse shouted otherwise whenever he ventured near her. There was not enough wine in all the keep to soothe lips that wanted this man alone.

"It is not *that* I fear, as you know too well from the poetry I've been writing." She breathed in the scent of him, wondering why he had moved so close. "But I've been raised between worlds, half merchant's daughter and half noblewoman. Instead of fitting in both societies, it seems I do not belong in either, and I dread tying myself to a man who will not embrace at least half of who I am."

"A woman of your talent does not belong in any tradesman's home." He stroked a finger down the side of her cheek and she knew all was lost when her thoughts scattered and then vanished, leaving her with only an answering hunger for response.

Her legs turned to liquid. She called up words to make an answer, but they were hardly a defense against his touch.

"I have no say in the matter." Her eyelids fluttered as he bent closer and she quivered at the feel of his breath on her cheek.

"But you do." He lowered his voice to an intimate pitch as his thumb paused beneath her lip to trace the outline of her mouth. "You are Lady Ivy of the troubadours, a class of intellectuals beyond merchant or noble."

Through her haze of desire, something inside her smiled. That naive, idealistic woman she'd once been sang out in approval of his gallant words. Or maybe her body simply sang out at his touch. Either way, one of them must have moved toward the other for they were suddenly entwined, arms wrapped about one another as their mouths met with reckless abandon.

Chapter Fifteen

Roger had beaten back celebrated knights and mercenaries with the force of his blade, and still he could not summon enough might to move away from Ivy tonight.

Enveloping her in his arms, he greedily sought the softness of her curves, the feel of her beneath his fingers. Last night he had used up the last of his restraint where she was concerned. Tonight he would not bother to try.

He knew from the moment she had confessed a reluctance to marry and implied a desire for *him* that he had no choice but to claim her for his own. He might not possess the lovesick inclinations she preferred in a husband, but he admired her and, God help him, he wanted her.

Many a union had been based on less.

He would make her see that he'd be better for her

than some hard-hearted tradesman or a struggling young knight who would resent her father's money even as he tied himself to the wife who could help him secure it. Roger didn't need her money, and his reputation as a knave didn't scare her. His noble status and service to the king would protect her from Henry's wrath toward the women who'd served Eleanor at Poitiers.

Their union would be practical. Beneficial to both parties. And—hellfire—it might just burn him alive, if the heat surging through him proved any indication.

He tunneled his hands through her hair. The candlelight gave the fair locks an ethereal glow as they spilled over his arms.

"Ivy." He whispered her name for the pure pleasure of speaking it aloud. "I will never be satisfied with only a taste of you tonight."

Better to warn her so she could still flee if she chose. But her hands remained as greedy as his own, her fingers separating the ties of his tunic to bare his chest to her gaze. Her lips.

"I hope you indulge in much more, my lord." Her tongue flicked against his skin. "I have been sorely disappointed that you are not living up to your reputation as a knave."

"Then you may congratulate yourself for having brought out the worst in me." He hooked a finger into her bodice and tugged the fabric loose. Looser.

Her breasts overflowed the confinement as he

worked her kirtle down her shoulders, exposing more of her. She gave a helpless cry as he bent to claim one taut peak with his mouth.

Hunger for her made him too rough, too hurried, for a woman who deserved every tenderness. Cursing himself for the need that had been barely banked the night before, he forced himself to be more gentle with the kisses he swept down between the mounds as he squeezed the soft flesh in his hands.

"Nay," she protested, spearing her fingers through his hair as she arched against him. "I am not as delicate as I appear."

Any hope he'd had of softening his touch burned away in a tide of desire as he raked her half-fallen garments down her body, stripping her bare so that she only had to step out of her pile of clothes. Vaguely, he was aware that her stockings remained gartered about her lower legs.

High round breasts heaved softly as he fixed his attention on the sweetly curved shape of her. A cinched waist and rounded belly. Flared hips that twitched shyly at his stare.

Or perhaps they merely wriggled for his touch. Her shifting thighs retained secrets still shielded from his gaze by silky blond curls.

His breathing grew more labored every moment he looked at her, his legs leaden.

"You are a sight to behold." The gruff note in his voice was possessive.

"I'd rather be a sight to touch." She reached for his hand, but her words propelled him forward.

He seized her at the waist, lifting her against him to carry her toward the curtained bed across the room. She tore at his tunic as they moved, her nails scratching lightly at his skin as she tugged his tunic up his chest. They fell onto the bed in a pile of linens and half-torn bed-curtains, since they hadn't bothered to fully open the drapes.

"Oh!" She bit her lip as she peered up at the torn fabric, but he didn't even spare a glance at the damage.

Pulling off his tunic, he drew her to him again.

"It's better this way," he murmured into her ear as he propped pillows beneath her back. "Fallen drapes let more light in so I can see you."

"Look all you want, but do not stop touching me." Winding her arms about his neck, she stretched up to press the full length of her voluptuous young body against the hard planes of his own.

"Never." He breathed the vow into her ear before capturing the silken shell in his teeth to nip her lightly.

She shivered beneath his slow assault, his lips questing lower along her neck, pressing lingering kisses into the hollow of her throat, the valley between her breasts and the seductive curve of a hip.

"The wanting—" she squealed with surprise as he placed a kiss along the inside of her thigh "—it is so much more urgent than I ever dreamed."

He paused in his delightful discovery of her body to meet her gaze and found her frank interest to be more enticing than any sexual trick from a well-experienced bedmate.

"You know too little of urgency to make such a statement," he assured her. His pulse pounded through his lower half so hard he was damn near seeing stars from the dizzying lack of blood to his brain.

Still, he would apply all his effort to the task of giving her even half the pleasure he would take. Bending low over her hips, he breathed warmly on the silken curls at the juncture of her thighs.

She whimpered in answer and he found he could not wait another moment to touch her. Taste her.

Securing her bare bottom in his hands, he savored the secret heart of her with his tongue. The scent of her enflamed him, as he urged her closer, nearer that peak that he could feel in her trembling legs. She writhed against him, but he held her fast, knowing that precipice loomed a scant heartbeat away.

When her release came, it shuddered through her along with an unholy cry, her pleasure echoing through the whole chamber as she dug her nails into his shoulders.

Levering himself up to recline on the pillows beside her, he found her still trembling with the aftermath of her fulfillment. She hooked a finger into the waist of his braies, tugging them down with awkward movements in her haste to undress him.

"I want all of you," she confided in a throaty plea, her green eyes wide and desire-dazed as she gripped his jaw. "I will not go through my whole life without knowing the feel of real passion."

Heat raged through him, burning away all rational thought until he was left with only the need to possess Ivy, to bind her to him in the way no other man ever would.

Unfastening his braies the rest of the way he vowed to use caution this night to lower her chance of conceiving. He wastrel ways had taught him a few tricks on that count.

He stretched over her, holding himself above her for one long moment as he stared down into her eyes. The expression there undid him as much as any kiss or any touch. For that one moment, she looked at him with the same rapturous glow she took on when she spoke of her courtly lover hero. And he wanted to be that man. To protect her perception of him for one more night—a few precious days, perhaps—before he foisted himself on her in an arrangement she would surely resent.

Ivy struggled to capture all the details of the moment. Perhaps she sinned gravely by not at least pretending some maidenly reluctance, but she could not tear her fascinated stare from Roger's bared skin, his muscular form braced above her as his thighs wedged themselves between hers. She would commit every nuance to her mind, since she knew this final consummation would never make it onto parchment. This moment would be hers alone to savor.

Her legs still trembled from the sweet rapture she had experienced. They fell apart easily for him now, welcoming him to lie between them. She started when his sex nudged her, the silky heat of his taut skin a decadent contrast to the heavy, hard weight of him.

Her eyes slid closed as he eased his way inside her, her slick heat welcoming him even though the fit remained snug, stretching her more with each breath.

"Hold on to me." He shifted his weight to guide one of her arms around his neck, showing her what he wanted. "It will hurt only for a moment, I promise."

Before she'd had time to comprehend his words, he already had her wrapped around him, his one arm supporting her lower back as he thrust more deeply. The pain he'd promised was sharp but swift, fading into pleasant awareness of him buried deep inside her in a union that felt sweet and sinful at the same time.

"You are mine," he whispered in her hair, the words inciting a primal shiver within her.

She would never belong to him legally because of their different social stations, but perhaps they were forever bound in spirit now. At least, she would be to him. Tenderness for this man swamped her, urging her to indulge every moment of pleasure she could before they parted ways forever.

"The sting has faded," she told him, realizing that he seemed to be waiting for some sort of sign from her, since he'd held her very still after he'd pierced her maidenhead.

"Are you certain?" He peered down into her eyes, the candlelight reflected in a bead of sweat along his brow.

He must be holding back for her sake.

"Absolutely." She unwound her arms from his neck to trail her fingers down his back. "And I demand that you show me everything. Give me everything. You must be my tutor this time."

"With pleasure." He withdrew from her partly and then surged deeper.

Heat wound about her womb and then radiated out through her limbs. And despite the daze of passion that clouded her thoughts she began to understand the rhythm of this pleasure, the currents of heat that ebbed and flowed between a man and woman. Every withdrawal sharpened the need, heightened the hunger. Each new thrust gave more satisfaction, propelling the whole dizzying joining toward some sublime completion.

She pushed her hips up to meet his next thrust, speeding the fulfillment and earning a ragged growl from Roger. He was the smooth-tongued charmer no more, but a warrior in pursuit of pleasure for them both. His fierce aspect coupled with his groan made her realize she might provide as much thrill for him as he gave to her, but she could not think to be unselfish now. Not when that sublime completion loomed so near.

And then he bent his head to kiss her and she was lost. His tongue teased her lips and swept inside, mirroring the sex act so neatly that she would never be able to bestow a kiss again without remembering this moment, this man buried deep inside her.

She flew apart at the thought, her womb contracting and her body squeezing. Only this time, the feeling was all the more wonderful with him inside her to share the sensation.

He must have found that lush heat as seductive as she did, for he shouted out her name in one last thrust before he spilled his seed inside her, bathing her newly initiated womanhood with his life force.

For one insane moment she prayed that she might retain some small piece of him to carry with her, some physical reminder of their one night together and the thought-stealing passion they could create.

But that was a foolish notion, since Roger had been devastated by another expectant woman in his past. He would never allow Ivy to walk away from him if he thought there was any chance she carried his child, a fact she would have to come to terms with after allowing her desires to rule her.

But assuming they had conceived no babe, he would be free to wed a woman of his own class, a woman who would not be an unhappy reminder of all he'd given up. And she would be free to…

To what? She couldn't even contemplate the future now when all she wanted was to enjoy this taste of sweet bliss for as long as she could before she returned home to duty. Obligation. And an eternity of pining for a life she could never have.

"I don't understand."

Ivy's words rang in his ears the next morning as he left the great hall. He hadn't expected a joyous outcry at his announcement that they had to leave for London today, but he had hoped she might at least understand his predicament.

Spinning on his heel at the doors leading into the courtyard, he hoped to settle this here before they lost any more time.

"I am sorry for the haste." More sorry than he could express to her, since he feared saying too much about his plans to wed her in spite of her fears of marrying outside her own station in life. He could not risk her running off or plotting against him before he'd spoken to her father.

"So why must we rush?" she pressed, her slow smile suggesting things she would not speak aloud. "I can pack tonight and we can leave tomorrow morning instead."

"But Montcalm made a point of stopping here last night to threaten me." He had not forgotten William's warning and Roger knew the older man was not one to speak idly. "I fear he means to launch some sort of attack on my holdings near London, since he knows I'm here."

"But why would he warn you if he intended such

a thing? It makes no sense." She took a bite of a strawberry from her breakfast plate, the juice moistening her lower lip.

The urge to lick off the sweet liquid gnawed at him, but he harnessed it so that they could get on the road sooner. And celebrate his inevitable marriage as quickly as possible.

He would not make the same mistakes with Ivy that some other wretch of a man had made with Alice. Roger would ensure any child of his was taken care of and he would damn well make certain Ivy would never worry about her future if she wound up with a babe.

"Montcalm is a smart man. He will not take lands from me if he thinks the king will not support his maneuver. But now that he knows I'm not with the Henry in Poitiers or riding with the king to round up the displaced women of Eleanor's court, Montcalm will at least flex his might."

The man had every reason to hate Roger, but maybe marriage would make William back off, since it had been Roger's reputation as a wild and reckless man that had angered Alice's father the most.

But then, William had never known Roger's real reason for throwing himself headfirst into life for a year. Roger had been dealt the blow of Alice's faithlessness in addition to her death. And then there'd been the death of the son or daughter he'd never known.

Too much death and defection and betrayal. And all of it had to be kept quiet.

"So we hurry back to protect your lands." Ivy finished her berry and tossed her unbound hair over one shoulder, her informal appearance at the breakfast table increasing Roger's guilt for misleading her. She'd probably envisioned another visit to the bed they'd shared the night before—something he would have taken great pleasure from as well.

"And we return to inform your father that you are well." He had thought about this even before his night with Ivy. "Your sire will be worried about you as rumors of the disbandment at Poitiers spreads. And if he hears from his merchant friends that you were spotted in the company of a nobleman..."

The gossips would draw their own conclusions. Roger knew Ivy didn't want her father to have those kinds of thoughts, since she hoped to duck marriage for as long as possible.

"Perhaps you have a point." She straightened, the warm look in her eyes replaced by a small furrow on her forehead. "If he finds us together on the road, he will embarrass us both to no end about our obligation to each other. Such an encounter would be very unhappy for all parties concerned."

She flushed at the statement but appeared ready to move. How sad that her haste stemmed from her desire to walk away from him when, in fact, she would be walking toward their future together with each league they covered on their northern journey.

"Why don't you gather your things while I give last-minute directions to the men?" He would put his best retainer in charge here again until he could ensure Ivy's safety and the security of his larger holdings.

Even though he did not believe in Ivy's fairy tales about courtly love and high ideals, he had a future to build now and he planned to start today.

Chapter Sixteen

London beckoned with shouts and cheers from within the walls, a lively city even at sunset as Ivy directed Roger north along Fleet River toward her home. Her father maintained a small residence within the city to direct his trade, but when he'd taken her mother to wife, he'd built her a lofty house with fine gardens and river views just outside the city gates.

But its distance from London town did not isolate Rutherford House from the scents and sounds of city life. Even now, Ivy tried not to breathe too deeply, since the fishmongers worked late along the river to lure some elusive catch with other dead fish.

No doubt she could smell the scents of baked bread or fresh flowers from the homes and gardens along the riverbanks if she *tried*. But it seemed to Ivy as though the foul stench rose up in particular to match her mood. The whole day had a foul stench to it, since she would be saying goodbye to Roger shortly, perhaps never to see him again.

And if by chance her father was in residence tonight, she faced the humiliation of having him grovel at Roger's feet for the honor of a nobleman's company. Worse, her father would never be able to watch Roger leave Rutherford House without hinting broadly that Ivy would be a wife who would come with extensive wealth.

Little did her father know she'd already given Roger the best she had to offer. Quite possibly, she had given him the whole of her heart as well, since that vital organ seemed to be breaking at the thought of saying goodbye.

How far she'd fallen from her sweet ideals of courtly love. And yet, how much better she was for the education. Love was not a gentle inspiration to seek noble quests and achieve great accomplishments. The emotion that pulsed through Ivy was as dark and frightening as it was uplifting. Perhaps that was only because she'd had so little time to enjoy the magical connection to a man who could never be hers.

"We have reached my father's lands." She pointed to the line of pine trees that marked the property he'd purchased at a thrifty price from a vintner whose crops had failed most miserably, leaving him unable to afford the lavish lifestyle Thomas Rutherford craved.

The story had always reminded Ivy how quickly a man's fortunes could change when he was not protected by the crown with noble status. Merchants like her father and his colleagues could only rely on their own skills to find profit.

The foot traffic was lighter on this side of the city, although a few unambitious vendors still lined the roads with their carts and animals and children. They created a sprawl of movement and activity as the cobblestone street ended and turned to a wide dirt path.

"I am sorry the journey has been long and unrelieved." He peered over at her in the last pink and gold light from the sun as it tipped the trees to the west. "The past few days should have been easier for you after…" He shook his head. "I hope you have not been overly uncomfortable from all the riding."

When she realized he referred to their activities of a few nights prior and the possible aches a woman might experience as a result, she could hardly form a response. Her cheeks heated as she looked up at the house coming into view ahead.

"I am sure I'm fine." Although she certainly would have traded anything for another day or two alone with him. Another day to explore more of what a man and woman shared when they were not foisted upon one another by the constraints of vows and laws and obligations to fulfill marriages of duty. "But I must take the opportunity to warn you about my father before we arrive at his residence."

"There is no need." He kept his horse at a steady pace, seemingly unconcerned. "You have told me of his wish to see you wed and I have gathered from your other comments about him that he will gladly apply all his merchant wiles to the task of making a good marriage for you. I see no harm in that."

Surprised that he had perceived her father so accurately, and that he had remembered this fact that had embarrassed her all her life, Ivy hastened her horse's step to maintain pace with him.

"I only remind you of his matchmaking tendency to help ease your way out of my home, since he will solicit your company for food and drink." Ivy could not accept the torment of having Roger under her father's roof. He would be so close to her physically, yet there was every chance he could grow from her heart due to her father's lack of subtlety. He might well regret that he had ever touched her.

And that, she could not bear.

Her hand went to her belly as they rode the rest of the way, taking surprising new comfort from the notion that her lover might have left some piece of himself within her. She would not know for some weeks, but the timing seemed favorable.

Although—heaven help her—she could not imagine her father's fury if she indeed carried Roger's babe. She could not tell her father the truth for fear he would try to force Roger to marry her. And she could not lie to Roger about such a thing in light of the circumstances of his betrothed's death. Ivy would not give him any cause to worry that she would ever be so cruel or so foolish.

"I am not opposed to speaking with your father

this eve. I have been expecting as much." Roger guided his horse around a hedge that formed a small maze in the only garden her mother had shown any interest in while she lived.

Perhaps Rosamunde Burkshire Rutherford had sought to hide from her unwanted husband in the depths of the sweetly scented labyrinth.

"Will you return to your holding tonight?" Her chest tightened at the thought of him leaving and she wondered if she now appeared as besotted as every other female at Poitiers had once been with this man.

"Nay. My lands are still a few hours' ride north of here."

Good manners dictated she open her home to him, but in her heart she knew it would probably be kinder to let him seek other shelter, where he would not be harangued to wed a woman beneath him.

Candles burned throughout the lower level of Rutherford House as they approached the main entrance of the dwelling. Comparable in size to the fortified house Roger held on the other side of the channel, her home lacked a tower but boasted expansive living quarters hewn from rough limestone. The wealth of candlelight spilling out of the small windows suggested her father was indeed in residence this evening.

Roger halted his horse and leaped to the grass before holding out a hand for Ivy.

"I thought we might speak alone a moment before we go inside," she whispered, hoping no one would hear their arrival yet. "We may not have another moment to speak again before—"

"There will be time enough." Unmoved, or perhaps merely in a hurry to depart, Roger pulled her toward the doors. "The hour grows late."

Hurt at his abrupt dismissal, she wondered if her willingness to give her innocence to him had only proven her lack of noble morals or genteel upbringing. Perhaps her warm acceptance had revealed her as an unrefined woman, unworthy of his notice.

She pushed open the doors to her home and invited him in. All at once her father's cook, the cook's young son and her father himself appeared in the entrance hall, the house erupting with raucous whoops and hollers and laughter as her father and Belinda both raced to hug her and greet Roger.

"My girl!" Thomas Rutherford swung her around like a child, his enthusiastic greeting reminding her how much she loved him in spite of himself. He might be pushy and occasionally coarse with his words, but he loved her dearly. His broad forehead and thick, unkempt eyebrows set off kind blue eyes and a perpetual grin.

"It's good to see you, Papa, but we have a guest." She introduced the men and prepared herself for her father's obsequious proposals for a late supper while Belinda and her son hurried to the kitchen.

"We are so honored, my lord." Thomas bowed over Roger's hand and kissed a small ring bearing the Stancliff family crest.

And to Ivy, Thomas smiled like a mischievous boy. "You have done well despite your protests that you could never catch a nobleman's eye, didn't you, my girl?"

Ivy attempted to interrupt, but polite manners were no match for her father's brusque ways when he had sniffed a marriage possibility on the wind.

"She is beautiful, is she not?" Her father smiled indulgently and squeezed her shoulder.

"She is as lovely as her poetry," Roger acknowledged, his courtly manners in place now. "The queen found much to admire in your daughter's work, sir."

The small compliment might have been solely intended to make her father proud, but Ivy appreciated that Roger had placed more emphasis on her writing skill than her scant beauty, since any woman of substance would prefer to be remembered for her quick mind or a loving heart than for a fair face doomed to fade with age.

She could not think about how much she would miss his clever insights or she would soon fall prey to dark thoughts of all the other ways she would miss him when he left.

Belinda's son, a shy child of six years, returned with wine and cups. Ivy's father motioned for them to take seats about the hearth while he poured the libations for them all.

"Of course I'm very proud of my Ivy. I've long known she is a prize any man would be proud to call his own."

Sensing the inevitable direction of a conversation that would only bring her discomfort and—eventually—disappointment, Ivy rose to her feet again.

"I think we have a better vintage than this in storage, Papa." The wine was fine, but she would be easily excused from the company if her father thought his table might be improved for his illustrious guest. But since she needed to speak to her father, she bestowed a warm smile on him. "Would you help me retrieve it, Papa? I keep it up high."

She moved toward the storage area behind the larder, winding underneath the stairwell and hoping he followed. By the time her father joined her, she had already plucked a new cask from a shelf she could reach easily.

"Where is this infernal wine, girl?" he asked as he entered, his forehead wrinkling at the sight of her with a fresh cask in hand.

"I merely meant to beg you not to push Lord Stancliff when he has already extended such courtesy in accompanying me home."

"All the *more* reason to push him, my daughter." He yanked the cask from her hand, his shaggy eyebrows halfway up his forehead in his obvious surprise at her ignorance. "And I would not have to offend your delicate sensibilities if you had been able to cinch the lad's affections on your own."

"To what purpose? He is a high-ranking lord with

no need to barter an unwanted bride for gold when he has vast holdings of his own."

"Every man has a need for gold." His scowl communicated how frivolous he thought her. "And who is to say I am angling for you to be his bride? I might do you and your arrogant ways a favor by suggesting the fine lord make you his mistress. 'Twould serve me just as well if he saw fit to shower you with fine gifts or settle you in a home of your own."

Her blood chilled at the threat. Not just because it had been a crude thing to say, but also because— saints forgive her—she had already offered up as much to Roger by her own free will. What must Roger think of her?

"I have served the queen," she reminded him, anger chasing away the chill in her veins. "Surely I am worth more than a man's…leman."

"Aye, you've served a queen, but the gossips say Henry is marching her off to prison, so perhaps that association will not count for much." Scowling at her, he gestured her away with an impatient hand. "But you do not belong at the table when men discuss such matters. Excuse yourself, Ivy, and let us settle whatever we like where you are concerned."

With that he left, his footsteps echoing down the corridor, leaving her with only hurt and regret for company. Queen Eleanor would have never been so easily dismissed. But Ivy did not have Eleanor's importance or her daring at this moment when she would be parting from Roger soon—a thought that made her more heartsore than she ever would have suspected.

She could only dream of another place and time when she'd been so much happier. She could scarcely credit that earlier in the week she'd been melting into Roger's arms for the most profoundly exciting moments of her life.

And now she'd been dismissed from the table where he would visit with her father before saying goodbye. Would he pass a night in Rutherford House? Or would he find her father's wheedling too distasteful to bear for that long?

Stung at the thought of finding him gone in the morning without ever having had the chance to say goodbye, Ivy returned to the small hall to excuse herself. She might have withstood the hurt better had Roger even cast a longing look her way. But he drank his wine quietly and nodded good-night like a remote stranger.

For all that she'd thought they had shared, and despite her heart's new fear that she had fallen in love with him, the man did not spare her so much as a second glance.

Roger slipped out of Thomas Rutherford's home at first light, unwilling to delay his future for even one more day. He experienced some twinge of guilt at departing without speaking to Ivy, but he would return to her soon enough. Perhaps too soon for her liking.

Would she resent the arrangement he'd made with her father the night before?

The morning loomed warm already as he led his horse along the river to the main road north. He mounted with no rations, as he planned to reach his home quickly. He was eager to secure the lands he'd left for too long.

Her home had been different than he'd expected. From her exquisite garments, he'd anticipated a home rich with obvious wealth and all the adornments a tradesman could buy. But apparently Thomas Rutherford had only adorned his daughter with an eye to ensnaring a nobleman as a marriage prize. The man's house had been comfortable but not lavish, and Roger had been at ease with a man whose goals were clear and forthright.

He did not resent the man's obvious desire for a better future for his daughter. Ivy's mother had been a noblewoman, after all. Roger had settled upon a bride price easily enough, securing a generous dowry in return. But as much as he appreciated the additional gold and the promise of new swords from the respected silversmith in the future, Roger did not appreciate leaving Rutherford House without the woman who would be his bride.

And he damn well knew that Ivy would not be pleased to discover he'd made the arrangements without telling her. Without even asking her properly to wed.

As he reached the main road, however, he dismissed his restless sense of guilt and wrongdoing where she was concerned, since a familiar figure awaited him on horseback just ahead—a tall, fair-haired English knight whose unrelieved dark chain mail did not bear any family colors or crests.

"Forrester." Roger greeted the spy stiffly.

"Stancliff." He nodded with equal formality, although he appeared far more at ease. "I have been awaiting your arrival because I spoke with the king before Katherine and I made our crossing. Henry bid me to tell you that you have his unequivocal support in your claim to all the Stancliff ancestral lands."

"What sort of joke is this?" Suspicion would not allow him to believe the story. Roger kept his horse moving, forcing Forrester to hasten step alongside him if he wished to continue the discussion. "Since when are you Henry's messenger? I thought you were with Lady Katherine this week at Beauvais and no longer serving the king?"

That had been the news from the lord of Beauvais before Roger and Ivy had left his company.

"I wish it had been so easy to remain at Katherine's side." The sharpness in his tone belied the affable manner he'd adopted in Aquitaine. "Henry stopped at Beauvais Keep mere days after you departed. He had captured Queen Eleanor riding halfway across the continent dressed as a man to escape Poitiers. Henry said he will return to London as soon as he assembles as many of Poitiers' former inhabitants as he can find."

Thankfully, Ivy had escaped the mayhem just in time. But Roger could not help but think she might still require his protection if Henry sought more of Eleanor's women. How far would he search?

"And with all the controversy swirling about him, he still thought it important that you chase me down to deliver a message?" Doubt made him wonder what else Forrester might have in mind. "Are you here to look over my shoulder again? Or perhaps Henry wants to see how I run my keep now that he's had you observe how I run a spying assignment."

"That was hardly my idea." Forrester urged his mount faster to keep pace. "Would you have me deny our sovereign because the task he set for me offends you? Sorry, Stancliff, but I don't have enough standing in his eyes to disobey the man who said he only wanted me there in case you needed assistance. If he'd asked me to spit on his boots for a better sheen, you can bet your arse I would have offered him my best tunic for the job."

Roger had little wish to be appeased by a man he wasn't sure he could trust. But his story made sense.

"So you tell me my reward for a job well done is the right to keep my own lands." A clever way to employ inexpensive labor but Roger was too relieved on that count to care. "What was your reward, Forrester? You get to keep your own tunic? Or did he grant you something that might make you a more attractive candidate for Lady Katherine's hand?"

It was no surprise that marriage preyed heavily

upon Roger's mind this morning as they trotted through meadows and sparse woods, over rolling hills and past small country chapels. Sheep roamed the hills with sleepy shepherds to stand guard over them. All the world looked a little brighter today with the knowledge that Ivy would soon be his.

"No lands." Forrester squinted into trees up ahead. "And while I think the rewards will be plentiful one day, I fear Katherine will not remain unwed for much longer."

"You served your king so loyally that you were forced to implicate your own queen, and for that you receive naught but royal goodwill? That seems unjust." Roger had not appreciated Forrester's presence at Poitiers when he feared the man as a possible rival for Ivy's hand. Later, he had resented the other man's deception, although perhaps James had had little choice but to do as Henry bid.

But now he could see no reason to hold a grudge against him, especially since he obviously held Katherine de Blois in great affection and had no designs on Ivy.

Obviously the king trusted him, as did Ivy.

"The king has other matters on his mind, I fear. Those closest to him say he plans to do public penance for the death of his friend the archbishop." Forrester seemed willing to grant Henry latitude, and it was true enough that the king had much to prey upon his heart.

But Henry's preoccupation hardly excused a lack of reward for loyalty such as the kind Forrester had provided. And given Roger's lighter mood today, he suddenly could not abide seeing love thwarted by something so worldly as gold or land. A ridiculous notion took root in his brain.

"Perhaps Henry will forgive me if I offer you some small lands in his stead." The idea had merit. Forrester had proven himself loyal to a fault by doing Henry's work in Poitiers with no compensation.

Besides, granting lands to a deserving man might even buy Roger more royal gratitude, a commodity he would sorely need when Henry learned of his un- orthodox decision to flout marriage traditions by wedding a merchant's daughter.

Although, much as he feared Henry's reaction, Roger knew Ivy's resistance would probably be far more troublesome, since she had made her stance clear on the problems inherent in marriages across class lines.

"What jest is this?" Forrester eyed him with sus- picion. "I recognize well when a man does not think highly of me, Stancliff, and I'll warrant you are one of those men."

"I had reasons, but they have disappeared now in light of your attention to a woman who is not Ivy Ru- therford." Possessiveness swelled inside him at the thought of her. He had not anticipated how much he would miss her on today's excursion.

"I admire Ivy, 'tis true, but my heart has belonged to Katherine since I met her a year ago." The expres- sion on the burly knight's face testified to his words.

"I had hoped to force myself to notice a woman who might be more appropriate for me at Poitiers, but I fear it was too late for such a ploy to work."

"A damned bit of good luck, if you ask me, since I would never consider granting you authority over my Norman lands if I thought you harbored even a moment of warm sentiment for the woman who will be my wife."

"You're can't be serious." James swiveled in his saddle to look at him. "Holy hell, you are serious." He slapped his knee and whooped a hearty cheer. "May the saints smile on you, Stancliff. You are a bold man to defy convention so easily, but then Mistress Ivy is a woman of the highest principles. I wish you both every happiness."

"Thank you." Roger allowed himself a moment to enjoy the idea of his future, a future which he hadn't let the king approve and which Ivy might resent for the rest of her days.

But by God, someone besides him saw the merit in the unconventional union, and that lifted his spirits. He passed the rest of the trip in deep conversation with Forrester, working out a strategy for defense and new fortifications at the coastal property that had been in Roger's family for two generations. The property was strategically important and deserved more direct supervision from a seasoned knight who knew how to construct the best defenses. Roger would begin his new life as a staid, responsible liege lord by parceling off outlying lands to the most capable of men.

The decision settled comfortably on his conscience, and he knew Forrester would be far better fit to rule the lands than Alice's stepbrother, who would have received the holding as part of Alice's bride price. William Montcalm had driven almost as hard a bargain as crafty Thomas Rutherford for his daughter, granting Alice a generous dowry, but insisting on the installation of his stepson as Roger's vassal to improve family relations.

Roger would rest easier with a more experienced man in charge of lands that were so vulnerable. And so important to the king.

Once Roger secured his own keep, he would send for Ivy and attempt to offer her whatever he could to woo her into a marriage she didn't want. He only hoped the endeavor would not require any more of his heart than he'd already given her, since he feared the rest of it had died a year ago on the courtyard of Montcalm's keep along with Alice and her unborn child.

Chapter Seventeen

As the sun rose on the tenth day after Roger's word-less departure, Ivy walked the length of Belinda's garden, far behind the kitchen at Rutherford House. Efficiently planted, the small plot would provide food for half the year, from sweet peas that had already come and gone, to the last pear plucked before the snow came.

This patch of earth bore little resemblance to the elaborate plantings at Poitiers, but Ivy found herself drawn to the heavy greenery and neat rows because they brought to mind the queen's bower, where she had passed those first tremulous conversations with her silver-eyed knight. Inevitably, she ended her morning walks now in front of the pear tree, which brought to mind her first kiss.

Peering toward the road leading north, Ivy won-dered for the tenth day if Roger would return, as he'd apparently promised her father. She'd scarcely believed her sire's news that a man of Lord Stancliff's significance wanted to marry her. But her disbelief was quickly followed by guilt for having led him to her bed. Had he thought marriage was the only answer to their one night of passion? Had he thought she'd maneuvered him into an impossible situation?

Perhaps as his courtly love tutor, she should have known better. Hadn't she preached the art of restraint in those first conversations?

Leaning against the trunk of the tree as she looked for signs of movement on the road ahead, Ivy admitted that her bout of guilt had been short-lived, too. She'd experienced a twinge of regret for the first few hours after Roger had departed. Then, her worries had been plowed away by anger that he would not even speak to her directly about a potential union.

He knew how she felt about her parents' disastrous marriage. Had he purposely not mentioned his wish to seal their fates? Her father had dismissed her fears as foolish, saying his marriage had not been as bad as all that and that Ivy had merely been a sensitive child who did not understand the passionate tempers of her parents. He'd even gone so far as to embarrass her completely by implying that their tempers were not the only passionate aspects of their marriage and that Rosamunde had been happy enough for a woman whose parents had forsaken her.

And while his version of their past had made Ivy rethink some of her old notions about love and marriage across social boundaries, she still felt Roger's absence keenly and resented the fact that he'd never spoken to her of any future together.

Now, she withdrew her parchment scroll from under her arm and considered her latest poem, a romantic epic with a hero who was decidedly more brash and arrogant than lovesick and worshipful. No surprise, perhaps, considering her fascination with a certain errant knight who wasn't nearly as errant as the world thought.

When she heard the pounding of hooves on the road from the north, she hardly dared to look beyond the scroll to see the rider. She'd been disappointed too many times in the last few days.

She waited for as long as her curiosity could be silenced and then—finally—she stole a peek beyond the parchment. A man rode hard toward her, his face all lean angles and intensity. He looked vaguely familiar, but she could not place him. She thought about calling out a greeting, thinking that she might be able to identify him if she heard him speak, but he charged too near, too quickly.

What was this?

Her limbs froze as her thoughts raced. Surely this man, this stranger, meant her no harm. Yet he bore down on her, closer, chasing away her doubts with a sudden rush of cold fear. The wind around her picked up, blowing her skirts and hair in a sudden gust, as if heaven itself begged her to flee.

Dropping her parchment on the ground, she broke

free from her stunned thoughts and turned to run, but a great arm scooped her from her feet as she let out a scream of protest.

Ten days after he'd left Rutherford House, five days after he and James Forrester had parted, Roger was alone in him empty keep, save for retainers elsewhere in the building.

Tonight the wind was Roger's only company. The small holes between random stones in the tower created a whistling, mournful cry as gusts howled past.

Some foul-tempered recess of Roger's brain insisted he would not even hear such noises if he'd brought Ivy here with him. He would be listening to her sweet cries of pleasure as he made love to her in his bed instead of noticing every hiss of the wind.

No doubt, Stancliff Keep lacked warmth after his year of neglect. His father's death, followed so closely by his betrothed's betrayal and tragic passing, had left him incapable of caring about life and lands. He vaguely remembered selling off a few tapestries from the living quarters to finance his relentless travels. His search for anything that would take his mind off of failing Alice and her unborn babe.

And although he had not succeeded in finding something to relieve his mind, he had found some-*one* in Ivy. Her romantic leanings that at first had seemed so naive to him at least assured him she believed love existed. And he would prove to her that it could be found within marriage.

He might not be the idealistic man he'd been during his first betrothal, but Ivy had at least reinstated his faith in honor. And, judging by his morose longing for her as he wandered the echoing halls of his keep, he almost feared she'd revived his ability to care.

Deeply.

The realization shook his foundation far more than the wind pounding the walls. He could not spend any more time securing his keep. He would leave tomorrow morning—no, tonight—to retrieve the woman who had resurrected him.

He sprinted down the spiraling staircase, heedless of the dark and wind now that he had a new goal. New clarity. He did not see the man-at-arms rushing toward him until he all but collided with him.

"Pardon, my lord." The young man held up a sealed parchment as if to excuse his haste. "A messenger arrived for you at the east gate some moments ago, but the lad rode off before he could claim a coin or a meal. Most peculiar in this weather, don't you think?"

Peculiar indeed. Only now as he lifted the parchment did it occur to him he had no light with which to read it. He'd been stumbling around in the dark like—devil take him—a lovesick idiot. Perhaps Ivy had crawled far deeper beneath his skin than he had realized.

A slow grin tugged at his lips while he moved into the hall still ringed with torches from the meager meal he'd shared with his men. The grin faded as he spied the wax seal of the Montcalm family on the scroll. Tearing it open, he unfurled the parchment and read the words it contained.

> You robbed me of Alice. Now I return the favor with the merchant's daughter. I only hope she holds your son the way Alice held mine.

Fury and fear mingled with disbelief. This came from the Montcalm household? Alice's own family?

His feet already in motion, raw terror filled his throat at the thought of innocent Ivy in the hands of some vengeance-seeking lunatic. But he would not fail her the way he'd failed Alice. He might not be the kind of hero who filled the pages of courtly love poems, but after waging plenty of Henry's wars, he could bloody well be the kind of hero who wielded the deadliest sword this faceless enemy had ever seen.

Ivy could not help but think that if this had been one of the sweet ballads she'd written, a gallant knight would ride out of the hills at any moment and wrest her from the brooding, tortured soul who forced her out onto the battlements of some remote tower a few hours north of Rutherford House.

No wonder Gertrude had laughed at Ivy's creative efforts. To think anyone would save her was not only naive, it was foolish.

Possibly deadly.

Rain fell in earnest now as the brute with the blade

in her back nudged her onward. She tripped on a loose stone, and although she could have caught herself, she allowed her body to drop to the ground. Stalling for time. She would think of some way to save herself and—possibly—the life she might already carry inside her. She could not be certain of a babe, but her courses had not followed their usual moon cycle.

Heaven help her, she would not allow anything to happen to Roger's child. Fate could not be so cruel to punish the man she loved that way.

"Get up." The man with the knife—Stephen, she'd discovered, who had accompanied Montcalm to Roger's Normandy lands—nudged her fallen form with his boot as the rain splattered across her cheek.

The gesture struck her as odd, an action performed by someone who did not wish to touch her. Her captor did not strike her as evil so much as—devastated. A lost soul. As Montcalm's stepson, the man apparently had grown up with Alice and had claimed to love her since childhood. He'd hidden their affair from his stepfather since he feared the elder Montcalm would not approve, even though Stephen was not related by blood to Alice.

"I cannot rise," Ivy protested, flinching dramatically and curious to see if this strange man would lend her a hand or if he would force her onto a foot she'd pretended to injure. "I think I've broken it."

Her fingers clutched small stones and dirt as she struggled to stand, her leg unharmed but the rest of her body truly aching after jouncing on horseback to this hidden tower. She'd struggled with the man for many leagues until she realized she only wasted valuable strength.

She had regained some of it now and she would not hesitate to use it. To fight at the crucial moment to ensure his twisted plans did not come to fruition. This was no pretty poem. This was her life and she would be a worthy heroine of it.

The man hesitated, his angular face twisted with indecision and anger, until another masculine voice broke their silent standoff.

"Stephen!" The enraged bellow drifted up to the battlements from the ground below.

Roger.

Hope and disbelief warred within her. Ivy did not believe in courtly love anymore, so she couldn't possibly have imagined Roger's voice unless he really had come for her. Or so she hoped. And it gave credence to her hope that his voice was not lifted in gentlemanly ire or lovelorn angst, but rather fired through the storm like a vocal weapon.

This wasn't some sweet and tender knight of wooing words and poetic phrases but a fearsome man who protected her with body and soul, so much more powerful than bended-knee declarations and empty praise. The humanity of a real man was far more magnificent than her fanciful dreams had been. She should have seen that deeper beauty—that the strength of a true hero—was more poetic than any pretty words.

Ivy raised her eyes to her captor and saw Stephen's shoulders tense before he stalked to the edge of the parapet.

"Stancliff," he shouted down, although he kept his eyes and his blade closely trained on Ivy. "You have come in time to witness my nightmare. A nightmare about to become your own."

"You think you can ease your own sorrow and regret by spreading it to others?" Roger's disgusted tone conveyed his low opinion of Stephen even better than his words. "Are you so small a man that you could not challenge me for Alice when you had the chance to declare yourself? Are you so small a man now that you cannot come down here and skewer me instead of lashing out at a defenseless woman?"

"You will find yourself skewered soon enough," Stephen taunted, wrenching Ivy along the ground with one hand, his aversion to touching her apparently past. "Right after you experience the same horrors I've endured, you faithless wretch."

Stephen's fingers bit into her arm as he hauled Ivy closer. She stopped pretending her foot was broken, since he seemed all but oblivious to her pain anyhow. The scent of his sweat and fear made her belly roil in protest. His skin was slick and cold against hers where he held her. Slowly she rose, stalling again, but she could not resist the chance to see Roger's face after the long days apart. The long nights of wondering if she'd dreamed their intense connection. She would only look for a moment, and then she would prove to Roger and her captor both that she was not the defenseless woman they thought.

She might not hold a knife like Stephen or a sword like Roger always wore, but as a once-shy merchant's daughter, she'd always been skilled at making herself disappear so she might observe life from afar.

Could she elude this man for a few crucial moments?

If nothing else, she still held a fistful of dirt from her fall. A small defense, but she would gladly grind the grit into the man's eyes when the moment was right.

As she peered down from the battlements, waiting for that right moment, Ivy discovered the man at the base of the tower was not Roger, even though he wore Roger's colors and bore his standard.

She knew it could not be him the moment Stephen forced her to the waist-high ledge. Even with the driving rain and the low-lying mist, she could see the figure below possessed a noble bearing but lacked Roger's height. He did not hold himself in the saddle in the way that Ivy had come to recognize well during their long hours of travel from Poitiers to London.

Surely Roger had been there a moment ago, since she knew his voice. Somehow, he had vanished since he'd spoken, leaving another man in his place. Did Stephen realize it?

"I am so sorry, my lord," she cried into the howling wind, hoping her trick would deceive Stephen into thinking Roger lingered below for a few more moments. "I should have stayed within the walls of my father's house."

The dark-haired figure below shaded his eyes as he looked up, as if to keep the rain from his vision. A sensible ploy to hide his identity while— perhaps—Roger climbed the tower.

She prayed so.

"I love you." She hadn't meant to proclaim her innermost feelings here. Now. But the sentiment seemed too important to hide when Roger deserved to know. He might not be the listener below, but perhaps he could still hear her.

If anything were to happen to her today, she would have him know that she went to her grave loving him. That she'd finally come to understand the appeal of a man who wielded a blade rather than empty words.

The knife pinched her back again as Stephen gripped her. Lifted her. Horror made her vision swim as she realized he hefted her onto the ledge.

Her feet braced against the wall, refusing to go. She prayed for some of Roger's strength to infuse her shaking limbs and found it as she tossed her handful of stones and grit into Stephen's face, blinding him for a moment.

All of the sudden, the knife and the arms that held her were gone. She slipped backward, away from the ledge, arms flailing as she fell hard upon her hip into a deep puddle atop the battlement.

Pain radiated through her legs in jarring response and the shouts of men fighting filled her ears. In a rain-filled blur she saw Roger circle Stephen, their swords drawn, but she dared not stay to witness their battle. Not if there remained any chance she carried Roger's heir. A worthy heroine might know when to help in battle, but she also knew when to protect her babe. Her warrior hero's babe.

Slipping behind the big wheels of a catapult aimed beyond the tower walls, she prayed with every fiber of her being for Roger's safe deliverance.

At last she'd seen the beauty of a real knight. She only hoped her awakening had not come too late.

Rain and sweat rolled down Roger's temple as he battled the ox of a man who had tried to hurt Ivy. The same man who had hurt Alice by not declaring for her. By denying her his protection when she'd needed it most. And this brute said he loved her? Roger worked his sword arm harder at the thought. What good was love if you could not embrace it and claim it for your own?

The way Ivy had proclaimed love for him, even though he didn't deserve her.

He could not think about that now or he'd lose focus in this slippery contest of strength and skill. Wind howled past his ears as Roger knocked his opponent's sword from his hand, sending Stephen Weymouth's weapon hurtling over the parapet walls to clatter on the stones far below.

Roger had backed him against a low wall, close to the spot where the man had tried to force Ivy onto a wet ledge, where she could have slipped so easily. Fury bubbled in his veins, simmered behind his eyes.

He raised his sword to the man's throat, settling the tip into the soft flesh beneath Stephen's chin. The other man took shallow breaths, avoiding the blade as much as possible as he swallowed and gasped.

With his opponent secured, Roger finally spared a glance around the parapet to look for Ivy in the driving storm.

He saw nothing. No one.

Dark memories of Alice on the ledge, his failure to save her, pummeled him.

"Ivy!" He shouted her name with all the force his lungs could muster while his gaze scoured the battlement for signs of her.

"Here." She arose from behind a catapult wheel, her graceful form unfolding slowly as she waved her arm urgently—shakily?—to reassure him. "I'm here and I'm unharmed."

Relief shot through him as he drank in the sight of her, his anger cooling just a little. His knees damn near buckled with gratitude.

Thank God she was safe. Whole. Soon to be his.

He never should have left her at Rutherford House

alone. He couldn't have lived with himself if anything had happened to her.

"Stancliff."

William Montcalm's voice emanated from somewhere behind him. Roger had ridden to Montcalm's holding first to interrogate the old man about the message he'd received with his family seal. And William—no doubt recognizing the genuine fear in Roger's eyes—had offered to help him find Stephen. Montcalm had led him here, to his stepson's sole holding.

"You cannot save him," Roger threatened the old man now, his blade deliberately nicking Stephen's skin. "Your sorry excuse for a stepson would have killed Ivy if we had not stopped him."

And that alone required his death. But his behavior toward Alice weighed against him, too, doubling the man's need for punishment.

"He was always close to my daughter." Montcalm's voice loomed nearer. The anger Roger had been accustomed to hearing it had been replaced by despair. Guilt. "I married his mother when they were naught but ten or twelve years old. I never thought his care for her extended beyond brotherly affection."

Roger could glimpse the old man now from the corner of his eye. Montcalm knew better than to interfere with Roger's right to justice.

And yet, as Roger glanced back to Stephen Weymouth's face, he found the man's lip trembling. Weymouth's eyes held a haunted look Roger knew well. It was the same one he'd spotted in his own reflection many times during his months of hollow revelry that never quite hid his guilt.

How could he kill a man who'd already been punished so gravely by Fate?

"Alice was your daughter longer than she was my betrothed," Roger shouted to Alice's father through the relentless fall of rain. "What justice would you seek for her death?"

"If it were my decision to make, Stancliff, I would have him sent to the Templars in far-off lands. Let him use his sword for God's glory while he prays for mercy all his days for what he did to my daughter."

Stephen—quiet throughout his battle with Roger—now spoke softly, seemingly mindful of the blade still resting against the vulnerable softness of his throat.

"She said she loved me, but she would not dishonor her father or her betrothed by forswearing her promise to marry him."

Roger wondered if it were true or if she'd merely been confused about her feelings for the man who'd been close to her as a girl. But it hardly mattered now. He only knew that so much heartache could have been avoided if Alice had spoken to him. Her promises had been more important to her than honoring passion, a mistake Roger would not make. He had already forsworn himself to Eleanor by breaking his vow not touch Ivy, but that pledge had been too difficult to keep.

He was a better man for having broken it.

"Very well then, old man." Roger lowered his sword slowly, never taking his eyes off Stephen as he called to Montcalm. "If you can promise me he will depart England at first light and no later, I will convey your stepson into your keeping, but for my mercy I claim this tower and the garrison that goes with it for Ivy Rutherford to hold as her dower lands."

And for the first time in a year, Roger walked away from death and dark thoughts of what might have been. Would his fierce battle with Stephen have already lessened Roger in Ivy's romantic eyes? She'd held so fast to her beliefs about how a chivalrous man should behave. Roger had turned his back on all notions of courtly gallantry tonight, even if he chose to show his opponent some small mercy now.

But even if Ivy never understood him, he had learned something from her, since in his youth he would have never walked away from a foe at his mercy. Ivy had helped him find his soul again. Turning his back on Stephen as that man sank to his knees weeping, Roger turned toward Ivy and a future he could only pray she still wanted.

Chapter Eighteen

Ivy launched herself into Roger's arms the moment he dropped his sword, but she could not speak to him here in the shadows of his past. *Their* past, now. She pulled him through the rain down the tower steps, away from Montcalm and his stepson, who had pledged on his mother's life to leave the country forever.

"We can light a fire in the hall," Roger called to her as she hurried across the vacant courtyard adjoining Weymouth's small keep. "You will catch your death in the rain."

She smiled to herself, thinking how unlikely she was to perish from a cold after she had survived Stephen's attempt to drop her from a forty-foot tower.

"I would rather not venture into his holding." The thought of Stephen made her skin turn colder than the rain ever could.

"'Tis your holding now, Ivy." He surrendered and allowed her to lead him into the woods surrounding the tower. "Your place to retire, should you ever wish to run off and start your own court of love away from your husband."

She slowed her step as they ducked under tree branches, the ground padded by years of fallen pine needles. Thick foliage protected them from the rain, and the trees were high enough to allow them to move about freely. She guessed that deer probably favored the place as a resting spot, since a narrow dirt path led into the copse and away from it in the other direction.

"I cannot imagine ever feeling at home in a place that contained such frightening memories for me." Suppressing a shudder, she feared she would have nightmares about a fall from the tower for a long time.

"You will feel at home at Stancliff Keep," he promised, ducking beneath a low branch as he stepped over a damp log.

The thought of visiting his home sent an unexpected thrill dancing along her skin despite all the fears and upheaval of the day.

"I'm sure that I would. Besides, if I ever create my own court of love, I should wish to have my husband by my side to enjoy all that I learn, so there would be no need to find a separate residence. That is, if I can ever find a husband who is not some despairing minstrel falling at my feet in praise of my beauty." She attempted a curtsy in her wet skirt, well aware that any scant beauty she possessed had been washed away in the driving rainstorm. "I would much prefer a husband who can come to my aid when I falter."

"I wouldn't have *had* to come to your aid if I had been by your side in the first place." His silver-eyed stare warmed her inside and out as he drew her close.

She sensed the frustration he felt was only anger at himself for not protecting her the way he thought he should have. She could not be incensed at that kind of anger now that she understood it. His wish to guard her only made her feel all the more fortunate.

"You could not know that Alice's lover sought vengeance after all this time." She sidestepped a leak in their forest canopy, solving her problem my pressing herself even closer to him. "He seems like a man with a broken spirit, so perhaps his time with the Templars will give him new direction. New hope."

"I find I cannot care whether he has hope or not." He tightened his grip on her waist. "I only care that he remains gone."

"I admire you for showing him mercy he did not deserve." Emotions swelled inside her as she looked into his eyes and, surprisingly, still found shades of her courtly love hero wrapped up inside this fearsome warrior. "Thank you for finding me."

"When I made it up the tower steps and saw him shoving you out on that ledge..." He shook his head, speechless. "I don't plan on ever having to search for you again after today, since I will never leave you long enough for you to disappear."

"My father will have something to say about you taking up so much of my time when he seems to think I should be finding a suitable husband this year." She didn't know where she found her nerve to tease him as boldly as the ladies at Eleanor's court once had, but now that they were safe and dry and, most importantly, together, she felt a lightness of spirit she couldn't remember ever experiencing before.

"Believe me, your father will profit grandly from my affection for you, but I received the better half of the deal, my lady." His perfect smile had charmed women far and wide, but she knew this one was meant only for her.

Still, hearing his old endearment, his insistence that she was a noble lady, brought a bittersweet pang of regret that she did not have the rank he deserved in a wife.

"I only wish I could have remained in Eleanor's court long enough to gain the recognition that might have brought me the noble standing your family name merits." She had not spoken her fanciful yearning aloud to anyone at the court, but she had nursed the secret dream long enough to mourn its loss.

"I have been thinking about that." He smoothed away a dripping lock of her hair, drying her cheek with the edge of his palm. "And it occurs to me you sought to impress the wrong royal with your poems."

The trees cut the wind here as well as the heavy rains, but still she found herself swaying toward him for his warmth.

His strength.

"I don't understand." She tipped her chin into his hand, so grateful for his touch after too long apart. "The king doesn't even like the arts."

"He may not spend a lot of his coffers on patronage, but he has no wish to be thought of as the sovereign with no culture in his kingdom. Perhaps if you applied yourself to making Henry a manly hero in some epic poem about his battles, you might find yourself rewarded with no funds or patronage, but your choice of empty noble titles."

"Do you think so?" Ivy bit her lip to hide the ridiculous smile that tickled her cheeks, since an empty title would suit her splendidly. "You make it sound so easy."

"I've come to recognize the king as a crafty sire, and I happen to know his crown could use a bit of artful praise after his quarrel with the queen and the matter of the archbishop." He traced the outline of the smile she could no longer hold back. "And while I'm glad the notion pleases you, Ivy, you will always be the most praiseworthy woman I know and I will love you whether you are a tradesman's daughter, an outlaw poet or a grand noblewoman with the king's blessing."

Her heart soared at his words and she wrapped her arms around his neck to revel in his declaration. Perhaps she would be the recipient of pretty phrases now and then, even if she had gladly forsaken her dreams of a courtly lover for a knight who was strong and true, fierce in his love for her.

"Truly? I am beloved of Lord Roger Stancliff, the most notorious heartbreaker in all of Christendom? The man whose reputation makes maidens swoon in fear and married women swoon with ardor?" She remembered that first day she'd spent with him and all the fanciful notions she had built around him before she knew anything about him. Little did she know then how much more deeply a woman could come to love a man. A *real* man with passions to match her own and strengths she hadn't fully appreciated.

"I think my reputation was exaggerated by your contemporaries, but the part about you being beloved—that much is very true."

Hearing him confess his love for her was even better the second time. She wondered how much more it would mean to her a week from now. A month from now. Nine months from now?

"I think I may swoon myself, my lord, for that is very good news." She did not wait for his kiss but stretched up on her toes to brush her mouth over his. His lips welcomed her warmly, and she had to pull away before she grew too inflamed to speak the rest of what she needed to say. "And I might have some good news for you in the next sennight, as well. In fact, it is the kind of good news that might make you wish to marry me sooner rather than later, if you can find the time."

Wrapping her fingers about his wrist, she moved his broad hand to span her flat belly and savored the warmth of his touch upon her, permeating her wet surcoat and girdle. She could not be fully certain of her condition yet, but her heart was sure enough that she wanted to share the news.

She could tell the exact moment when he understood the message, for his fingers and his mouth stalled in harmony. He pulled back to look at her.

"What is the meaning of this, lady?" Clutching her shoulders, he steadied her to meet his gaze.

"The meaning is that we may have become a family more quickly than we intended, and the Church may wish to give us its blessing." She didn't even try to hide this smile, since the joy inside her was deep-rooted and ready to bloom. "And perhaps we should wed before my father discovers the news, lest he raise the bride price still higher."

She knew her father would be generous in her dowry as well, but her words had their intended effect when Roger grinned.

"You cannot know how happy you've made me, Ivy. Not just today, and not just because we might be a family already. But even before Stephen's note arrived, I realized I needed to retrieve you from your father's house because I couldn't wait another day to see you."

"Eleanor was right when she said we had things we could teach each other." She hadn't forgotten the queen's prediction that Ivy would have as much to learn from Roger as he would from her. "Maybe she saw something between us before we even knew it was there."

"You give your queen too much credit." His fingers returned to her waist now, almost as if to remind himself of their future together. "I knew something was there the first day I spied you in the bower and wondered how I would survive getting to know you without falling in love with you."

"You thought no such thing, you brazen knave." One day she would confess to him how much she had lost her heart to him before she knew his identity. "You gave no thought to love back then."

"Ah, but I think about it a great deal now. And I must have taken the notion to fall for you sometime between then and now, and I'm so grateful that I did, Lady Ivy." He kissed her sweetly at first, his mouth persuading her in ways that had nothing to do with words and Ivy fell a little more in love with her hero.

She would write an epic for the king soon. But once she'd secured the title her future husband had bestowed on her already, she planned to finish the work of her heart, the story of the valiant knight Roger Stancliff and the lady who loved him for all of his days.

Experience the anticipation, the thrill of the chase
and the sheer rush of falling in love!
Turn the page for a sneak preview of a new book
from Harlequin Romance
THE REBEL PRINCE
by Raye Morgan
On sale August 29th wherever books are sold

"OH, NO!"

The reaction slipped out before Emma Valentine could stop it, for there stood the very man she most wanted to avoid seeing again.

He didn't look any happier to see her.

"Well, come on, get on board," he said gruffly. "I won't bite." One eyebrow rose. "Though I might nibble a little," he added, mostly to amuse himself.

But she wasn't paying any attention to what he was saying. She was staring at him, taking in the royal blue uniform he was wearing, with gold braid and glistening badges decorating the sleeves, epaulettes and an upright collar. Ribbons and medals covered the breast of the short, fitted jacket. A gold-encrusted sabre hung at his side. And suddenly it was clear to her who this man really was.

She gulped wordlessly. Reaching out, he took her elbow and pulled her aboard. The doors slid closed. And finally she found her tongue.

"You…you're the prince."

He nodded, barely glancing at her. "Yes. Of course."

She raised a hand and covered her mouth for a moment. "I should have known."

"Of course you should have. I don't know why you didn't." He punched the ground-floor button to get the elevator moving again, then turned to look down at her. "A relatively bright five-year-old child would have tumbled to the truth right away."

Her shock faded as her indignation at his tone asserted itself. He might be the prince, but he was still just as annoying as he had been earlier that day.

"A relatively bright five-year-old child without a bump on the head from a badly thrown water polo ball, maybe," she said defensively. She wasn't feeling woozy any longer and she wasn't about to let him bully her, no matter how royal he was. "I was unconscious half the time."

"And just clueless the other half, I guess," he said, looking bemused.

The arrogance of the man was really galling.

"I suppose you think your 'royalness' is so obvious it sort of shimmers around you for all to see?" she challenged. "Or better yet, oozes from your pores like...like sweat on a hot day?"

"Something like that," he acknowledged calmly. "Most people tumble to it pretty quickly. In fact, it's hard to hide even when I want to avoid dealing with it."

"Poor baby," she said, still resenting his manner. "I guess that works better with injured people who are half asleep." Looking at him, she felt a strange emotion she couldn't identify. It was as though she wanted to prove something to him, but she wasn't sure what. "And anyway, you know you did your best to fool me," she added.

His brows knit together as though he really didn't know what she was talking about. "I didn't do a thing."

"You told me your name was Monty."

"It is." He shrugged. "I have a lot of names. Some of them are too rude to be spoken to my face, I'm sure." He glanced at her sideways, his hand on the hilt of his sabre. "Perhaps you're contemplating one of those right now."

You bet I am.

That was what she would like to say. But it suddenly occurred to her that she was supposed to be working for this man. If she wanted to keep the job of coronation chef, maybe she'd better keep her opinions to herself. So she clamped her mouth shut, took a deep breath and looked away, trying hard to calm down.

The elevator ground to a halt and the doors slid open laboriously. She moved to step forward, hoping to make her escape, but his hand shot out again and caught her elbow.

"Wait a minute. *You're* a woman," he said, as though that thought had just presented itself to him.

"That's a rare ability for insight you have there, Your Highness," she snapped before she could stop herself. And then she winced. She was going to have to do better than that if she was going to keep this relationship on an even keel.

But he was ignoring her dig. Nodding, he stared at her with a speculative gleam in his golden eyes. "I've been looking for a woman, but you'll do."

She blanched, stiffening. "I'll do for what?"

He made a head gesture in a direction she knew was opposite of where she was going and his grip tightened on her elbow.

"Come with me," he said abruptly, making it an order.

She dug in her heels, thinking fast. She didn't much like orders. "Wait! I can't. I have to get to the kitchen."

"Not yet. I need you."

"You what?" Her breathless gasp of surprise was soft, but she knew he'd heard it.

"I need you," he said firmly. "Oh, don't look so shocked. I'm not planning to throw you into the hay and have my way with you. I need you for something a bit more mundane than that."

She felt color rushing into her cheeks and she silently begged it to stop. Here she was, formless and stodgy in her chef's whites. No makeup, no stiletto heels. Hardly the picture of the femmes fatales he was undoubtedly used to. The likelihood that he would have any carnal interest in her was remote at best. To have him think she was hysterically defending her virtue was humiliating.

"Well, what if I don't want to go with you?" she said in hopes of deflecting his attention from her blush.

"Too bad."

"What?"

Amusement sparkled in his eyes. He was certainly enjoying this. And that only made her more determined to resist him.

"I'm the prince, remember? And we're in the castle. My orders take precedence. It's that old pesky divine rights thing."

Her jaw jutted out. Despite her embarrassment, she couldn't let that pass.

"Over my free will? Never!"

Exasperation filled his face.

"Hey, call out the historians. Someone will write a book about you and your courageous principles." His eyes glittered sardonically. "But in the meantime, Emma Valentine, you're coming with me."

Introducing…

nocturne

a spine-tingling new line from Silhouette Books.

These paranormal romances will seduce you with dark, passionate tales that stretch the boundaries of conflict, desire, and life and death, weaving a tapestry of sensual thrills and chills!

Don't miss the first book…

UNFORGIVEN

by *USA TODAY* bestselling author

LINDSAY McKENNA

Launching October 2006, wherever books are sold.

SNIBC

Silhouette® Desire®

Introducing an exciting appearance by legendary *New York Times* bestselling author

DIANA PALMER
HEARTBREAKER

He's the ultimate bachelor...
but he may have just met
the one woman to change his ways!

Join the drama in the story of a confirmed
bachelor, an amnesiac beauty and their
unexpected passionate romance.

**"Diana Palmer is a mesmerizing storyteller
who captures the essence of what
a romance should be."—*Affaire de Coeur***

**Heartbreaker *is available from Silhouette Desire*
*in September 2006.***

Visit Silhouette Books at www.eHarlequin.com SDDPIBC

Harlequin® Historical
Historical Romantic Adventure!

An unexpected liaison...

MISTAKEN MISTRESS
Margaret McPhee

To her spiteful aunt, Kathryn Marchant
is little more than a servant: she does
not deserve a place in polite society.
That's about to change, when Kathryn
accidentally falls into the arms of the
most notorious rake of them all.

"A fresh new voice in Regency
romance. Hugely enjoyable."
—Bestselling author Nicola Cornick

On sale September 2006.

*Available wherever
Harlequin books are sold.*

www.eHarlequin.com   HHMM29415

If you enjoyed what you just read,
then we've got an offer you can't resist!

Take 2 bestselling love stories FREE!

Plus get a FREE surprise gift!

Clip this page and mail it to Harlequin Reader Service®

IN U.S.A.
3010 Walden Ave.
P.O. Box 1867
Buffalo, N.Y. 14240-1867

IN CANADA
P.O. Box 609
Fort Erie, Ontario
L2A 5X3

YES! Please send me 2 free Harlequin Historicals® novels and my free surprise gift. After receiving them, if I don't wish to receive anymore, I can return the shipping statement marked cancel. If I don't cancel, I will receive 6 brand-new novels every month, before they're available in stores! In the U.S.A., bill me at the bargain price of $4.69 plus 25¢ shipping and handling per book and applicable sales tax, if any*. In Canada, bill me at the bargain price of $5.24 plus 25¢ shipping and handling per book and applicable taxes**. That's the complete price and a savings of over 10% off the cover prices—what a great deal! I understand that accepting the 2 free books and gift places me under no obligation ever to buy any books. I can always return a shipment and cancel at any time. Even if I never buy another book from Harlequin, the 2 free books and gift are mine to keep forever.

246 HDN DZ7Q
349 HDN DZ7R

Name	(PLEASE PRINT)	
Address	Apt.#	
City	State/Prov.	Zip/Postal Code

Not valid to current Harlequin Historicals® subscribers.

Want to try two free books from another series?
Call 1-800-873-8635 or visit www.morefreebooks.com.

* Terms and prices subject to change without notice. Sales tax applicable in N.Y.
** Canadian residents will be charged applicable provincial taxes and GST.
All orders subject to approval. Offer limited to one per household.
® are registered trademarks owned and used by the trademark owner and or its licensee.

HIST04R   ©2004 Harlequin Enterprises Limited

eHARLEQUIN.com

The Ultimate Destination for Women's Fiction

Visit eHarlequin.com's Bookstore today for today's most popular books at great prices.

- An extensive selection of romance books by top authors!

- Choose our convenient "bill me" option. No credit card required.

- New releases, Themed Collections and hard-to-find backlist.

- A sneak peek at upcoming books.

- Check out book excerpts, book summaries and Reader Recommendations from other members and post your own too.

- Find out what everybody's reading in Bestsellers.

- Save BIG with everyday discounts and exclusive online offers!

- Our Category Legend will help you select reading that's exactly right for you!

- Visit our Bargain Outlet often for huge savings and special offers!

- Sweepstakes offers. Enter for your chance to win special prizes, autographed books and more.

Your purchases are 100% guaranteed—so shop online at www.eHarlequin.com today!

INTBB104R

HARLEQUIN *Blaze*

"Super-
steamy!"
—*Cosmopolitan*
magazine

New York Times bestselling author

Elizabeth Bevarly

delivers another sexy adventure!

As a former vice cop, small-town police chief
Sam Maguire knows when things don't add up.
And there's definitely something suspicious happen-
ing behind the scenes at Rosie Bliss's flower shop.
Rumor has it she's not selling just flowers.
But once he gets close and gets his hands on her,
uh, goods, he's in big trouble…of the sensual kind!

Pick up your copy of

MY ONLY VICE

by Elizabeth Bevarly

Available this September,
wherever series romances are sold.

www.eHarlequin.com   HBEB0906

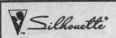

INTIMATE MOMENTS™

Don't miss the next exciting romantic-suspense
novel from *USA TODAY* bestselling author

MARIE FERRARELLA

**Risking his life was part of the job.
Risking his heart was another matter...**

Detective Sawyer Boone had better things to do
with his time than babysit the fiercely independent
daughter of the chief of detectives. But when
Janelle's world came crashing around her, Sawyer
found himself wanting to protect her heart, as well.

CAVANAUGH WATCH

Silhouette Intimate Moments #1431

When the law and passion
collide, this family learns
the ultimate truth—that
love takes no prisoners!

*Available September 2006
at your favorite retail outlet.*

Visit Silhouette Books at www.eHarlequin.com   SIMCW